Celibet

Stacy McWilliams & Sienna Grant

Celibet

**By
Stacy McWilliams & Sienna Grant**

Stacy McWilliams & Sienna Grant

Celibet

Copyright

Copyright © 2020 Sienna Grant & Stacy McWilliams

All rights reserved. No part of this publication may be reproduced, distributed, or transmitted in any form or by any means, including photocopying, recording, or other electronic or mechanical methods, without the prior written permission of the author, except in the case of brief quotations embodied in critical reviews and certain other non-commercial uses permitted by copyright law. For permission requests, write to the author, addressed places, events, and incidents are either the products of the author's imagination or used in a fictitious manner. Any resemblance to actual persons, living or dead, or actual events is purely coincidental.

The authors are in no way affiliated with any brands, songs or musicians or artists mentioned in this book.

Editor: Eleanor Lloyd-Jones
Cover: Shower of Schmidt Designs
Formatter: Maria Lazarou - Obsessed by Books Designs

Stacy McWilliams & Sienna Grant

Contents

COPYRIGHT	III
CONTENTS	V
ACKNOWLEDGEMENTS	IX
BLURB	XIII
CHAPTER ONE	- 1 -
BETH	- 1 -
CHAPTER TWO	- 11 -
CHARLIE	- 11 -
CHAPTER THREE	- 19 -
BETH	- 19 -
CHAPTER FOUR	- 26 -
CHARLIE	- 26 -
CHAPTER FIVE	- 33 -
BETH	- 33 -
CHAPTER SIX	- 43 -
CHARLIE	- 43 -
CHAPTER SEVEN	- 48 -
BETH	- 48 -
CHAPTER EIGHT	- 65 -
BETH	- 65 -
CHAPTER NINE	- 76 -
BETH	- 76 -
CHAPTER TEN	- 82 -
BETH	- 82 -
CHAPTER ELEVEN	- 90 -
CHARLIE	- 90 -
CHAPTER TWELVE	- 96 -
BETH	- 96 -
CHAPTER THIRTEEN	- 105 -
CHARLIE	- 105 -
CHAPTER FOURTEEN	- 109 -
BETH	- 109 -
CHAPTER FIFTEEN	- 117 -
CHARLIE	- 117 -
CHAPTER SIXTEEN	- 121 -
BETH	- 121 -

CHAPTER SEVENTEEN	CHARLIE	126
CHAPTER EIGHTEEN	BETH	132
CHAPTER NINETEEN	CHARLIE	139
CHAPTER TWENTY	BETH	144
CHAPTER TWENTY-ONE	CHARLIE	151
CHAPTER TWENTY-TWO	BETH	155
CHAPTER TWENTY-THREE	CHARLIE	160
CHAPTER TWENTY-FOUR	BETH	166
CHAPTER TWENTY-FIVE	CHARLIE	172
CHAPTER TWENTY-SIX	BETH	178
CHAPTER TWENTY-SEVEN	CHARLIE	187
CHAPTER TWENTY-EIGHT	BETH	194
CHAPTER TWENTY-NINE	CHARLIE	202
CHAPTER THIRTY	BETH	207
CHAPTER THIRTY-ONE	CHARLIE	213
CHAPTER THIRTY-TWO	BETH	217
CHAPTER THIRTY-THREE	CHARLIE	224
CHAPTER THIRTY-FOUR	BETH	229
CHAPTER THIRTY-FIVE	CHARLIE	235
CHAPTER THIRTY-SIX	BETH	242
CHAPTER THIRTY-SEVEN	CHARLIE	249

Celibet

- CHAPTER THIRTY-EIGHT .... - 253 -
  - BETH .... - 253 -
- CHAPTER THIRTY-NINE .... - 259 -
  - CHARLIE .... - 259 -
- CHAPTER FORTY .... - 264 -
  - BETH .... - 264 -
- CHAPTER FORTY-ONE .... - 269 -
  - CHARLIE .... - 269 -
- CHAPTER FORTY-TWO .... - 275 -
  - BETH .... - 275 -
- CHAPTER FORTY-THREE .... - 281 -
  - CHARLIE .... - 281 -
- CHAPTER FORTY-FOUR .... - 287 -
  - BETH .... - 287 -
- CHAPTER FORTY-FIVE .... - 292 -
  - CHARLIE .... - 292 -
- CHAPTER FORTY-SIX .... - 298 -
  - BETH .... - 298 -
- CHAPTER FORTY-SEVEN .... - 305 -
  - CHARLIE .... - 305 -
- CHAPTER FORTY-EIGHT .... - 310 -
  - BETH .... - 310 -
- CHAPTER FORTY NINE .... - 317 -
  - CHARLIE .... - 317 -
- CHAPTER FIFTY .... - 322 -
  - BETH .... - 322 -
- CHAPTER FIFTY-ONE .... - 330 -
  - CHARLIE .... - 330 -
- CHAPTER FIFTY-TWO .... - 335 -
  - BETH .... - 335 -
- CHAPTER FIFTY-THREE .... - 342 -
  - CHARLIE .... - 342 -
- CHAPTER FIFTY-FOUR .... - 347 -
  - BETH .... - 347 -
- EPILOGUE .... - 353 -
  - CHARLIE .... - 353 -
- PLAYLIST .... - 362 -
- AUTHOR BIO .... - 364 -
- SOCIAL LINKS .... - 366 -
- AUTHOR BIO .... - 367 -
- SOCIAL LINKS .... - 369 -

Acknowledgements

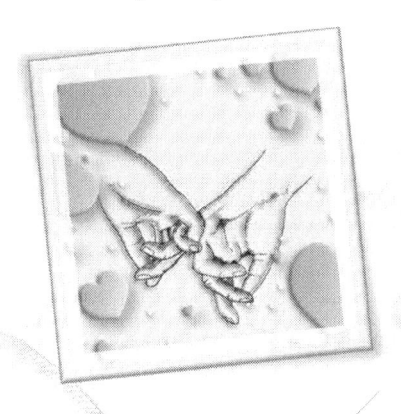

Well, it's that time again...

I was honoured when the lovely Stacy asked me to write a book with her, and once she'd told the premise for the book, I knew I wanted to be a part of it. I knew I needed to make Charlie my own.
Beth and Charlie are such wonderful, fun characters and I'm so happy I got to be a part of their story... thank you so much Stacy for asking me to work with you.

There's so many people that make a special they are like Christmas elves working away in the background polishing it up so without a further ado...

A massive thank you goes out to Eleanor Lloyd-Jones, our editor for making it readable. You're worth your weight in gold. And also for the beautiful cover you designed. You're amazing!

Stacy McWilliams & Sienna Grant

Maria who formatted for us. You really do make the books pretty. Thank you for the time you spend on them.

Also to our very sprint group I don't think we could have got this finished so quickly without your constant support, so thanks guys.

I also want to say a massive thank you to our beta readers and arc readers for taking a chance on us as a duo rather than a single writer. It really does mean a lot. I know this year has been hard on so many people but you and the readers that support us make it a whole lot better. We couldn't make this little a hobby a dream without you guys helping us.

Lastly my family and friends. I love you guys from the bottom of my heart.

I hope you enjoyed Celibet and if you did tell your friends about it. We'd love to hear their feedback.

Much love...
Sienna ♥

To Sienna, thank you for bringing Charlie to life. I never imagined how amazing you'd make him and I'm so, so grateful to you for working with me and not strangling me when I blew things up and changed the direction. You are a star and I can't wait to do it again.

Celibet

To my family, friends and especially my hubs and boys, I love you dearly.

To our readers, thank you so much for believing in me, and in us. Thank you for letting our words into your hearts and sharing this amazing book with your friends. We are truly grateful.

And that's it. Sienna has covered the rest, but thanks again for everything to our arc readers, beta readers, cover designer, editor and formatter. You guys are amazing.

Stacy ♥

Stacy McWilliams & Sienna Grant

Celibet

Blurb

When Beth gets dumped by text, she's more irritated about being left without a ride, than losing her boyfriend of six years. With not feeling the heartbreak you are supposed to feel after a breakup, it tells her all she needs to know about that relationship.

When her best friend and roommate Charlie, returns from Paris, after filming his debut movie, having also been screwed over. Then it's time to get the drinks out.

One drunken night, a scorching kiss later and the Celibet is made.

Can they stay single for twelve weeks?

Will their attraction to each other break their pact, or can they resist temptation?

Stacy McWilliams & Sienna Grant

When fate intervenes and friendship turns into more, who will win the bet?

Chapter One

BETH

It was almost six pm, and I was just about to finish my working day. I was craving a large glass of wine and was looking forward to seeing my boyfriend, Warren, tonight. He was taking me to the OXO tower to celebrate our fifth anniversary.

I was wearing a grey wrap around dress with my brand new, shiny black Louboutin's, and I had my very pretty Marc Jacobs handbag with me.

The last half hour had dragged on, and I was sitting at the reception desk, waiting on the last patient to leave the office so I could close the door and lock up for the doctors.

My mobile chimed with a message as Mrs Smith walked at a snail's pace from the doctor's office. I could hear her slow shuffling footsteps echoing through the empty hallway. I couldn't check it until she was gone. Dr West was so strict about us checking our mobiles while patients were still in the building. An eternity later, or so it felt, she finally approached me to make three appointments: one for herself and two for her son for later in the week.

"And you'll text Gerry to remind him that he has appointments?" she asked me for the sixth time.

I smiled at her. It was now four minutes past six, and she just wouldn't leave. "Yes, Mrs Smith. It's an automated system now and a text will be sent before the appointment to remind Gerry to attend."

She nodded at me and turned to walk away but paused just as I was about to release the breath I was holding.

"You have lipstick on your teeth dear!" She grinned, and her long, grey hair swished behind her as she walked even slower towards the door.

I couldn't even check my teeth because I could tell that Dr West was behind me.

"Bethany, I need you to grab my Dictaphone from my desk and close down my computer."

He didn't wait for my answer, and when I turned back to look at him, he was gone.

I was finally alone.

I picked up my mobile and turned it onto my camera, and sure enough, there was a traitorous smudge on my teeth. I cleaned it off with a tissue and closed the booking system down before turning my PC off for the night. I was so glad it was the weekend, and I couldn't wait for dinner. I was starving.

Celibet

I checked all the examination rooms, shut down his computer and grumbled to myself as I collected his Dictaphone that he could have just brought to me, but not Doctor West. He liked to treat me like a paid servant who was just out to do his bidding. I shook my frustrated thoughts off as I stepped out into the hallway and began to make my way down the corridor, closing and locking each door with the master keys before placing them into the safe.

Eventually, it was time to leave, and I remembered my text as I puzzled over where Warren was parked. I couldn't see his red MG anywhere. The car park was poorly lit, and on a wet December night the ground was slippery. I moved along the pavement slowly, and when I reached the end, I knew his car wasn't there.

Grabbing my mobile, I checked the message from earlier: five fifty-three pm.

Sorry, Beth. I can't do this anymore. We're over.

That was it.

I tried to call him, but after one ring it went straight to answerphone. I couldn't believe it. Dumping me by text was the lowest of the low, and he hadn't even had the decency to answer me.

What a wanker.

I dialled for a cab and fumed as I sat on the low wall that bordered the doctor's surgery as I waited. It was shaded and kept most of the wind off me. After ten chilly minutes, my cab arrived and I climbed into it gratefully, texting my besties as I clipped myself in. Callie was working at Bar C and Marcie was out with her fiancé. I didn't text Charlie because he was currently wining and dining some movie star in Paris, his current squeeze, and I didn't want to ruin his weekend.

I didn't cry—I wasn't a crier—but I was bloody furious.

How dare he?

Part of me wanted to confront him, but another part of me wanted to forget about him and this humiliating day, so I directed the cabbie to take me back to my Notting Hill flat. The drive was half an hour long, and the cabbie chatted nonsense at me, but I wasn't paying that much attention. I knew we had a bottle of wine in the fridge, and I decided to order a takeout since my dinner plans were now ruined.

As I finally arrived home, my mobile went again. It was another text from Warren the Wanker.

Don't call me again. I won't answer. We are over.

I didn't reply. I just changed his name to Wanker and paid my cabbie.

The doorbell went as I poured myself a large glass of red wine, and I jumped, sloshing some on my dress.

"Damn it!" I cursed as I rushed towards the door. The day was shit, and I just wanted it to be over. I quickly paid

Celibet

the Chinese delivery man and shut the door as my neighbour, Bessie, opened her door. She was one of the nosiest people alive, and she knew I was supposed to be going out with the Wanker. I couldn't face the inquisition from her, and I needed to get my favourite dress off, sharpish, if I ever wanted to wear it again, which wouldn't happen if Bessie caught me.

I unwrapped it as I walked through to the sitting room and then I dumped the bag of Chinese onto the coffee table before heading through to the kitchen. I grabbed a pair of sweats and a T-shirt that were mostly dry from the clothes horse and pulled them on as I put the washing machine to the lowest setting and threw my dress inside before closing the door.

I grabbed my glass and a fork before heading back through to the living room and plonked myself on the sofa, taking a sip of my wine and wondering why I wasn't more upset about the fact that my boyfriend had just dumped me.

I really wasn't that bothered about it, and that was what bothered me. I knew I never loved him, not really, but I was just annoyed that he hadn't even had the decency to take me to dinner before he had decided that it was over.

Dumping me by text was a low blow. What a fucking coward!

I picked up my chicken chow Mein and spilled some of the sauce from the container all over my lap, leaping up from the sofa and knocking my wine glass all over our new Laura Ashley cream rug.

Fuck my life.

I rushed into the kitchen and began spraying white wine all over the rug, praying that the mark would come off.

My chow Mein sat forgotten on the floor as I scrubbed at the rug Charlie and had just gone halves on. He was going to murder my clumsy arse—he was going to murder me then bury me in the bloody rug.

Wine, I decided, was not my friend. In fact, wine and I were done for the night. I took my glass into the kitchen and poured myself a large gin. I deserved it. I sat at the dining table in the small kitchen to eat my meal and drink my gin (which turned into multiple gins) and by the time I went to bed, I was merrily drunk.

I didn't hear my mobile go, and I didn't hear the knocking at the door.

I was done with men. Men were all useless, idiotic freeloaders who didn't want you unless you wore a size six and looked like a barbie doll. I wasn't a barbie doll: I had curves and my hair was way too wavy to fit into that category, although it was blonde: a dirty blonde. A darkish, almost brown blonde, and I loved it.

Screw men and their idiotic ideas of perfect. I was happy being a curvaceous size twelve and no man was going to change me. I drifted off to sleep and dreamed of Sam Heughan and kilted men.

When I woke up the next morning, I decided to go visit Scotland on my next holiday. My gran and papa lived in Inverness, and I hadn't been there since I was a little girl, so I looked to see how expensive it would be to get there and texted my dad to ask if it would be okay if I went up for a few days.

Dad was having a hard time since Mum had passed away. She'd only been fifty-six when they'd discovered breast cancer, and she'd just gone into remission when a brain aneurysm took her from us. It was awful we'd just began to feel like she was getting better and then bam, she was gone, just like that. We all missed her terribly, but my dad was lost. He'd retired from his professor's job to care for her and now didn't know what to do to fill his days.

My mobile went and I started at the ring. I took a moment to compose myself because thinking of my mum always made me emotional.

"Hello…"

"Hey girlie, how are you? I can't believe Warren did that to you. What a bloody piece of shit. How could he?"

Callie could go off on one when the mood took her, and by the sound of it, she was going off on one on my behalf.

"I never really thought you guys were any good together. I mean, I had a bet going with Macie that you would have dumped his ass by Christmas, but I never saw him dumping you. You always seemed so happy with him though, but he was a bit smarmy and smug.

She paused, sucking in another breath without letting me speak.

"Beth, why didn't you tell me you weren't getting on? I could totally have been there for you?"

"I would've done, if I'd known …"

She shrieked, and I held the phone away from my ear as she began cussing him out, and after a moment, I wanted to hang up. I didn't want to deal with it. At all!

"Look, Callie, he's a wanker, plain and simple, and he's a coward. He didn't even answer my call last night—"

"Oh my God, are you serious?" She cut me off and went off again, but I wasn't listening, not really, because my dad had just texted back, assuring me that it would be great if I went to Scotland.

He'd never liked Warren, assuming he was only with me because they had money, but it was my parents' money. Not mine. The only thing I'd let them do was to buy me a flat because otherwise, I'd have needed to have left London since the house prices were so high, and I didn't have anywhere else I wanted to live.

I'd come to London from Wells in Somerset seven years ago and had started to study at the London Academy of Music and Dramatic Art. After I finished my degree, I'd had dreams of gracing the Broadway stage or winning something like Britain's Got Talent or X Factor, but I didn't have the drive to succeed, ending up working as a receptionist in a Newham doctors' surgery instead. It wasn't the best job, but it paid my bills and allowed me to retain some of my independence. I did have a trust fund, and money from when my mum died, but I didn't use it. It was all in a separate account, and I kept my card at my dad's house in Kensington.

"Bethany! Are you listening to me?"

Callie's voice broke into my thoughts and I realised I hadn't been paying the slightest bit of attention to her for the last few minutes. Oops. "Sorry, no. I spaced out, but you were going on a bit, Cals."

"Humph," she muttered before starting again. "Well, never mind that. Get dressed. Jay, Lou and I are coming over, and we're going shopping today."

My heart hammered in my chest. I didn't want to go out. I wanted to stay in and hide under my duvet and not think about the real world. "No, Callie. I want to stay home."

"Tough," her tone was firm, and I knew that no matter what I wanted, I was going out.

"We'll be there in half an hour, so get up and get showered or I'm dragging you out, no matter what you look like." She hung up and I sat staring at my phone, wishing a meteor would crash into my room and take me out.

Callie was a nightmare at shopping, and Jay was even worse. I would always, always overspend when I was out with them and end up living on beans on toast for a fortnight after. Maybe, I thought, I should get my dad to transfer me some emergency cash, but then he'd want to pay for everything, and I'd get all stressed out because he never offered Lucy or Connor money.

Lucy, my sister, was a pharmacist who lived in Cornwall with her doctor husband, Phillip. Connor, my big brother, was an engineer, and was married to the gorgeous Maxine. They lived in Dubai with their two gorgeous boys who I missed terribly, but I couldn't afford to go out there more than once a year and Maxine refused to come back to

London. She hated it, so I always had to make the trip out there.

I wished Charlie were home. We could have some fun in town, go shopping and hit a few bars along Regent street. God, I missed my best friend, but he was having a blast in Paris, sleeping with his co-star, the last I'd heard, and filming this movie.

I couldn't wait until it was over, though, and he was home with me. He'd kick off when he heard about what that douchebag had done, but truth be told, Charlie had never liked him much anyway.

Chapter Two

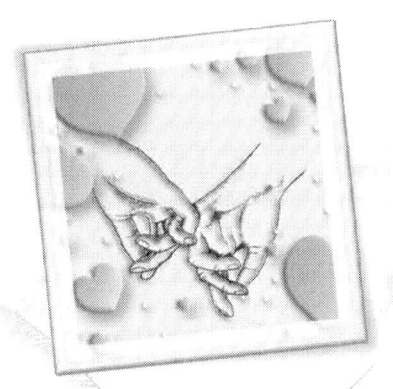

CHARLIE

It was almost time to fly home. Three days, and then I could finally go back to our flat. I missed Beth. Her incessant chatter, cheerfulness and smile made my days better. I hadn't spoken to her in days.

She was my best friend. She was always there when I needed her, and I needed her desperately just now. I'd just found out my girlfriend had been screwing around behind my back, probably had been ever since we'd started going out. Could you call her my girlfriend? I don't even know. My eyes closed as I lay on my hard hotel bed. The events of earlier were swimming around my head as I willed my exhausted body to try and sleep.

Jessie Lewis was an actress, the hottest starlet in Hollywood just now, but she was a stone-cold bitch. I'd come back early from filming after we'd been rained off and caught her in bed with the sound guy.

My heart had dropped, and I'd known I just wanted my own bed and home comforts. She hadn't even apologised. She'd just smirked at me over his shoulder as he plunged into her on my bed. I wanted to beat the fucking shit out of him, but sixty-two hours of filming had exhausted me. I just hadn't got the energy.

"Get out!" I hissed at them, and Jack the sound guy turned to look at me.

"Aww don't be like that darlin'! Come join us!" said Jessie as she grinned and patted the bed beside her.

I stared at them wide-eyed and shook my head. "No. No way. I don't need this shit. Get the fuck out of my room, now."

Jessie laughed and rolled away from Jack. He stood and gathered his clothes from the floor, but Jessie just sauntered towards me, ignoring him.

"Come on darlin'. It's just sex. I'm not built to be faithful." She ran her finger down my cheek while rubbing her tits against me. "Life is too short."

I wanted to strangle her, but I kept my cool and stepped back. My back hit the dresser as I'd held up my hand to stop her from coming any closer. "Stop. Stop Jessie! Just go." My teeth clamped together as I hissed again. "And if you wanted to fuck behind my back why didn't you use your own fucking room?"

"Because sweetheart, I thought we shared this room."

"Well, sweetheart... not any fucking more. Now leave!"

Jack walked over and tugged on Jessie's arm, but she shook him off and her eyes stayed trained on me.

"Are you sure darlin'?" She winked with a smirk plastered to her face. Her Texan accent became more pronounced as she spoke, and I nodded once.

"Yep. I'm sure." I kept my voice low; I knew it sounded more lethal than anything, and Jack the prick hadn't got the balls to say anything to me. I may have been exhausted, but if he said anything at all, I'd find the energy to put his fucking head through the wall if need be. This way was better.

Her eyes widened and she stepped back, watching me quizzically as she picked up her robe from the floor, tying it around her waist and not quite believing that I, had just turned down a threesome with the mighty Jessie Lewis. Well get over it sweetheart!

"Your loss. Don't come crawling back. As soon as I leave this room, we're over."

"Good. Get the fuck out." I didn't look at them as she and Jack started to leave the room, but I couldn't

leave it there either, "Oh, and it's your loss Jessie, not mine."

As soon as they were gone, I walked towards the bathroom and stripped off. My jeans stuck to my legs and my socks were soaked through. Playing a demon in a movie with Jessie as the heroine was fun and all, but it was bloody freezing, and I was so over her fucking prima donna drama.

I hadn't actually cared that she'd been cheating on me. I had been too tired to give a shit about anything other than the hot water that had run down my back as I stood in the shower once they'd left.

I'd grabbed five hours of sleep on set earlier, but it hadn't been enough. I was exhausted. The days had been so long.

As I ran my fingers through my hair, pushing it back out of my face, I thought about Beth. I missed her and I wanted to call her, but I knew she'd be out with her dickhead of a boyfriend. I really hated him. It made me wonder what she actually saw in him. He was a total douche and a user, but she was stubborn and refused to see the bad in people. It made me angry. I was her friend, one of her best friends, and I wanted to look out for her.

Tucking my hands behind my head, my body finally relaxed into the mattress. All the tension from earlier started to lift as I thought of home. I missed it so much.

Being on set was good and all, but nothing could beat your own bed, and after what had happened tonight, I couldn't wait to get back there. As I closed my eyes, all that was there in my mind was the vision of Beth running around the flat we shared. We'd laugh as we watched Friends on the sofa, and she'd make me laugh at her clumsy-arse behaviour. I don't think I'd ever met a woman as clumsy as she was.

Finally, I began to fall asleep in a much happier place.

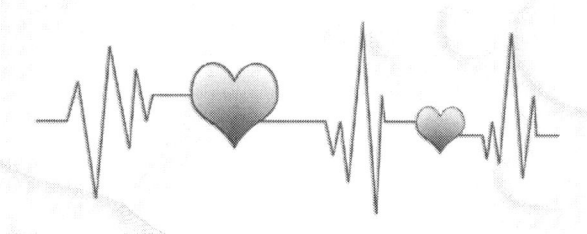

As soon as I opened my eyes the next morning, everything came flooding back like a tidal wave washing over me. Maybe I'd made a mistake not placating Jessie—maybe I should've gone and found her to tell her I was sorry… Ugh.

I sighed out loud.

No. She would have walked all over me and acted like I was the one that was in the wrong. Not a fucking chance. But then, what if she spread shit around set about me? One word from her and I may never work again.

I rolled out of bed and clicked the switch for the kettle, making myself a coffee—a much-needed coffee. I hadn't slept great. It had come in fits and starts. First, I was thinking about going home and seeing my best friend finally, after weeks on end, and then Jessie would pop her smug fucking face up. It was like a dream that suddenly turned into some kind of thriller. I'd felt like I was being tugged from pillar to post, and I'd had no idea what to do about it. She had suddenly turned into the zombie we'd been filming earlier that day, only uglier.

Taking that first sip was like standing in the first downpour of rain after a heatwave: nice and refreshing and somewhat awakening. It wasn't long before I was halfway down the mug when I realised that I hadn't looked at my phone since I'd gotten into bed last night. I plucked it from my pocket and sitting right there on my screen was a missed call from Beth.

"Fuck," I said to the empty room.

I sat on the bed and with my back against the wall and, holding my mug in one hand, pulled up Bethany's number from my contacts, clicking the green button.

I hoped she hadn't called me for anything really important because I'd feel like a right dick for missing it.

I held my cup against my bottom lip as it rang out at her end, and finally hearing her answerphone message, I gave up and hung up. It couldn't have been too important, but if I were being honest with myself, I just wanted to hear her voice.

Fuck, why was I being such a female?

Gulping down the rest of my coffee, I set the mug on the bedside table and stood, grabbing my suitcase from beneath the bed, throwing some of my clothes into it. We only had a couple days left of filming at the most anyway,

Celibet

so decided I may as well start packing. By the time the movie was over, so would my career be if Jessie Lewis had anything to do with it. She'd hang me out by the balls just to make herself look good, but she needed to look out: I wouldn't be leaving without a well-earned scrap, and if Jack, the saggy ball sack, had anything to say to me, he'd be munching on the concrete floor while he searched for his teeth.

I pulled back one of the curtains and saw the rain had finally stopped and that the sun was shining. The skies were a powdery blue, and it lifted my spirits a little. I pushed away the niggling doubt I'd had when I'd first woken up. I was a positive person and there was no way I would let her knock that. I wasn't going to let Jessie drag my name through the mud; I'd done nothing wrong.

I took my light blue jeans from the wardrobe, pulling them up my legs and fastening them up before putting a white T-shirt on. While I'd been here, I'd managed to get a tan, between filming and of course rolling around in the sheets with Jessie. The colour of my arms stood out against the white cotton material, and I styled my dark hair with some wax.

Once I'd sprayed my body with Lynx body spray and applied some of my favourite Boss aftershave to my face,

I was ready to face the world and the diva that was Jessie Lewis.

Chapter Three

BETH

Forty minutes after the phone call, my buzzer went, and I let Lou, Callie, and Jay into my flat.

"Are you not ready yet?" Callie asked as they walked into the flat and sat down.

"Nope," I muttered, leaving the room, and wandered back into my bedroom to finish blow-drying my hair. I didn't want to go, but now that they were in my flat, I was a little more excited.

"Beth, come on," Callie wailed from the couch, and I rolled my eyes at my gorgeous, exotic friend. With her gorgeous, dark skin tone, sky blue eyes and beaded hair, she was always the first ready, and no matter how hard I tried, I could never quite reach her level of sophistication.

A few minutes later, I was putting on my lipstick before grabbing my clutch, checking to see if my cards were in it and walking into the sitting room, where I walked smack bang into the wall, bursting my nose and groaning as liquid squirted from my nose all over the white walls of the flat.

Now Charlie was really going to laugh at me. I'd spent hours painting tiny flowers onto the wall in the hall as Charlie had stood behind me and laughed, pointing out the flaws, but they were cute and quirky, just like me, and now they were covered in blood. I quickly leaned forward and held the bridge of my nose as I moved along the hall to the bathroom, ignoring the drip, drip, drip of blood as I walked. I waited for the tsunami of blood to stop pouring and then cleaned myself up, rolling my eyes as I saw my white, eyelet lace top was covered in what looked like a murder victim's blood. I peeled it off and winced as I saw my gorgeous Victoria Secret bra was pink when it should have been white.

Seriously, I was so over this shit.

I rushed back into my bedroom, stripped my bra off and pulled on another one followed by a pale pink cashmere wrap around top, as Callie came into the room.

"Jesus, look at your face."

I glanced in the mirror and saw my cleaning job hadn't been that good: I had dried flecks of blood on my cheeks, my lips, and my chin.

"You look like a bloody vampire. I take it that's your blood trailing along the hall?"

Celibet

"No. I decided to sacrifice a small goat this morning. Guess I forgot to clean it up." I set about cleaning up my face with a baby wipe, and Callie rolled her eyes, muttering under her breath.

"Oh, hardy har har. You're so funny, Beth, but can we get a move on please?"

"Fine, fine, let's go."

We left the apartment and walked to the train station, laughing, and joking along the way.

The shopping trip did wonders for my mood but wasn't kind to my bank account or my credit cards. It was so much fun, though, and I splurged on a Donna Karen dress that was a deep pink and ruffled down the front, a pair of Kurt Geiger heels and some gorgeous underwear. We grabbed McDonalds for lunch, but all decided that we would go out for dinner.

Jay booked at table at The Ledbury, and we laughed and joked as we made our way towards it. Her current squeeze was the maître 'd, and he gave us a great table. The food was simply divine, and I didn't even regret the pasta, garlic bread, mushroom starter, and chocolate mousse cheesecake that I ate, nor the copious amounts of very expensive wine I drank. The company was excellent, and we were all tipsy by the time the bill came. It was a rather expensive dinner, but it was worth it.

I handed over my card for the waiter to take my share of the bill—one hundred and forty-seven pounds to be exact—but he tried my card and then shook his head. I couldn't understand why my card wasn't working, and my face began to heat in mortification. I didn't have enough left on either of my credit cards to cover the food since I'd put my shopping purchases on them, but I knew I should have had enough money in my account to cover me.

I ducked into the bathroom to check my online banking and almost dropped my phone in surprise when I saw that my two thousand, two-hundred-pound bank balance had somehow been depleted and that there was only seventy-four pounds and twenty-two pence in my account. My mouth went dry and my head hammered as I tried to work out where my money had gone. I knew my friends couldn't cover me, so I swallowed my pride and called my dad.

As the ringing happened, I re-checked my bank balance and saw that it was down to fifty-nine pounds and thirty pence, but I hadn't bought a thing.

"HELLOO!" my dad yelled, and my phone slipped from my shaking fingers, bouncing along the tiled floor as my dad called out again.

"Hello, Bethany, can you hear me?"

I crawled along the floor and scooped it up, putting it to my ear and wincing as my fingers caught on my earing.

"Hi, Dad. I can hear you. No need to yell!"

He chuckled and on hearing his voice I wanted to cry.

"Dad, I need… I'm sorry… but can I… can you…"

"Bethany, what's wrong darling?" His words almost broke me, and I could feel the tell-tale burning in my throat as I tried to speak.

"Dad, my money is missing. I… I had a few thousand in my account to cover bills and stuff, but it's gone and I don't know where and I'm out for dinner and I can't pay

Celibet

because I've maxed out my credit cards and my trust fund card is at yours and I'm so embarrassed."

My dad didn't speak, but I could hear sounds as I spoke in a rush, mortified at having to ask my him to help me out but also mortified to be sitting on a bathroom floor, almost crying, because I couldn't pay for lunch.

"Okay, send me your bank details and I'll send you some cash, but call your bank and stop any transactions after you pay for lunch, then you can work out where your money is going."

"Thanks, Dad. I'm so sorry to have asked."

He sighed, and I could just picture his face as he sat at his writing desk, running his fingers through his hair with his grey eyes and knowing smile. My heart ached and I knew I needed to go see him soon because I missed him. My mum's birthday was coming up and I wanted to spend some time with him, so I'd taken a week's holiday to go to Kensington and see him, but it wasn't for another few weeks yet.

"Don't ever apologise for asking for help. That's what I'm here for. Now, send your details so you can pay your bill and then get on to your bank and find out who's spending your cash."

"Okay, I will. Thanks again, Dad. I'll call you tonight. Love you."

"You too. Speak to you then."

I quickly typed out my details and within minutes my dad sent me a text back saying the money was in my account. I quickly checked and rolled my eyes when I saw he had sent me five thousand pounds. However, my balance was only four thousand, eight hundred, and I hadn't done a thing. I quickly went out and paid my part of the bill, ignoring the questioning glances from my friends as I paid with the same card. Then, while they were packing up and finishing their drinks, I stepped outside and called my bank, stopping all transactions and explaining what had just happened. Within moments, I was transferred to the fraud team. The lady was lovely. She cancelled my card and put an agent onto my account to trace what had been happening with my cash, advising me that I'd hear back in a few days.

After that, my mood wasn't great, so while my friends all went out—even though they tried to talk me into it and basically said I was no fun when I declined—I made my way back on the train, thankful for my return ticket. I wasn't in the mood: I was pissed off and stressed out and had a headache forming. I was grateful to my dad for bailing me out. I knew I had my own money and Warren had despaired that I wouldn't spend it. I refused to live on someone else's dime. I was independent, strong and I didn't want to make my way in the world by relying on money that was only mine because my mum had come from a well-off family.

My dad was a working man, and he'd instilled that in me. Hard work, dedication and honesty would serve me much better than a couple of million in my bank.

I arrived home and checked to see if Charlie had text me, but there was nothing.

Celibet

I missed his special brand of craziness, and I picked up my phone, dialling his number and hoping to catch him between takes, but it just rang out. I set my phone down on the coffee table and sat morosely, missing him so much. If he'd been here, he'd have kicked my arse and made me go out or do something, but instead I sat alone, drinking a diet coke, and wishing my best friend would somehow magically appear and make me feel better.

I didn't envy his time away, though. He deserved it. In fact, nobody deserved a break more than him. He always worked so hard and tried to make sure we were all okay. He was our glue, and without him we were all loose flags, flapping in the wind.

Bored and irritated, I decided to watch an episode of Outlander and get lost in seventeenth century Scotland. I loved the costumes and the accents and the story (nothing to do with the tall, red-headed Scottish man who played the lead male... honest).

Three episodes later, I climbed into bed, my head buzzing as I pictured what it must have been like in those days without power, running water or roads. Jerking about on horseback was not my idea of fun, and as I closed my eyes, I pictured Sam riding along and decided that if I 'd been able to ride on horseback with him I wouldn't say no.

Chapter Four

CHARLIE

Everyone was just sitting around when I arrived on set just after ten. Grabbing myself a takeaway coffee from the big steel urn, I stirred some sugar into it and walked over to the others, saying hi. Nothing was said about Jessie, and when I looked around, I couldn't see her anywhere. While we waited for the diva to turn up, I decided to have a walk outside and take in the warmth of the Paris sunshine.

My head leaned back on the brick, and I closed my eyes, but my peace was soon shattered when I heard Jessie make her usual big entrance. The chatter got louder, and I could hear the director clapping his hands, probably to get the set's attention. When I heard my name mentioned, I thought maybe I should go in, too.

Celibet

"Ah Charlie, there you are. In position please." He clapped his hands again, right in front of my face, while wearing a stupid grin. I swore to God I was going to shove those hands right up his arse...

"We're going to re-shoot the scene from yesterday and take it from there."

Great...

I nodded and drank the rest of my piss-poor coffee, which almost scarred the back of my throat, and threw the cup into the bin.

Jessie sat in the corner with Jack as I got in position and did my re-shoot like the director had asked. Every time my eyes met with hers, she smirked and put her hands all over Jack. It was going to be one long-arsed day, especially when I knew my next shoot was with her.

Her antics didn't go unnoticed, though. The makeup and the wardrobe staff made a point of pretending they couldn't see what she was up to but still turned to me and gave me a look of sympathy. It was no secret that Jessie and I had been screwing, she didn't keep anything a secret, but I wished I'd had the common sense to turn her down in the first place.

Who am I kidding? And who in their right state of mind turned Jessie Lewis down? Maybe me and my big mouth. My plans to be the man in all this had fucked me over.

I needed to talk to Beth. She'd listen to my ramblings. She probably wouldn't advise me to walk away, though, since she was always getting walked all over by Warren the wankstain.

The lights around us shone brightly, and I sat in the chair while one of the girls did my makeup, sweeping the highlighter brush over my forehead and cheeks, and within minutes, I was done and up and out of the chair.

The director called 'ACTION', and I jumped into character.

It took two hours to re-do that shoot from yesterday, and I was sweating my arse off. I stripped the heavy costume from my body and got into the next one for my shoot with Jessie. The hair stylist sat me in front of a desk fan to cool me down for a few minutes and touched up my hair and makeup. At least the next costume meant me being bare-chested and I could stay in my jeans for it.

Jessie glared at me through narrowed eyes as she stood in front of me, but it didn't take her long to step into character as she slid her body up against mine. Her hand rested against my skin, and she pushed her face into mine and whispered, "You know you want me."

"How about we get this shoot over and done with," I snarled at her.

Her hand burned through my skin for different reasons. I didn't want them on me anymore—not like I had before anyway. There was nothing I'd loved more than having her slide her hands all over me, but now, all I saw was her doing the same to that ball sack. And how fucking long had she been shagging him? That was what I really wanted to know. Had it been a one off, or had she been shagging us both between shoots? That was probably why she'd wanted the threesome: so, she could have the best of both worlds.

Celibet

"CUT!" the director balled from the side-lines. "I don't know what's going with you two, but you'd better sort it out. Where's the chemistry gone, guys?"

What was I supposed to say? 'Oh sorry, but I caught her shagging the sound guy last night so it knocked me a little off kilter because all I really want to do is tell the main star of the whole movie what dirty little slut she is.'

I didn't think it would go down well, so instead, I stayed quiet and let him carry on.

"Go take a break and come back in fifteen minutes, and you better have your shit sorted or I'll be replacing you both."

I grabbed my T-shirt and pulled it over my head as I stepped outside. I leaned against the wall at the back of the same building as earlier and hid for five minutes. I didn't need Jessie coming to find me—I just wasn't in the mood for it. I took my phone out of my pocket and saw another missed call from Beth.

Knowing I had ten minutes to spare, I rang her back again, but after four or five rings, it went through to the answerphone again. We were just not getting a break. I decided to give up until I was done with filming and I'd ring her then. Once I pulled my big boy pants up and sucked in a deep breath, I went back inside and prepared to get this shoot finished.

The sooner it was done, the quicker I could get back home to London.

As I turned the corner, I came face to face with Jessie.

"You know, Charlie, the green-eyed monster isn't a good look on you."

"Jessie, I'm not one for big confrontations, and I've said nothing so far, but it was you who cheated on me... Or did you forget that?"

With her hand on her chest, she threw her head back and laughed. "Oh Charlie... Darlin', this is the movies: no one's faithful. Please don't tell me you thought this would go any further after filming got done?"

I felt my nostrils flare as she tried to ridicule me. She stepped up closer and pinched my chin between her finger and thumb, putting her cheek against mine. "I will miss you, though. You were the best so far..."

My head snapped to the side, and I made her loosen her hold on me. "Why don't we get this finished then me and you can pretend like nothing happened, and once there're thousands of miles between us, it'll be so much easier to forget I had ever met you." My body was wound up tighter than a coiled spring, and all I wanted to do was hit something. It wasn't like I was even sad, but I was still hurt catching them like that—in my fucking bed, too. The worst part of all this was how many people had been laughing at me.

Probably the whole fucking set.
Fuck it!

With renewed determination, I vowed to finish the filming. I was an actor after all: I could play a part and I would play it fucking well. Then, if she wanted to ruin my career, she could bring it fucking on.

Celibet

Four hours later, the scene was done. I had one more scene left for the following day and then I was heading back to London. Some of the guys were trying to plan a night out in Paris, but I wouldn't be there. I wanted to be fresh as a daisy for the last day of filming then I'd be getting my flight later that night.

I grabbed my T-shirt and pulled it back on, and once I'd said 'goodnight' to the others, I started towards my digs. A hand on my shoulder stopped me from going any further, and I spun around on my heel. I was surprised to see Jack in front of me.

Do these two not think I've had enough shit for today.

"Ha!" I couldn't hold in the laugh that burst from me. "What do you want, Jack? I'm warning you, I'm not in the fucking mood. I'm tired."

He held his hands up in front of him and took a step back—a very wise idea if you'd asked me. "Look, all I wanted to say was don't be too hard on Jessie: it was me that prompted it."

"Then I should fucking smash your face in for making me look a dick, is that what you're saying?" My fists balled so tightly at my sides; I felt my short fingernails digging into my skin.

"Woah. No. N... not at all." He stuttered like the piece of shit he is.

"Do yourself a favour and walk away, Jack. You've done what you aimed to do. This conversation is over." I didn't take my eyes from him—at least not until he started backing away from me. Only then did I turn around and return to my room where I packed up the rest of my shit and willed the next twenty hours or so to hurry up so I could get the fuck out of there.

Chapter Five

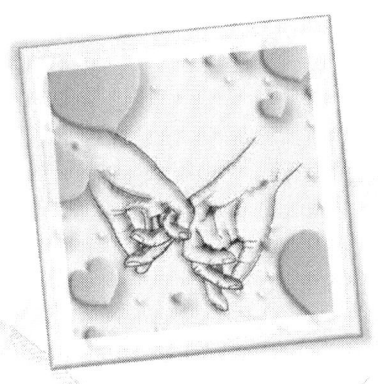

BETH

Monday morning dawned bright and clear, and my alarm went off at six am. I was on the eight till four shift this week, which meant I was to be at the practice to open up the surgery rather than be there to close it down. I didn't want to get up, but I knew I had to.

I had to work, and I had to pay my dad back for his help over the weekend. I just hoped my new bank card would arrive soon because I had a grand total of forty pounds in my purse and I had very little food in. I hadn't planned to be in all weekend, and since Charlie was still in Paris, we hadn't shopped.

I grabbed a quick shower and got dressed before rushing out to get the train to work, forgetting my purse, which in turn meant I'd be starving by the time I got home because I'd planned to pop into Greggs to get a sandwich on my lunch. I just hoped there was still some cake leftover, or I'd have nothing to eat until half five.

My stomach was growling at me, and I checked my handbag again—a black Primark one this time—feeling like I'd won the lottery when I found two pounds and fifty pence in there. I scuttled out to the local Sainsbury's and picked up a tuna mayo sandwich, a glazed donut, and a packet of crisps, which left me with a total of ten pence. I was thirsty, but I could drink the water at the surgery and have a coffee in the break room.

Brenda was manning the reception desk and she nodded at me. I put my stuff away and came back out to make sure they didn't need me before I had my tea break. It was only half nine and our breaks didn't usually start until ten.

"Hey, do you need anything?" I asked Marg as she sat typing furiously on the computer. She shook her head at me, waving me away. Brenda however walked back towards us and I stifled an eye roll. She hated being on reception. She didn't mind taking calls, but she hated dealing with the public.

"Be a lamb and mind the desk for a bit?"

I didn't ever argue with her, even though she'd just started for the day. Marg had been on reception while I popped out to the shops and I was hoping I could take my tea break, but Brenda always had to go first, even though she didn't start till half eight and I'd been there first.

I walked to the desk and my stomach dropped because of who was standing at the desk: none other than Warren's

Celibet

mother. She had her back to me and was chatting with another of our patients, Mrs Grant.

"Yeah, we all knew it wasn't going to last. I mean, he's going through his master's in computing and she's just a receptionist. Plus, she's not his type. His type is model thin and she's fat and unattractive."

Mrs Grant looked at me, and I could feel my face heating. I wished the ground would open up and swallow me whole, but it didn't happen.

"And you know what the worst thing is?" She paused for dramatic effect, and I could feel everyone's eyes on me at this point. "She was a stone-cold bitch. He asked to move in with her and she said no. Even though she knew he was studying and even though she knew he needed to concentrate on his studies, she wouldn't let him stay with her..."

Yep, that's right. I'd turned down his request to come and live with me—rent free, I might add—and that made me a bitch because he didn't want to pay his way. He wanted to freeload off me and Charlie, and I'd refused to let that happen.

"Ahem." I cleared my throat refusing to be intimidated, and she turned to me.

"Oh, hello." Her tone was frosty, but her smile was wide. "I have an appointment with Dr Finchley at ten."

I didn't care that she didn't like me, but I refused to be made a fool of in my place of work. "Okay, that's fine. Take a seat."

She glared at me and walked away, leaving a cloud of Chanel No.5 in her wake. My face was hot at hearing her berate me, but I decided to just let it go. Part of me wanted to tell her that Warren had been too lazy to go to classes and hadn't been going to Uni for a few months, but I knew it wouldn't achieve anything. It would make me as petty as her, and I couldn't be bothered with the drama. She wasn't worth my time or the effort, but it was easier said than done, since she was now calling me frigid and telling Mrs Grant and a few others in the reception area that I was self-conscious about my weight and that I was a huge turn-off for her son.

"Her body jiggles. Almost put me off my lunch when we all went to the beach in Dorset for the day. I couldn't believe how much she wobbled in the middle."

I could feel my eyes burning as memories of that trip came to mind. Warren had convinced me that we were going on a romantic day out, so I'd fuelled up his car and we'd driven to Dorset to spend time at the beach, but when we'd arrived at the hotel it became clear that we were to be staying with his parents and his siblings were all there.

We'd booked the Hilton on the beachfront for the night, and I had been looking forward to a night away with my boyfriend, but instead it was him and his whole family.

It had been dreadful. His mother had expected to be treated like a queen, his father had drunk more than anyone I'd ever met and became more and more unpleasant and Warren's siblings had argued and squabbled the whole weekend.

Celibet

I'd paid most of the money for the break and it was awful having his mum glare at me when I appeared in my bright blue bikini with my sarong around my waist. Her eyes had narrowed when I'd refused to pay for more than my own drink, and Warren had glared at me when I told him I wasn't paying for dinner for his family.

The rest of the day had been uncomfortable, and I'd ended up faking a migraine to escape him and his family.

The noise of the desk phone made me jump, and I started, picking it up as the whole waiting room turned to stare at me. I quickly dropped my eyes and caught a glimpse of my reflection. My face was beet red as I scrambled to pick up the phone, dropping it twice on the desk before I managed to get a hold of it and brought it to my ear.

Dr Finchley's voice barked down the line. "Send my next patient in! Where have you been for the last five minutes while I've been buzzing the desk?"

"Sorry, Dr Finchley. I was miles away." My voice was low, and I knew I was going to get a telling off. Evan Finchley hated tardiness and had a low tolerance for bullshit.

"Well, if you would like to keep your job then perhaps you could focus on it, rather than being miles away."

The line buzzed in my ear and I replaced the receiver, checking the system to make sure I called the correct person through Mrs Graham. Great. Just great. It was Betty the Bitch.

"Mrs... Um... Mrs Graham!" I called, my voice wobbling as everyone turned to look at me.

"Yes?" she spat at me and then her eyes widened maliciously.

"The doctor will see you now." I watched as she stood and sauntered towards me, smirking with an evil glint in her eyes.

"You know your bra is showing, dear! I'd maybe wear something a bit more appropriate for work." Her voice carried across the waiting room, and every eye was on me at this point.

I glanced down, horrified, and sure enough my pearl buttons had popped open. It must have happened when I was scrambling about for the desk phone. My red, lacy bra was on show for the world to see. My cheeks got even hotter, and I quickly set about buttoning my blouse and pulled my cardigan on as Betty the Bitch walked away, smug as you like.

The next half hour dragged on as I waited for Brenda to get back from her break. She always took liberties, but because one of the doctors was her brother-in-law, she always got away with it.

Just as she returned from her lunch, Dr Finchley appeared and beckoned to me to follow him. He was an old dragon, and he had a real dislike for me.

"Bethany, I've had a few complaints from patients about you showing your bra off today. I really don't think that it's appropriate, do you?

I knew exactly who'd complained, and I wondered if my face would ever return to the pale colour it normally was or if it would stay permanently bright red and blotchy.

Celibet

"I'm so sorry," I muttered quietly, and Dr Finchley glared at me without speaking, so I continued. "It was an accident. My blouse popped open and I didn't realise. It won't happen again."

"See that it doesn't. Now get back to work!"

I stood and rushed towards the door, gripping the handle, but turned to face his computer and spoke again at me over his shoulder,

"And Bethany…"

"Yes, Doctor?" I turned back and he glared at me again.

"Watch your attitude with our patients. I shall be writing you up a formal warning this afternoon as a few of the patients did not appreciate the manner in which you spoke to them while on the reception desk. You are the face of this surgery, and if you cannot conduct yourself in an appropriate manner then I'm afraid we shall have to let you go."

"Okay, sir," I muttered, with my eyes full of tears.

I hadn't said a word, even though that old bat had been goading me, and now I was getting a written warning for nothing. I wanted to tell him to shove his job, but I really liked it normally and got on famously with the staff—the two other doctors in the surgery were lovely. Dr Morgens and Dr Little were both amazing and the nurse on staff. Suzie was hilarious—but the two older doctors were old school. Although only Dr Finchley was a director of the practice, both he and Dr West were awful to work with.

I scurried out of the office and rushed to the loo to wipe away the tears that had leaked from my eyes. I stood for a moment, breathing in and out, trying to calm myself down, but my hands were shaking, and I was mortified about earlier. I left the bathroom to see Betty the Bitch still sitting in the waiting room, and she grinned maliciously at me.

"You are nothing, but a jumped-up little tart, and I hope that the doctor took you down a peg or two."

I ignored her—or at least I tried to—but she followed me to the door of the reception area.

"My son could always do better than you, you little trollop."

I let the door shut on her face and leaned against it, shaking. Marg, who'd heard the commotion, came straight over to me, and gave me a hug, causing me to burst into tears against her rather large chest.

"There, there pet. Don't let her get to you."

I nodded and she patted me on the back before stepping back.

"Why don't you get off for your break?"

I gave a weak smile as I stepped around her, heading for the breakroom at the back of the office. I sat down after I made myself a cup of coffee, and just as I lifted the cup to my lips, Dr Finchley came in with a face like thunder.

"Did you close the door in one of our patients faces?"

His face was ruddy, and spit was flying everywhere. His furious gaze had me pinned to the chair as Doctor Morgens walked into the break room.

"How dare you? You cannot go around treating patients that way. Never mind the warning, you're fired. Get your stuff and get out."

Celibet

My body was frozen to the chair and I couldn't move. My eyes were still bright red, and my nose was blotchy or at least that was how I looked in the mirror over the sink. Dr Morgens stepped in front of me and turned to face Dr Finchley.

"Evan, hold on. You don't get to fire someone without hearing their side of the story…"

"Come on, Liz. You cannot be serious. She cannot treat our patients like that and expect to get away with it. It's appalling."

"And do you know why she did that? She has worked here for over two years and we've never had a complaint about her from a patient, yet today, the same patient has made three separate complaints about her. I just think we should get her side of the story before we fire her."

Dr Morgens turned to face me and came over to sit beside me. "Beth, what's going on?"

Her tone was gentle and her gaze kind, so I looked at her and promptly burst into tears again.

"Oh, for goodness sake," Dr Finchley exclaimed behind her, but Dr Morgens didn't move. She sat and waited for me to get control of myself.

"The lady complaining about me is my… my ex's mother. She's been horrible to me since she arrived here this morning, saying that I'm fat and useless and making snide remarks about me…"

Marg walked in as I was speaking and cut me off. "Yeah, I heard her. She was following Beth back from the loos saying she was a trollop. In all my days, I have ever heard a patient speak to one of us like that."

Dr Finchley swallowed and turned away from me. "Is that true, Bethany? Why would she behave like that towards you?"

I nodded and tried to swallow, but there was a lump the size of a golf-ball in my throat.

Dr Morgens turned to face Dr Finchley and I took a few deep breaths.

"See, Evan, sometimes you need to ask questions and not just assume guilt. Beth, why don't you take the rest of the day off and come back tomorrow. You can't possibly work in this state."

Dr Finchley glared at her, but she held her ground, and as the other partner in the practice, he knew when he was beat. "Yes. Good idea. Let's leave this sordid mess behind us, but Beth, try not to bring your personal life to our practice again or you will be fired." With that, he spun and left the room, and I released the breath I was holding.

Dr Morgens squeezed my arm gently and then stepped towards the percolator. She poured herself a coffee and picked up two chocolate biscuits before walking to the doorway. "Beth, go home and relax and don't let him scare you. You'll have a job here as long as you want one."

Chapter Six

CHARLIE

"Cut!" the director called. "And that's a rap!"

Thank God that was over and I wouldn't have to cross paths ever again with Jessie Lewis. I gathered my things into my arms and was all set to walk away. A couple of the guys had stopped on their way past me to congratulate me on a great ending scene after I'd saved the world from a zombie apocalypse. Not my type of film, but hey, you have to take what's available at the time. I'd needed the money, and it had meant I got to work with Jessie Lewis. Yeah, if I had known then what I knew now, I'd have said hell fucking no.

I shook the director's hand and thanked him for putting up with me for the last few weeks, making my way through the makeshift set. Before I had even got out of the door, a small hand caught a hold of my arm, stopping me. I looked back over my shoulder and caught her dark hair swishing around her.

"What do you want Jessie? I have to get going." I turned slowly and waited for her to say what she needed to say.

"Were you going to leave without saying goodbye?" She placed her hands on her hips and cocked her head to the side as she looked up at me.

"I was hoping to." I shrugged, not really caring if I hurt her feelings or not. She hadn't spared mine when she had shagged ball sack in my bed.

"After the time we spent together... I thought you'd care more than that."

"Are you actually fucking crazy?" I shook my head, not quite believing what I was hearing. "You know, I'm glad I got to meet the real Jessie Lewis 'cause now I can go home and forget you ever existed." I bent over her and kissed her cheek. "Thanks for teaching me that film stars are nothing but sluts." A smirk formed on my mouth as I watched her mouth drop with a shocked O. "See ya 'round." I turned back around and left.

As soon as I walked into my bedsit, I threw the remainder of my things in my case and rang a cab, moving around the small box room, gathering up the things I could put in my flight bag and leaving things like toiletries as we had those at home. I threw the key on the side, lifted my large rucksack onto my shoulder and walked out.

Once I'd checked in at Charles De Gaulle airport, I took the elevator up to the departure lounge and strolled

Celibet

through duty free. As I was browsing, I stumbled across Beth's favourite perfume. I should know it: she'd practically choked me with once, she had sprayed that much of it. I picked up the 100ml box of Daisy by Marc Jacobs and passed it over to the assistant, smiling. She wrapped it in some paper and tied a ribbon around it before putting it into a bag. Once I had paid, I thanked her and went over to the alcohol. I grabbed a bottle of scotch, a bottle of pink gin and some vodka to take back with me then took a seat in the departure lounge, waiting for my flight to be called.

I was more than ready to get on that plane. I decided to get my phone out and try Beth again. The sound of the beeps down my ear, though, told me she was on the phone this time…

What the fuck, Beth. Get off the fucking phone.

When I couldn't get a hold of my flat mate, I decided to text my mum. It had been a while since I'd called her. She had made me promise I'd only text her when I came to France.

"Don't waste your credit on me, dear. As long as I know you're safe."

Yeah, I rolled my eyes, too. I loved her, but she was a worrier. She'd worried when I said I was moving out. She'd worried when I said I was going to become an actor and then she'd panicked even more when I'd said I was coming to Paris to shoot a film.

Opening my messages, I pulled up her number.

Should be boarding the plane soon, Mum. Will ring you in the morning. Love you.

I had thought about just texting Beth, at least then we wouldn't have kept missing each other. As I was pondering, I heard the 'bing bongs' overhead and listened for my flight but they never mentioned it. I looked at my watch, knowing I should get called soon and then sat back in the chair with a sigh. Someone who was sitting in the same line of chairs as me began to moan about his flight being delayed, and not wanting to be nosy, I got up and walked towards the monitors. Right there in HD colour was my flight: **DELAYED**.

Fucking great!

I'd turned around, huffing my frustrations as I walked back to my chair and sank into it. God knows how much longer I was going to have to wait.

Plucking my phone back out of my pocket, I pulled up Beth's number telling her my flight had been delayed. All I wanted to do was go home and get some proper sleep in a decent bed.

A few hours later, my flight was called.

Thank fuck for that. That's it I'm not going anywhere else for a while.

I had enough money sitting in the bank to get me by for at least a couple of months. I had, had my fucking fill of travelling and planes and shit. I got my passport from the front pocket of my rucksack, gathered my bags, and joined the queue for passport control.

Once I was on the plane, I found my seat, lodged my bags in the overhead compartment and pulled my Air Pods from my pocket. My eyes were closed before we had even taken off, and all I got was the muffled sound of the pilot's voice as he told us which route that he would be taking back to Heathrow.

I didn't give a shit which route he took, I just wanted to get home.

Chapter Seven

BETH

Twenty minutes after being dismissed from work, I was on the train, munching on my tuna sandwich as I sat in the window seat watching the world go by. The train was quiet since it was only just two in the afternoon, but there were a few pensioners and some shoppers dotted about. I glanced around and continued to eat, all the while thinking about what a shit morning I'd had.

There was an hour's delay on the line, so I sat reading my favourite book on my kindle and munching on my crisps until the train began moving again, but as we pulled into the station, I began to get cramps in my stomach. My legs wobbled as I bolted towards the station loo's, but the doors were locked, and it was only as I stepped back that I noticed the out of order sign.

Celibet
Great. Just fucking great.

I walked as quickly as I could in my pencil skirt with heeled boots, but my stomach was clenching painfully, and I just hoped I would make it home to my second floor flat.

As I reached the corner, my body tensed with pain, and I let one go, mortified to realise that there was a little wetness in my knickers. I all but ran the rest of the way home and halfway up the stairs when another painful cramp hit and had me doubling over. I tried to hold it in, but my body had other ideas and I let another one go, wincing as I felt the tell-tale leak of moisture.

I rushed up the rest of the stairs and let myself into the bathroom to be met with an explosion of shit as soon as my ass hit the toilet seat. I pulled my boots, soiled knickers, and tights off, and doubled over as another wave of cramping happened.

Eventually, it seemed my bowels were sated, and I left the bathroom, only to return a few moments later. This happened three times before my stomach finally settled. My feet dragged me into my bedroom, and I stripped out of my work clothes before pulling on a fresh pair of knickers, and jammie bottoms. Scooping up my skirt and gathering my underwear and tights, I threw them all into the washing machine then crawled back to my room before climbing into bed.

I must have dozed off because my ringing phone woke me. Jumping up to get it, I slipped and landed in a heap on the floor, missing the call.

It started to ring again moments later, and I rushed out into the hall, searching through my handbag and pulled my phone out of the pocket at the back just as it stopped ringing again. I rolled my eyes seeing two missed calls from Charlie. I was about to call him back when my phone started to ring again, this time with an unknown number.

I cautiously answered. "Hello…"

"Hi, Ms Matthews?"

"Yes, that's me."

"This is Lindsay calling you back from the fraud team at Barclays Bank. Is this a good time to talk?"

My mind began racing as I assured her it was and answered my security questions.

"Okay, now that's done, I can tell you that there was a large Amazon order placed on Saturday? Was this you?"

An amazon order? I didn't really use Amazon and my dad was a technophobe, but Warren was always on Amazon. He would one click all the time and I did often wonder how he was paying for it. Now I knew.

"Wait, no it wasn't."

"Are you sure? There are three separate transactions on amazon from Saturday?"

"No, it wasn't me."

"Okay what about the shopping purchases Saturday afternoon? There were a few purchases made in Karen Millen, Kurk Geiger and a charge in the Tetbury?

"Yes, those were me."

"But you are certain the amazon purchases weren't?"

"Absolutely positive."

Celibet

My head was swimming as I came to the realisation that it was Warren. He'd clearly ordered stuff from Amazon, the day after dumping me. My head was swimming. I couldn't believe it. Then I remembered a while ago that he'd said something was wrong with his card and could he try my card to order something for his class. I hadn't thought anything of it, and I'd sent him my details to let him get it.

That prick was using my bank card to buy shit and I was fucking furious about it. No wonder I was skint. How the fuck did he manage to do that without me noticing?

"It would appear so. There was also a rather large purchase made from TUI!"

"He bought a holiday?" I questioned in disbelief. "Oh my God."

"Yes. This wasn't you either?"

Her tone conveyed her disbelief, and I knew it was almost unbelievable that I hadn't kept track of my money, but I didn't. I was dreadful with it. I always thought I had more than I did, and I always ended up overspending.

She advised me to go through my account and highlight any purchases that I hadn't made and send them to her.

"Now you have my email address you can email me bank statements with highlighted sections on what you haven't spent."

"Yes, thank you so much, Lindsay. I'll do it now!"

The call ended and I began going through my online banking. There were two mobile phones being paid from my account. I checked and cancelled the extra one, then I saw a payment to Arnold Clark, and I realised he had set up his car to come out of my account. I cancelled that one, too, and his car insurance, car tax and his gym membership.

I checked each one and sat with a notepad and pen. He'd managed to swindle me out of seven thousand pounds on bills and that wasn't even including the Amazon orders that had constantly been coming out of my account. Over the space of a year, increasing amounts of my money had been used to fund his lifestyle. I remembered his login for Amazon, and logged in and checked, cancelling the recent orders for a dining table, iPad, lawnmower, a new bike, and a garden set. It had started off small and was almost unnoticeable at first, but then over the last few months more and more of my money was going to fund his fucking lifestyle.

He knew I rarely checked my bank account and that I always had spare cash in there because I hated to rely on my dad, so I usually had four thousand pounds in my account that I didn't touch. I'd noticed in July that my account balance was nearing three grand, but I'd just gone shopping and I'd assumed I'd overspent, plus Warren had used my card in a few stores and told me he'd send the cash back, but he hadn't.

I couldn't believe that I'd let him do that to me. How I hadn't noticed was beyond me, but I was sure as shit cancelling everything on my account that wasn't mine. If he wanted shit, he'd have to find a way to pay for it himself.

Celibet

My blood was boiling, and I wanted to call him, but I knew that I shouldn't, so I held off. My fingers ached from highlighting a full year's worth of bank statements, and after I scanned and emailed the documents back to the fraud advisor, I called my dad. I wanted to tell him about the money that Warren had been stealing, but I held off telling him the extent of it. I told him Warren had used my card to buy stuff and that I hadn't realised, but that he was going to pay me back.

"Why hasn't he paid you back already?" My dad was sharp as a whip and never missed a trick.

"He uh... he didn't realise he hadn't paid, and he spent the money?" I hated lying to my dad, but I knew he would lose his mind if he found out about the amount of money Warren the Wanker had stolen from me.

"So, he basically stole from you?" He always had an uncanny ability to read my mind.

"He... uh..." I wanted to lie, but why should I? I hadn't done anything wrong. "Basically, yeah. My bank is on it, and it's being treated as fraud, but I don't know how long it'll take for me to get the money back now that we're broken up and I likely won't get it all."

"Oh, you're over?" He couldn't hide the note of glee in his voice, and I knew he'd never really liked Warren but had put up with him for my sake. He'd stopped Warren from visiting when he found out about the wanting to move in thing.

"Yeah, we're done, Dad."

"And?" My dad was worse than a woman, nosey to a fault!

"And I'm fine about it. To be honest, it wasn't really working out. He was too needy and too much of a mummy's boy, so I'm glad it's over."

"Good, darling. That's good. I'm glad. He was never good enough for you anyway."

I wanted to tell him about what had happened at the surgery that day, but I knew I couldn't. It wouldn't be fair to burden him with it, and he didn't need to know how close I'd come to almost losing my job.

"Okay. Thanks, Dad." I was about to speak again when my phone buzzed against my ear. "Dad, I'm sorry. I need go. My phone is ringing. I'll see you in a few weeks for Mum's birthday."

Every year, I went home to my parents for my mum's birthday, only this year we would be celebrating by going to a freezing cold graveyard and laying flowers instead of giving presents to my mum. It didn't seem like much of a celebration, but I was determined that Dad wouldn't be alone. He'd only wallow, and so would I, so it was best if we wallowed together and maybe we could raise a wee sherry to her, even though it was disgusting stuff, and spend the day remembering her.

My mum had been a character. She put cheese sauce over our pudding once, and another time put custard over her cauliflower. She hadn't been a great cook, but she'd been a wonderful mother, and we all had a marvellous childhood because she was a born storyteller.

Celibet

We'd gone on adventures through the trees, searching for wood nymphs and leprechauns and fairies. My mum's dad was Irish, and he used to tell her tall tales of his homeland, which mum had then passed down to us.

My dad said bye, and I quickly answered my phone without checking to see who was phoning me.

"You cold-hearted bitch! How dare you treat my mother that way? What has she ever done to you, apart from be nice to you?"

Ah, Warren.

I hadn't a clue what he was talking about, but I was done being his punching bag. "Right, I'm going to just stop you right there. I haven't got a clue what you are talking about, and to be honest with you, I don't care. Your mother is a horrible person, and I really don't wish to continue speaking about this. I don't really want to speak to you either, so do me a favour and fuck off!" I hung up and dropped to my knees, shaking on the floor. I wasn't a fighter, but when I had to, I would always stand up for myself.

He tried calling back, but I just ignored him and went into the bathroom. A nice bubble bath would go down a treat. Part of me felt relieved that I knew what a colossal dick he was, but as I angrily sloshed too much bubble bath into the tub, I realised I was more angry with myself that I'd stayed with him for so long.

"Harumph," I hissed, sitting down on the floor and placed my head in my hands. It was aching, and I knew it was going to get worse because I had to call a lawyer to deal with the fact that he had been defrauding me for the longest time. The bathroom began to fill up with steam, and I closed my eyes, leaning back on the tub, ignoring the persistent buzz of my phone against my leg.

I wanted to look at it, but I also didn't want to deal with him anymore, so I ignored it and waited until my bath was full.

My stomach was still a little sore from earlier, but I ordered a nice takeout and open one of the bottles of wine from the fridge as soon as I was a bit more chilled out. Each of my limbs relaxed in the bath, and when I was wrinkly and feeling floaty, I climbed out of the bath, realising that in my haste to draw myself a bath, I'd only gone and forgotten the bloody towel.

I heard the front door slam, and I jumped about a mile in the air, landing awkwardly as my feet slipped under me, and I thumped down on my knee. I stood and shook my legs out, dripping more water onto the floor. Picking up my mobile, I dashed out of the bathroom, dripping water all over the marble floor of the bathroom and the wooden floor in the hallway, calling for Charlie as I went.

"Charlie?"

No answer, so I tried again louder this time.

"Charlie are you home? You won't believe the weekend…"

I stopped speaking as the door to the sitting room opened and Warren strolled out. Damn it. Fucking damn it all to hell. I had only gone and forgotten I'd given him a bloody key. I quickly pressed record on my camera and held it facing away from me towards him.

Celibet

He moved lithely towards me, like a cat stalking his prey, and I shrank back away from him.

"What are you doing here Wa... Warren?" I'd almost called him Wanker, which made me snort and he glanced at me in disdain.

"Well, you wouldn't take my calls, so I had no choice but to come over here to talk to you." His eyes kept darting away, and I realised it was making him uncomfortable that I was naked. I was also freezing, and goosebumps rose on my arms and legs, but I ignored it. If it made him uncomfortable, then all the better.

"I don't want to speak to you. Please leave." I knew it was pointless to demand, but I wanted him to know that he wasn't welcome.

"Not until you talk to me. I need to tell you some stuff." He swallowed and glanced around nervously, but I stood my ground.

I refused to be intimidated in my own home by the guy who had dumped me via text message. "Fine. Talk and then leave. Make sure you leave your key though."

He glanced again at me and tugged at his collar. "Don't you want to get dressed."

I was already dry by this point and my teeth were starting to chatter, but I wasn't about to let him alone to wander about my flat. God knows what he would take.

"Nope. I'm fine." I crossed my arms across my breasts, hiding the fact that my nipples were so erect they could cut glass, and stood glaring at him, waiting on him to start speaking.

"Fine. Here goes. I need to… erm…" He stuttered and spluttered, and I stood, tapping my foot in what I hoped seemed like impatience, but in reality it was because I was fucking freezing and I didn't want to give in and have to go put clothes on.

"Well it's like this… I kinda… erm… You know how…" He took a deep breath and plundered on. "I kind of took out a loan in your name and it was due to come out today, but for some reason the direct debit failed and…"

I could hear the blood pounding in my ears as I glowered over at him and my hands were shaking, not with cold anymore, but with complete and utter fury. "You did what?" My voice came out eerily calm, and I wanted to swing for him, but I stood stock still as he nervously twirled his hands around and around.

"We'll I was trying to… Never mind… I just need you to know that I changed the address today and that you'll be getting all the correspondence from the company."

My fists clenched in fury and I waited for the punchline. "This has to be a joke. You've been stealing from me for ages and now you've put me into debt? Are you fucking serious?"

He glanced nervously behind him and shrugged as I waited for a response.

"How much? How much money did you take out in my name you absolute fucking moron?"

He swallowed and shifted from foot to foot as he stared at me. "Ten… ten grand." His voice was low, and I wondered why he was suddenly here telling me all of this.

Celibet

"Why are you here? Why are you telling me about this?" Me questioning his motives was clearly something he had wanted to avoid because he began edging backwards towards the door and I moved towards him.

"Well, my mum advised me..." His words stopped me in my tracks as I questioned myself. His mum knew about this... of course she did.

"Your mum advised you what?"

He had reached the handle of the door and was half turned away from me. "She told me I could get done for fraud, and I don't want that, so she said I should come clean and get you to pay it off and then that'd be it. All over."

This time my pulse was thundering in my ears. "Are you fucking serious? You expect me to pay ten grand back that I never spent, you absolute walloper?"

He turned towards me and an evil smile lit up his face. "Yes, because if you don't, I'll share the photos and videos I've got of you. You know the ones I'm talking about..." He ran his eyes up and down my body and I shuddered in revulsion.

How I had ever found him attractive I didn't know.

"So now you're trying to blackmail me?"

"I wouldn't quite call it that..." His eyes lingered on my breasts and he smirked as he caught my glare.

"What would you call it then?"

"Gentle persuasion. You see, all the money that I've spent of yours, I'll just say you let me use your account. Who are they going to believe: a girl who was recorded doing a strip tease or me, a stand-up member of the community?"

My fingers strained as I got closer to him. I wanted to hit him. I wanted to murder the fucking lying little weasel, but I was recording this, and if I retaliated, I wouldn't have a leg to stand on, so I held myself back, even though it was killing me.

"Get out of my house!" I screamed at him. "Leave the fucking key and get to fuck! I never, ever want to see your ugly fucking face again!"

He shrugged and turned the handle, stepping into the sitting room and then I heard the front door click. As soon as he was gone, my adrenaline left me, and I slumped to the floor. After a few minutes sitting there plotting his murder, I began to shake. I wasn't sure if it were the cold or the fact that he'd threatened to share private images.

I stood on shaking legs and carried myself to my bedroom. I crawled under the covers and lay in bed for a few minutes, shaking like a leaf in a hurricane. My eyes burned with tears. I fucking hated him, and then I remembered that I'd pressed record when he'd stepped into the hall.

I picked up my phone and checked, surprised to see it was still recording. I stopped it and watched the video.

It was perfect. The camera was facing right onto him and you could see his face the whole time. Even when I'd folded my hands, I'd kept my phone facing him, which was quite by accident because I'd completely forgotten I was filming.

Celibet

I lay there for a few minutes, trying to think what to do with the recording when I remembered that Callie's ex was a copper, and they were still on good terms. Chris was a friend, but not a close friend, and I weren't sure if I was allowed to call him. Instead, I called Callie. The phone rang and rang then clicked onto voicemail. I checked the time and saw it was only just after six, but she was probably at work. Two seconds later this was confirmed as she texted me.

Callie: Hey babes, what's up? I'm at work and the big man is in so I can't talk. Can text though. Xx

My reply was instant.

Hey, Calls. Is it okay if I text Chris and ask him to meet me for a drink?

I saw the little dots flash as she typed, and it took a few minutes before she texted back.

Callie: Yeah course it is. I'm not his keeper, but can I ask why?

I pondered how much to tell her. Callie was a badass, and she would kick Warren's arse for what he'd done. I decided to tell her part of the truth and hope she'd let it go.

I need some advice about some shit Warren's pulled. Figured Chris is the best guy to go to since he's a cop. Xx

Callie: Ah okay, gotta go. Big man coming out. Have fun with Chris, and by have fun I mean get some. He's awesome in the sack lol. Call ya tomorrow. Xx

I laughed and searched through my phone book for Chris's number. I didn't even know if he'd be up for meeting me, but I knew his station was near, so if he were working, he would be close by.

Nerves overtook me, and my fingers shook as I typed the message.

Hey Chris, it's Beth, Callie's friend. Are you free for a drink later tonight? I need some advice about something. Xx

As soon as I sent the message, I cringed. Chris was a Triple T. Callie and I had come up with a ranking system for guys with Triple T's being the best. Tall, toned and tatted or tanned, and Chris was tall, with light brown hair,

green eyes, and a gorgeous smile. He also had a body made for sin and had tats all up his arms. I'd actually drooled the first time we'd met him.

We knew a few triple T's. Charlie was one and so was Dominic and Quentin, but Warren wasn't. In fact, Warren was as far from a Triple T as you could get.

My blood began to boil again as I thought about Warren, and I was full of rage at what I'd let him pull on me. The fuckin' prick.

I stopped myself thinking about him by imagining Chris topless and then remembered the time we'd gone to the beach. Wanker had flipped when Chris and I had flirted by the beachside bar, just after he'd broke up with Callie.

While I was thinking about how gorgeous Chris was, my phone vibrated in my hand, and I dropped it in fright. I seriously needed to get a grip.

Chris: Sure, I'm at work till seven, though, so do you wanna meet me at the station and we can go from there. X

I smiled and thought that' it was perfect as I replied telling him I would be there. I got up and walked over to my wardrobe to try and see if I had anything suitable to wear. I didn't want to dress up too much and have him think I was a slapper, but I also didn't want to dress too formal and have him think I was a school ma'am.

My silver scoop neck top would do, but with a skirt or jeans. I took my mid-thigh denim skirt out and matched it with my top, but when I tried it on, it looked like I was going on a date as a hooker, because I didn't have any underwear on yet.

My black, see-through top was there, and I grabbed a black vest to wear underneath. Next, I picked out some nice lacy, black, and silver underwear and pulled out a pair of black tights.

Dressy, but casual.

Once I was dressed, I sat in front of my vanity and put my long hair up in a messy bun. It was curling at the ends because of the bath and I didn't want to straighten it. I put on a little light makeup, drawing my eyebrows on because I was fair and had none, and doing my eyes always made me feel like I looked good. Next, I put on some lippy and I was ready to go.

Chapter Eight

BETH

I grabbed my mobile and my handbag and put on my leather, heeled boots. I glanced around for my black leather jacket, but I couldn't see it anywhere and I was sure I'd left it in the sitting room. My phone buzzed in my hand as I walked to my room door and I had to laugh as I read the message. It was from Charlie.

Charlie: Flight's bloody well been delayed. Apparently, there's a problem with the plane. Just my bloody luck. C xx

I rolled my eyes as I typed a reply. It really was his luck. Charlie was the unluckiest person with travel ever. He'd either a) get delayed, b) get lost, c) lose his luggage or some combination of all three. One time, he was flying back from Rome and got lost on his way to the airport and missed his flight. It cost him three hundred pounds to get home. Another time, he flew to Spain, lost his luggage on the flight out and then they lost it again on the flight home. He was cursed.

OMG! You're actually cursed. Is it the flanges? Haha xx

We'd watched that episode of friends a few weeks ago, so I was sure he'd get the joke, but apparently, I was wrong as his next message arrived a moment later.

Charlie: Oh my God! I actually looked around there for someone to ask. Planes don't have flanges, do they? C xx

Sometimes I worried about him. Sometimes I really worried about how he managed to adult, not that I was doing much better with my knack for letting my boyfriend fraud me. Charlie would shit a hedgehog when he found out.

Charlie: Wait is that not in an episode of friends? Oh my God it is. It's the one where Rachel is leaving! You bitch. I actually had to think about that! C xxx

I started laughing at him and walked into the sitting room, finding my jacket flung carelessly over the armchair.

Charlie, you crack me up. What time will you be back?

He didn't reply straight away, which gave me a moment to check that Warren the Wanker had indeed left his key. He had. It was thrown on the floor next to the door.

Charlie: I'll be back about two am. Rain check on takeout?

Sure thing. See ya tomorrow.

Charlie: See you tomorrow. Xx

I quickly checked the time and saw it was almost quarter to seven, so I pulled my jacket on, shoved my phone into my bag and picked up Warren's discarded key from the floor. I quickly searched my bag to make sure I had lipstick,

perfume and the little cash I had in there, and once I was satisfied that I had everything I needed, I left, closing the door after me with a snap.

I rushed down the stairs and left the building, heading west and wincing as my feet slipped a little on the icy pavement. Heeled boots and ice were not compatible, and I ended up walking the fifteen minutes to the station like a penguin to keep from falling.

I was five minutes late, and I met Chris standing outside.

"Hey, Beth, how's it going?" He smiled over at me and I could see relief in his eyes.

My answering smile was bright but was quickly followed by a squeal as I slipped on a patch of black ice and went careering right into his side. He grabbed me around the waist and my body responded. Desire coiled in my stomach, but I shook it off and righted myself.

"You safe to walk in those things?" he asked, and I grinned up at him.

"Nope," I answered, popping my p as my eyes scanned up his body. He was more muscled than before; I licked my lips as my eyes roamed up his chest to meet his eyes.

He shook his head and glanced around. "Where do you wanna go?"

I mulled it over and my stomach chose that moment to growl loudly, making us both laugh…

"So, food first?" He nodded down the street and we began walking towards the end of it. My stomach flipped

Celibet

as my feet slipped and slid underfoot, and eventually Chris linked arms with me and kept me upright.

We reached the corner where a Wetherspoons sat and he gestured to it. "Do you want to go in here? We can get food and chat and it's usually pretty quiet?"

I nodded and we began walking inside but both froze on the pavement outside as Warren the Wanker walked out with a blond girl hanging onto his arm. Warren's eyes widened, but he didn't really know Chris. They'd only met that one time and he didn't know what Chris did for a job. He glared at me, but left without saying anything, then came back and snarled at me.

"You don't wait long, do you?"

Warrens hissed words and viscous glare had me shrinking back a little, but I refused to let him intimidate me.

"Watch yourself with this one mate!" he called to Chris, and then he turned to face my as he spoke again. "She's a frigid bitch with no respect for anyone. I'd swerve if I were you."

Chris glanced at me and then stepped up in front of Warren. My pulse raced as he glared down at him, but he only smiled coldly. "I think someone has a case of sour grapes. Getting dumped is no fun, but I can take care of myself and I don't need a fuckwit like you to tell me what to do." With that, he stepped back and smiled at me before taking my hand and leading me inside. We both ignored Warren's protests that he was the one who dumped me, and that Chris was making a mistake.

Once we'd found a seat and chosen our food, Chris went to the bar and ordered. He returned with a large glass of Merlot for me and a pint for himself. Taking a sip, he sighed and leaned back on the chair. For a moment, we were quiet, but then he pushed forwards and pressed a kiss to my lips.

I almost fell out of my chair in surprise, but he pulled back with an evil smirk and I heard the pub door slam at my back.

"What was that?" I muttered a little breathlessly. That kiss had turned me on more than Warren had managed in three years.

"That douche was coming in here, so I decided to give him a little show. You want to tell me the story there because he doesn't seem like he deserved you." His green eyes widened and framed by his dark lashes, he looked delectable.

I licked my lips to hide my dry mouth and took a sip of my wine to give me a moment to collect my thoughts. "I started dating Warren when I was seventeen. He is two years older than me and I fancied him rotten. We met at a nightclub and hit it off."

Chris's eyes widened as he took a sip of his pint.

"He was lovely at first—so attentive—and all my friends were jealous. Then, I went to uni and we somehow ended up staying together. He became more selfish and told me over and over that I needed to lose weight, that I wasn't attractive enough and that he could do better, so eventually I started to believe him. I still dressed the way I wanted to. I ignored his criticisms of me and just plodded along in the relationship." I paused to take a sip from my wine and then glanced over to Chris. His fist was clenched on the table, and he was staring behind me. Swivelling around in my chair, I glanced around, wondering why he was glaring, but then I spotted Warren and his date at the bar.

I turned back to Chris and he drew his eyes off them and nodded at me to continue.

"Well, Friday night I was waiting to go out for dinner with him when a text arrived, and basically he dumped me."

"By text?" Chris asked and I nodded once, my cheeks heating in mortification.

"Yeah, by text. At first, I was a little pissed off, but I knew it hadn't been right ever, so I wasn't too bothered, but I was a bit annoyed that he'd text me when I was due to finish work and left me without a lift home."

Chris leaned closer and whispered in my ear. "He's sitting a few tables away, trying not to look over here, but failing miserably."

I laughed and sat back, feeling nothing but amused. I leaned closer to him and he put his hand on my leg, squeezing gently.

Just as I opened my mouth to speak again, our food arrived, and we both sat back to eat. He'd gotten a burger with onion rings and chips and I'd gotten pasta with garlic bread.

We sat in companionable silence as we ate, and I almost forgot Warren was there. As we finished off our food, I sipped my wine, thinking about how to tell Chris about Warren and his threats of blackmail. Seconds later, it

turned out that I didn't have to say a word because Warren approached our table and, ignoring me completely, he began talking to Chris.

"Dude, you might want to watch out for her: she's a slapper. She did a strip tease for me, which she filmed and then shared with her friends. She always sends her friends pictures of herself in her underwear, like she's some kind of model…"

Chris stared back at him, stone-faced, and didn't say a word.

Warren saw he was having no effect on Chris, turned to me and hissed. "Remember what we talked about. You tell anyone about anything, and those pictures and videos go viral."

Chris sat bolt upright as Warren walked away. "Okay, so he's threatening to release pictures and videos of you. You know that's illegal right, and we can charge him with online bullying and blackmail?"

I put my hand on Chris's arm and he turned to look at me. "Yeah, I know. That's why I wanted to speak with you. Why don't I get us another drink and then I can tell you all about why I wanted to meet up?"

He nodded and took out his phone, typing something as I wandered to the bar. I was back within a few minutes and Chris was nowhere to be seen. I spotted him a few moments later with some guys, and I sat back, patiently waiting on him returning.

Celibet

Five minutes later he was back, and he sat down slowly. "Okay, you were going to tell me about why you wanted to meet up."

My eyes roamed over his body, and I wanted to say that I wanted to fuck him, but I wasn't sure if he'd be open to that, so I knew I needed to tell him the real reason. My eyes met his and his eyes darkened slightly, but he nodded at me and I began speaking in a low voice, checking around me to see if the Wanker was about.

I finished telling him and lifted my drink to my lips.

"So, he's been stealing from you, taking out things in your name and is now threatening to share images about you unless you keep quiet?"

"Basically, yeah..."

"Do you have any evidence of this?" He lifted his sweater over his head, showing a little of his toned stomach and one of his tattoos, and for a moment I was completely distracted.

"Hmmm, what?" I muttered as I drank his arms in. I'd always had a thing for arms, and his were totally gorgeous. My mouth watered and I leaned back licking my lips again. Chris picked up his pint and took a small sip and I watched as the muscles bunched and strained on his forearm.

"So, do you?"

I must have shown my puzzlement because he smirked at me and leaned over, brushing a strand of hair from my face, and whispering in my ear again.

"Keep looking at me like that and I won't be able to give you any advice." His eyes roamed over me and he ran his hand down my cheek and along my shoulder, giving my arm a gentle squeeze. His touch caused butterflies to erupt in my stomach, and I moved a little closer to him.

"Evidence," he asked me breathlessly as he sat back, shaking his head as though to clear it and I sat up, back in the here and now.

"Yes, I have this," I muttered holding up my phone and showing him the video. He watched and then picked up his pint, downing it.

"Come on. We're going to the station. This is all the evidence you need to make sure he never bothers you again."

He reached for my hand and pulled me up. I quickly grabbed my bag and jacket and he marched us from the pub and back towards the police station. It took half an hour for me to make my statement and I emailed the evidence to the desk sergeant. As soon as he said I was free to go, I was out of there like a rocket, but Chris wasn't waiting for me. Part of me was disappointed, but it was probably for the best. He was Callie's ex after all.

I walked outside slowly and began heading back to my flat when a voice behind me called my name. My heart thundered in my ears as Chris jogged up the pavement towards me.

"Hey, sorry. I asked the desk Sergeant to let you know I'd popped out for a minute and to ask you to wait for me." He glanced nervously at me and twisted a ring on his right finger. "Did you want to go home already?"

I pondered what to say for a moment and then spoke. "No, I thought you'd left, so I was heading home."

Celibet

"Well since I didn't, do you fancy more drinks, I'm off work tomorrow, and I don't want to go back to my empty flat just now."

"Lead the way, officer." I tried to joke with him, but he turned back towards me with fire in his eyes, and I shuddered. He reached out and linked his fingers with mine as he led me back towards the pub that we'd had dinner in, but we didn't go in. We walked a few feet further and he stopped outside a piano bar. It was quiet with only a little melody floating outside.

I followed him in, and we sat at a booth in the back, not speaking until we sat down. He shrugged his denim jacket off and slipped it over the chair before sitting down.

"What do you want to drink?" I asked him, getting ready to stand and go to the bar, but he reached out, putting his hand on my leg giving me an oh so gentle squeeze on my thigh that made me squirm.

"No. This is my treat." His eyes met mine, and I could see the promise of things to come in his smoky green depths. He stood and walked to the bar. I couldn't take my eyes off him and watched as his denims hugged his arse as he stood chatting to the waitress at the bar.

A few minutes passed and he turned back towards me, catching me staring at his arse.

Chapter Nine

BETH

My face heated, and I quickly turned to look around as he made his way back to the table. He placed an uncorked bottle of wine and a glass on the table before leaving returning with something in a glass with coke. He also brought two shots with him. Shots were a bad idea with me, but I wanted to let go, and I knew that I'd regret it if I didn't drink it.

He lifted my hand, licked the back of it and poured a little salt onto it, holding my left hand with his right. He picked up the shot and knocked it back before licking the salt from my hand. I visibly squirmed and he smirked at me, before turning his hand over. I copied his actions, wondering how he'd made it look so effortless. I licked along his hand and watched as his lips parted slightly. Then,

Celibet

I poured way too much salt on before I lifted my shot and necked it.

Bleurgh, I thought, as the tequila burned its way down to my chest, but then I leaned back over and licked the salt from his hand. As I sat back up, he captured my mouth in a fierce kiss that had our teeth clashing. My chest heaved as he sat back and took a sip of his drink.

I couldn't pour my wine because my hands were shaking so badly. I ended up spilling some on the table and he laughed at me, so I flicked it towards him.

His look of outrage made me laugh and he kissed me, more gently this time, but in a way that made my knickers wet.

As we broke apart, I turned to take a sip of my wine and he ran his hand up and down my spine, making me tingle all over. My heart raced as I sat, allowing him to stroke my back, and when he slipped his hand down and squeezed my arse, I almost dropped my drink on the table. I drank the wine quickly because I wanted what was going to happen afterwards to hurry up.

Twice more Chris went to the bar and returned with more shots of tequila, and each time, we performed the same little ritual. I was well on my way to drunk when he leaned over and asked if I was ready to leave.

"Yes, we should go now."

He nodded and stood, gesturing for me to walk in front of him, but as soon as I was on my feet, I staggered to the side and he ended up with his arm wrapped around my waist, holding me up. I was drunk, but not wasted, and we walked along, passing a kebab shop on the way back to mine. We both stopped and stared for a moment, but I didn't want to say we should go inside first, so he did.

"You hungry?" He nipped along my neck and pressed his lip to the underside of my ear as we stood looking inside the shop.

"Yeah, I am, but not for food."

He nibbled again at my neck and we continued the walk back to my place.

As soon as I opened the door to the block of flats I lived in, he scooped me up and marched up the stairs with me, placing me down gently at my front door. I fumbled with the key and almost dropped it, but I managed to get it into the lock. The flat was quiet because Charlie wasn't back yet, but I led Chris to my bedroom by the hand. He rubbed circles on my hand as we walked. I opened my bedroom door and Chris spun me around, pulling me into his chest and lifting my face.

"You sure about this, Beth?"

His uncertainty was sweet, but I was completely sure, so I stood on my tiptoes and pressed my lips firmly to his. After a moment's hesitation, he kissed me back and then wrapped his hand around my neck, holding me in place. He walked me backwards until we were right against my bed and then he stepped back a little. His hands moved along the bottom of my top and over my abdomen, making tiny goosebumps appear in his wake.

I slid my fingers lightly across his taught stomach, and he hissed a breath out when they reached the top of his jeans.

Celibet

He lifted his hands and removed my jacket slowly then lowered his hands to my waist, tugging my tops up and over my head. His eyes widened as he took in my black and silver bra and he ran his fingers along the edge of it before slipping his fingers inside each cup and twisting my nipples gently.

My fingers were still on the loops of his jeans, but I didn't move while he was exploring. Seconds later, he removed his fingers and pulled me towards him. He slammed his lips down onto mine and thrust his pelvis towards me, hitting me in the stomach with his straining erection. My body burned with desire as I submitted to his bruising kisses.

I popped open the button of his jeans and dragged the zip down before sliding his jeans and boxers down. His penis glistened with moisture and I was impressed with his length, but more so with his girth.

Running my hand up and down his penis had him thrusting forwards into my hand, and I gave him a gentle squeeze as his hands tugged at my skirt and yanked it up. He tore at my tights and pushed them down my legs, before reaching down to his jean's pocket and grabbing a packet of condoms and tossing them onto the bed. He still had his top on, and I wanted to take it off, but when he stood back up, he was ripping the packet of condoms open and tearing the foil apart.

I watched in fascination as he pulled the condom on and moved back towards me. His fingers shoved my knickers aside, and he slipped his fingers along my slit.

I was soaking.

"So wet for me, Beth."

I ran my hand along his penis as he slipped his fingers inside and started pumping them in and out. I could feel my body coiling in response, but just before I orgasmed, he stopped, spun me around and pressed me face down on the bed.

Seconds later he thrust his way inside me and thrust hard. It was heaven and hell. His penis hit me right where I needed it to, and the friction of my bed against my clit had me spiralling. He drove into me at a punishing pace and twisted his hand in my hair, tugging slightly which tipped me over the edge. I splintered apart and was only vaguely aware of him pumping into me a few more times before coming himself.

As he pulled out of me, he gave me a little tap on my arse, and I squirmed. I'd never had that before, but I kinda liked it. I turned to watch as he dragged his boxers and jeans back on, but I still couldn't move

"That was great. Thanks, Beth." He turned to leave, and I sat numbly, watching as he walked towards the door.

"Stay!" I almost shouted it at him as he turned the handle. The word came out without conscious thought, but I definitely wanted to ride the Chris train again before the night was out.

"You sure? It will only be for the night though: I don't do relationships."

"Yeah, I'm sure. I don't need another relationship right now. I just want some good, no strings sex." My voice quivered as I spoke. I'd always been a relationship girl, but

Celibet

that was in the past. For now, I decided, I'd just need to be content with a casual fuck.

"Okay, I'll stay. You got anything to eat? I'm starving."

I shoved myself up from the bed and pulled my skirt down, reaching over to take my boots off and kicking them away from me. I then dragged my tights off and walked to the door where Chris was still standing.

"I'm not sure. I think we have some eggs, but that's it."

"It's only half ten. You want to order some food?"

"Sure, what do you fancy?"

We looked at each other and both said, "Kebab" at the same time.

I walked over to the bed and picked up my handbag. My phone was right at the top, and within moments I'd ordered two kebabs with salad and sauce, a portion of chips and a portion of chicken pakora, plus a bottle of coke. I figured that would fuel us up for the night. I had to work the next day, but I didn't care. After the way that bloody doctor had treated me that morning, I would be going in hungover and not giving a shit about it.

Chapter Ten

BETH

Chris stood by the door, and after I'd ordered the food, we went through to the living room to watch some TV. As we sat on the sofa, I went into the kitchen and uncorked one of the bottles of wine, bringing it and two glasses through.

Chris sat up and smirked when he saw it. "You sure we need more alcohol?"

I shrugged and poured us both a glass, handing his over to him as I sat down with mine. "What do you want to watch?" I asked him, turning the TV on.

"How about something on Amazon Prime?"

"Lucifer?" I asked as I scrolled through the shows. I glanced over at him and saw he was shaking his head, so I continued searching.

Celibet

"How about that?" He was pointing at Outlander and I nodded.

"You ever seen it before?"

Shaking his head, he took a small sip of wine and leaned back on the sofa. I curled up beside him and began the first episode, but as soon as the good bit started, where Claire falls through the stones and meets Black-Jack, he started talking.

"That's so unrealistic. How would that even be possible?"

I wanted to strangle him because Outlander was one of my favourite shows, and I didn't want him to spoil it by pointing out the inaccuracies or by saying that it was unrealistic. I loved it. I loved the fact that it was fiction and that Claire struggled as a Sassenach in the highlands of Scotland.

Before I could tell him off, our food arrived, and I went out to it. I returned and placed the bag onto the table, turning Outlander off and putting Netflix on. Friends was the last thing I'd watched there, so I started up an episode as Chris opened the bag and shared the food out.

We ate, drank wine, and watched friends, laughing at Monica dancing about with a turkey on her head. After our food, we watched a few more episodes and finished off the bottle of wine.

He leaned over as I sat fiddling with my empty glass and plucked it from my hands, placing it gently on the side table. I turned slightly so I was facing him a bit more as the atmosphere in the room electrified. He ran his hand up my arms and tugged me towards him. Our lips met and he his hands roamed down my back, cupping my arse and giving it a squeeze. His fingers sent shivers down my spine as he slid his tongue along my lips. I opened for him and our tongues clashed.

I moved around to sit on his lap, and he tugged me down onto his erection, making me squirm as the denim rubbed against my swollen clit. I ground down on him as he cupped my arse again, thrusting against me as we kissed even more fiercely.

He yanked my skirt up and smacked my ass. I moaned as he moved his lips along and pressed kisses up and down my neck, nipping at my collar bone. His fingers wandered up to my vest and he lifted it up, dragging it and my top over my head and tossing it to the side. I leaned back so I could return the favour and I tugged his top up, throwing it behind me.

His fingers wandered into my bra and he scooped my boobs out, lowering his lips and sucking my left nipple into his mouth before biting down gently and then sucking again. Fire raced through me and I ground down even harder onto him as his fingers twisted my right nipple while his mouth sucked on my left. His other hand went back down and pulled me down even more tightly on top of him. I was tingling all over and my body responded to his touch like a violin responds to a musician, but just as I was approaching the big O, he stopped and moved me off his lap.

"Bed," he muttered, and I stood on shaking legs, following him through my flat to my bedroom. He moved

Celibet

into the room like he owned the place and kicked off his shoes, jeans, and boxers.

My mouth watered as I took him in. His toned arse was the first thing I saw as he reached down to his jeans and took out a few condoms, throwing them onto the bed.

He turned and sat on the edge of my bed as I stood indecisively by the door. His eyes blazed as he stared at me and he leaned forwards. His cock was rock solid, and my eyes widened as I watched him run a hand up and down it.

"Strip!" He commanded, and I jumped a little, turned on by both his tone and the fact he was ordering me about. I liked it more than I cared to admit.

I ran my hands along my stomach and shoved my skirt down, undoing the button and taking down the zip. He licked his lips as it dropped to the floor and ran his eyes up my body at a leisurely pace that had my nipples pebbling and heat pooling between my thighs.

My hands were in the waistband of my knickers, and I slid them slowly down, stepping out of them in what I hoped was a seductive fashion. I watched as Chris's eyes widen, and he reached his hand out towards me, beckoning me closer to him.

Willingly, I walked towards him, and when he ran his hands up my legs, cupping my arse, I wanted to jump onto his cock and ride him hard. He paused for a second and then smacked my arse hard before rubbing the spot. I gasped at the contact, and he smirked at me.

Moisture began to trickle onto my thigh, and I squirmed in front of him. He traced his finger down my crack and pressed against my puckered hole. I writhed against his touch and he smacked me again, moving quickly and shoved me down onto my knees between his legs.

His fingers from one hand tangled in my hair as he used his other to guide his cock into my mouth. It'd been a while since I'd given a guy a blow job. I just hoped I'd be good enough. Sex with Warren hadn't included oral, and I'd usually gone for a shower afterwards to get myself off since he'd never really seemed to manage it.

I shook my head a little to clear it and then licked at the tip of Chris's penis. He moved up and I opened my mouth and sucked the head. As I came back up, he hissed and twisted my hair a little, making me go down further. I wrapped my lips tightly and ran up the underside with my tongue.

I wrapped my hand around him and gently squeezed as I worked my way down and then back up his shaft. He pulsed in my mouth and thrust harder before he tugged on my hair.

"Stop!"

His command made me pause, and I glanced up at him.

His eyes were blazing down at me and his cheeks were flushed. "Stand up!"

I quickly stood, but my legs were shaking beneath me as I tried to get my balance. I opened my mouth to speak, but Chris shook his head, tapping my arse again.

"Lie on the bed on your stomach."

"How far up the bed?" My question earned me another smack, and I squirmed as more moisture pooled between

Celibet

my legs. Chris stood and stepped around me, gently pushing me onto the bed.

"Move back!" He tapped my legs and I shuffled back to the edge of the bed, turning my head to try and see him, but I could barely make him out.

"Close your eyes!"

His next command had me shivering all over, but I did as he said. I closed my eyes and waited to see what was coming next. I didn't expect the smack, so I yelped a little when he hit my arse, and he paused.

"I think you like this, Bethany. So, I want you to keep your eyes closed and just let yourself feel the sensations."

He did it again and I wriggled, but before I could collect myself his palm struck me again and I wriggled more. He smacked my arse again and again but not so much that it was painful. It was just a little sting, but I couldn't believe how much it turned me on. My heart was racing, and my clit was throbbing.

He ran his finger down my crack and then, before I could process what was happening, his mouth was there. He licked at me from behind and I almost convulsed off the bed.

He then slid his fingers up and stroked my clit before pressing his thumb into me and using his tongue on my arsehole. I writhed on the bed and he shoved his tongue in deeper and pressed harder against my clit

My stomach tightened and he continued to lick and finger me. His free hand roamed around and pinched my nipple gently before he twisted it slightly, almost to the point of pain, and I splintered apart around him. My body shook and shuddered on the bed as I came harder and faster than I'd ever come before.

I didn't get a moment to enjoy my orgasm before he flipped me over, ripped a condom with his teeth and pushed it on before thrusting into me hard. I was still riding my orgasm as he began pushing into me and his pelvis rubbed against me in the most delicious way as his lips found mine. He kissed me hard before biting down on my bottom lip and then sucking it into his mouth.

His lips wandered from my mouth and he kissed down my neck, right down to my chest where he tugged on my nipples with his teeth as he pounded into me. I could feel my body beginning to respond again, and as my toes tingled, he bit down on my nipple a little harder, which sent shockwaves through me. I fell apart around him, causing him to lean back his head and fuck me harder.

"Oh my God!" I muttered as I gripped his shoulders, digging my nails in and riding the wave of my orgasm. Chris grunted as he came apart and thrust into me a few more times before he flopped down on the bed beside me breathing hard.

"Wow!" I muttered as he lay there at my side, and he leaned over, capturing my lips in a kiss before muttering against them.

"Wow indeed."

For a few moments, we lay in complete silence and then he began running his fingers lightly over my stomach, under my breasts, over my nipples and down my arm. He turned on his side and faced me, watching me as he touched me. I began to respond, and after a beat, he leaned down, sucking my nipple into his mouth, and licking with his tongue. He then tugged on it and ran his fingers down my mound, parting my folds and sliding his finger along. His thumb pressed into my clit as he pushed his fingers inside and began sucking hard on my nipple.

I thrust my back off the bed as he continued to turn me on when my room door opened, and Charlie stood in the doorway.

His eyes widened and he spun away quickly, closing the door at his back, but in my shock, I tried to sit up, at the same time as Chris and I managed to headbutt him on the nose, bursting it and getting covered in Chris's blood.

He rolled away from me, holding his nose.

"Oh fuck! I'm so sorry, Chris!"

He nodded at me and held onto the bridge of his nose as I sat up slowly. I stood up on shaky legs and then glanced back at Chris once before running out to the bathroom to get a washcloth for Chris.

Charlie stood by the door to the sitting room.

"Hey Bethy-babe, guess my timing sucks as usual." His voice was low as I ran into the bathroom. He didn't turn to look at me (which I was grateful for), nor did he say anything else as I flew by him completely naked and rushed into the bathroom, somehow feeling awkward and irritated.

Chapter Eleven

CHARLIE

Tired and weary—firstly from the delay, and then from the flight, even though it was less than two hours—I dragged my case off the conveyor belt and began what felt like the walk of shame through customs, pulling my case behind me. If the person in front of me had walked a little quicker, I could have got through unnoticed.

I glanced at the customs officers who were standing behind the low counter, one woman and one man. There'd never been anyone here when I'd come through in the middle of the night before, but this is me, and the last couple of days really haven't been on my side, let's face it.

"Hold it." The female customs officer held out her hand, stopping me from going any further.

Fuck.

Celibet

I sighed heavily and moved towards the counter.

"Bags please."

I lifted my case onto the surface, and my rucksack, and folded my arms.

Her face was straight as she started to unzip the case, while keeping a stern eye on me.

"There's eight weeks of washing in there... you may have to excuse the smell. **Sorry."** I exaggerated the sorry for her benefit. That earned me another scowl. I rolled my eyes and instead thought I should shut my mouth before it got me into trouble. She pulled on some latex gloves and snapped the cuff. I felt my eyes widen, but she took no notice and started to pull a handful of clothes out, delving into my dirty washing, feeling down the sides of the case. I felt violated.

"Where are you travelling from today?"

"Paris."

"And did you pack the bag yourself?"

I tried to think of a funny comeback, but she'd have had me thrown me in a cell and questioned by the comedy police. "Yes." I nodded finally.

She pursed her lips at me and carried on dragging everything from my case.

"I hope you're going to fold all that back up?" I said with a smirk. "I spent all of ten minutes packing that."

Not even a crack of a grin. Wow.

She grabbed handfuls of my clothes and shoved them all back in the case then started on my rucksack. "Did you pack this yourself?"

"Yes." I answered, sighing again. "Can I just ask how much longer this is going to take? I obviously haven't bought anything into the country I shouldn't have, so I'd like to go home and go to bed."

She proceeded to dig her hand into my rucksack, and I watched with rapt attention as she began to pull the white carrier bag out with the spirits in.

"Before you ask, I bought those duty free, just like it says on the bag. Can I go now?"

She plucked my passport from the front pocket of my rucksack and opened it up, glancing between me and the picture in front of her. "Can you confirm your name?"

"Charlie Lewis James."

"Date of birth?"

"Fourteenth of the sixth, 1994."

Leaving all my belongings on the side she walked around the counter and pulled a wand out. "Legs apart and arms out."

"You know, you could say please; you'd get a much better response from people. Especially at…" I looked at my watch, "Three am." My head shook and my eyes rolled for the umpteenth time tonight.

"If you've got anything metal on yourself or change in your pockets can you remove it and also your phone if you have one."

I unfastened my belt and pulled it from the belt loops, dumping it on the side with a clatter, and took the loose change, my phone and wallet from my pockets. She cocked her head and placed her hands on her hips. Instead of antagonising her anymore, I did as she asked. She roamed

Celibet

the electronic wand over my body, started at my shoe then moved it upwards on one side and brought it down the other. Since there were no beeps, I guessed I was out of the woods, which I'd known I would be.

She turned the wand off and placed it on the counter again. Her face looked like it had been smacked with a fish or something.

"What no full body search? I'm game or if you are." I winked at her, smirking, but I could see the tension in her jaw as her teeth grinded together.

"Have a good day, Mr James."

"You sure you don't want my phone number, too? I mean you've already seen my underwear."

She took a step back and folded her arms across her chest.

I'll take that as no.

I piled the rest of my belongings into my case and zipped it up then did the same with my rucksack. "You too," I said sarcastically and forced a grin on my face, pulling my case from the counter and storming away from the grumpy customs bitch. As soon as I was out front, I got moved towards the first taxi that was in the loading bay and made sure he was free. With a nod of his head, I threw my luggage in the back of the black cab and gave him my address.

Finally, I reached home.

Once I'd gathered my luggage from the boot of the taxi, I pushed my key into the lock of the main door and dragged my bags in. I took every step up to the flat that I shared with Beth slowly. I was that tired, I could barely lift my feet up. After the drama with customs I was ready to say, **'fuck this day off'.**

The flat was quiet when I first walked in, but when I looked at the time and saw it was almost four am, it was no wonder.

Leaving my cases in the hallway I make my way towards Beth's room. I hadn't seen my best friend in eight weeks, and I was too impatient to wait. I hadn't seen Warren the Wankstain's car in the car park when I got dropped off, so she was either not here or he wasn't, which with the mood I was in was probably a good thing.

I tiptoed along the hallway and put my ear to Beth's door, still unable to hear anything other than soft sighs.

Twisting the handle slowly, I pushed the door open and what I saw in front of me had me stock still—frozen to the spot—and my eyes almost popped out of my head. I'm not sure what shocked me most: seeing Beth naked thrusting her back off the bed in ultimate pleasure or the fact that it wasn't Warren who was pleasuring her.

What happened next was something out of a 'carry on' movie…

Beth's eyes widened as they met mine, her body jolting, her arms flying up in the air and smacking exhibit number one straight in the nose. My hand slapped across my mouth as Beth bolted off the bed; it was only then that I realised I was still standing there watching.

I spun around as Beth rushed to get something to stop the bleeding and was moving towards me. I shifted from

Celibet

the bedroom doorway and leaned my shoulder against the frame of the living room door, scrubbing a hand over my face. She pushed past me with a scowl set on her face.

"Hey Bethy-babe. Guess my timing sucks as usual."

She wouldn't meet my gaze as she entered the bathroom.

I had no idea what to say to her.

Maybe sorry?

Would that work?

I was at a loss as to what would be the best to do, so I did nothing.

Armed with a whole toilet roll, she flew past me again, but this time I said nothing. Instead, I grabbed my case and quietly I disappeared into my bedroom, leaving it in the corner. I pushed the door shut and stood at the foot of the bed, letting myself fall. I buried my face down into my duvet and soon went to sleep.

Chapter Twelve

BETH

Chris managed to stem the flow of blood using toilet paper, but my bedding was covered in blood and the mood had well and truly soured.

"I think I'm gonna split."

I couldn't blame him, and I needed to strip my bed and go to sleep since I was up for work in just over four hours.

He dressed at breakneck speed and I walked him to the door with the embarrassment of getting caught from Charlie colouring my cheeks. "Thanks for tonight, Chris," I muttered as I opened the door and he stepped through.

"Yeah, it was great..." He leaned in and pressed a soft kiss to my lips before turning and jogging down the stairs.

I watched his firm ass as he moved and then I closed the door and leaned against it.

Celibet
Why was my life like a comedy sketch?

My jelly-like legs carried me to the kitchen, and I drank two pints of water before going to the bathroom and brushing the taste of tequila and regret from my tongue. I finally clambered into bed, remembering to set my alarm, and drifted off to sleep at a quarter past four.

My alarm blasted me awake at eight am, and I groaned as I rolled over, promptly falling right out of my bed, landing on the floor with an ungraceful thump.

"Argh," I screamed as I struggled to get out of the covers, which were currently holding me hostage, and my room door opened to show Charlie in just his boxers. His toned chest was on show and his eyes darted around the room.

When he saw me struggling on the floor, he snorted and turned to leave. I didn't realise that I was still naked—that my dressing gown I'd slept in had slipped open to reveal my whole chest.

"A little help please, Charlie?" I asked, and he spun back around, raising his eyebrow as he met me. I couldn't get my arms free, and my face was heating in shame as he stood and watched me fighting with the covers without moving.

"You sure?" he lilted, and I wanted to smack him as his eyes scanned my chest and lingered for a moment on my bare tits.

"Charlie, come on," I pleaded, and he grinned widely at me without moving.

"Oh, Bethy. Are you sure you want me to come?" he asked with an evil smirk that had me wanting to boot him hard in the balls.

My anger was beginning to get wilder, and I squirmed more on the floor, but the more I did, the tighter the covers got, and I couldn't get free. I really needed some help, but Charlie, for whatever reason, was reluctant to help me.

"Charlie," I moaned as my wrist began to ache, and he laughed as he stepped towards me. He stopped by my feet, and I tried to kick him, but the stupid fucking dick stepped back and left me completely tangled on the floor.

"Now, now, Beth. Chill. I will help you, but first you need to answer two questions. Agreed?" His light playful tone had made me spitting mad, but I knew him too well, and he wasn't joking around.

"Uh, fine. Shoot." I hissed at him, glaring up at him in annoyance and his smile got even wider, showing me the dimple on his cheek that made all the girls at university drop their knickers for him.

"Okay. One, did you cheat on Warren the Wanker? And two, who was the guy you slept with? He seemed quite familiar to me, but I couldn't quite place him after the carnage you caused on his face."

I glowered up at him and managed to kick him with my toes, but my foot began to cramp, and I howled as the pain shot up my leg.

Charlie leaned down and began to massage my feet, causing me to relax just a little as I contemplated burning him alive or stabbing him in the face with one of my stiletto heels.

Celibet

"I didn't cheat on Warren the Wanker. He dumped me last Friday," I began, and Charlie squeezed my foot tightly.

"Wait, he dumped you almost a week ago and you didn't tell me?" he asked, and a pained look crossed his face.

"I tried to, but you didn't answer. Now can you help me get out of this mess?" I asked, and he smirked at me. I glanced down and saw his sleeping serpent between the legs of his shorts. He was bigger than I thought, and he gave me another squeeze.

"Nope. Stop perving on my junk," he muttered in an amused voice as he dropped to his knees and closed his legs.

"Spoilsport," I began, and he stuck his tongue out at me.

Warren had always hated Charlie. He hated our friendship and how we could openly flirt with one another, knowing it didn't mean anything, and he was jealous of how close we were.

"Answer my second question, and I shall make like a genie and set you free."

"It was Callie's ex, Chris, and it was good. It was so fucking good."

"TMI, Bethy babe," he intoned, and he ran his eyes over my face again, down to my chest, before sucking in a breath. He dropped my foot and scuttled back away from me as he yanked on the blanket and loosened it from the bed. He then moved up until he was leaning over me, and for a moment, we stared at each other breathlessly. He tugged the cover from behind me and had me rolling across the floor, arse over elbow.

As I struggled to my feet, he left the room, chortling away, and I wanted to swing for him, but my alarm went off again and it was my 'move your ass, or you'll be late', alarm, so I couldn't go after him and kick his arse for holding me hostage in the blankets.

I got up and rushed to the bathroom, checking my face, surprised to see a red mark on my cheek and on my hair on the left side. I didn't have time to shower and the blood all over me made it look like I'd been involved in massacring Chris.

I scrubbed my face with a cloth and did my best to hide the blood that was stuck to my hair, by tying it up in a top knot and making a messy bun with bobby pins. When I was done, I dressed quickly and surveyed my room as I grabbed my cell. My bed was covered in dried blood, and I was sure my new grey, silk bedding was ruined, but I didn't have time to check or time to care. I had to move otherwise I'd miss my train and Dr West, or Dr Finchley would absolutely fire my arse if I were late, so I bolted towards the living room in search of my work pumps and my handbag. I was sure I'd left it in there the night before.

I ran into the living room, surprised to see Charlie still up and sitting on the sofa. He was sipping a coffee, and I could smell the mouth-watering aroma across the room. I eyed up his cup and was about to snatch it from him when he said, "I've made you one, it's in the kitchen."

He was an angel. A complete freaking angel.

Celibet

My handbag, jacket and shoes were all over on the chair, by the door and I sat down and watched him as he drank his coffee without really looking at me. His eyes never left his cup and as I shoved my feet into my work shoes, I took a grateful sip, noting as I did that Charlie had made my coffee exactly how I liked it, with milk and one sugar. Warren the Wanker had never made me a coffee right in our whole relationship. He'd been convinced that having sugar in my coffee would make me fat and refused to put it in. Even when we were out, he always made sure I didn't add any in myself.

I hadn't realised how insulting it was until now, and when Charlie asked me about him, I brushed him off because I really had to leave. I needed to run to the station, or I'd be late, but I could see something was bothering him. I would have to wait to find out what. I didn't have time to deal with it, so I rushed over, gave him a peck on the cheek and told him how much I'd missed him before I shot off out the door making my train with ten seconds to spare.

I was totally out of breath and sweaty as I sat on the train, and my stomach squirmed with the aftereffects of too much tequila and no breakfast.

I glanced down at my phone to see a message from the Wanker and one from Callie.

Callie: Hey, how did it go last night with Chris? Did you ride his cock all the way to orgasm central?

I giggled and was about to text back when someone tried to take my phone from my hand. I glanced up and saw it was the Wanker.

"What the fuck do you want?" I hissed at him and he glared at me.

"I want to know who the fuck you were out with last night and what the fuck you told him?" His eyes narrowed and I glared at him, rolling my eyes, and then laughing as he tried to look intimidating.

"My private life is none of your fucking business, so I'm asking you nicely to fuck right off."

He went to grab me when the guy to my left turned to him and gave him a glacial look. I watched as he froze and the man—who was about twice his size with muscles that went on for days—said in a deep baritone, "I think you need to get lost, mate."

Warren's eyes widened and he shot up from his seat, rushing towards the other end of the train as I turned and thanked my saviour. He gave me a smile and then went back to reading whatever it was he was reading.

I quickly text Callie to say I'd fill her in later and then sat and read a book for the remainder of my journey.

I was about halfway to the office when I got the feeling that I was being followed. I called Charlie, but his mobile rang out. Quickening my steps, I made it into the surgery with twenty-five minutes to spare. I'd planned on going to Greggs to grab something for lunch, but I couldn't shake the notion that someone was following me, but whenever I looked back, no one was there.

Celibet

I spent the morning a hyper vigilant mess, but I managed to perform my job effectively, even chatting with the patients and making jokes with them. However, I couldn't shake the feeling that something was off, and when I left for lunch, I got the same uneasy feeling. Rushing into Tesco, I picked up a sandwich and a bottle of water.

It was as I made my way back to the office that I saw him lurking behind a car, watching one of the entrances to the supermarket. I'd come out of the other door and I wasn't about to let him intimidate me, but my hangover was kicking in, and I knew I could do without the aggro. I left him there and made my way back to the office, texting Charlie as I did.

Charlie, Wanker is hanging about my office. Can you come meet me for finishing time please? B xx

He didn't reply straight away, and I assumed he was sleeping, but when it got to four pm and I still hadn't heard a word, I began to worry. I sat at the reception desk, chewing on my pen lid as my phone vibrated on the desk.

There were a few patients in the waiting area, so I scooped up my phone and asked Brenda to cover me while I took a coffee break. My palms were sweating. I had four messages from Wanker and none from Charlie. I didn't know what to think, and I was starting to worry that

Warren would burst into the practice because all of his messages were mildly threatening.

Warren: Beth what was that last night?

Warren: Beth, I'm going nowhere till you speak to me.

Warren: Beth, I'm sending those videos and pictures out tonight unless you come speak to me.

Warren: I know you saw me, and if you don't come out, I'll come in and I'll show your bosses those pictures.

Chapter Thirteen

CHARLIE

Once I'd unravelled her from the mess she was in, I walked out. There were a thousand scenarios running through my mind about what had happened between Beth and Warren the Wanker.

Why the fuck did he dump her?

What could Beth possibly have done for that piece of shit to dump her? She's one of the nicest people I know.

Something didn't add up.

I had thought about going back to bed, but I was too awake. Instead, I went into the kitchen and switched on the kettle. After not much sleep, I knew Beth would want coffee.

I thought about taking it to her, but I knew she had to get ready for work, so instead, I sat on the sofa and waited for her. Thinking back on our brief conversation this morning, I realised I must've made her feel like shit for pointing out that she hasn't told me but then, I hadn't told her about Jessie either.

I was about halfway down my mug when Beth walked in ready for work. No sign of blood anywhere.

She looked at my cup with pleading eyes, so I told her I'd already made her one. She rushed from the room coming back in just minutes with it cupped in her hands.

"Ah Charlie… I've missed you."

I plastered a grin on my face. "I've missed you, too." I study her for a moment. Her gaze flickered around before it landed on me again. "So, what happened?"

"With?"

"With Warren. Why did he dump you? I mean, you seemed well loved up before I left for Paris. It was sickening."

"Charlie, please. I don't have time for this right now, but I promise I'll tell you later." A pained look crossed her face as she gulped down the contents of her cup and put it down again with a thud sounding on the table.

Something had happened here, and I would find out, I'd make sure of it.

She leaned across and kissed my cheek. "I'm so glad you're home."

Within minutes, she'd grabbed her bag and was out of the door before I could even think about firing another question her way. The door closed with a slam, and my body sagged into the cushions of the sofa. I'd just have to get my answers later.

Finally, there was peace. I drained the rest of my coffee and trudged tiredly back to my room and got back into bed. I had plans to do absolutely jack shit today but catch up on some sleep first, then I'd unpack.

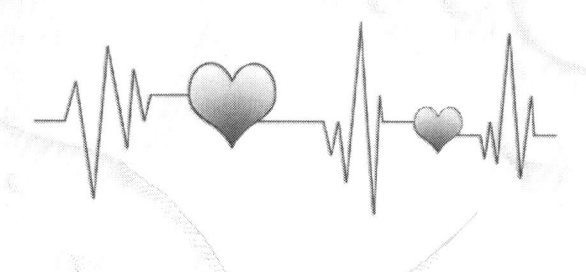

I swore to all that was holy if that vibrating happened once more, my phone was going for a flying lesson out of the fucking window. Nestling my cheek into my pillow, I kicked off the duvet and tried to go back to sleep. Just as I'd started to drift off and go back to my dream about Beth's boobs in my face, it happened again.

"ARRGH."

Hang the fuck on... Why was I dreaming about Beth's boobs?

Shaking my head, I rubbed the sleep from my eyes and grabbed my phone, unlocking the screen. There was a missed call from Beth and a message:

Beth: Charlie, Wanker is hanging about my office. Can you come meet me for finishing time please? B xx

Little Bastard!

Eyeing the time, I could see it was almost four pm already.

FUCK!

I opened the Uber app on my phone and booked a taxi for as soon as possible, and scrambling from the bed, I found a clean T-shirt in my wardrobe and a pair of jeans. I thought they were clean, but fuck knew they had been there since before I went off to Paris. Fuck it. They had to do.

Once I was ready, I ran out of the flat, taking the steps two at a time until I reached the doors, and shoved through to wait for the taxi. It pulled on to the car park and I jumped in, soon making my way to Beth.

Chapter Fourteen

BETH

I wasn't sure what to do. I didn't want to go out and meet him, but I also didn't want him causing a scene in my office. I glanced down at my phone again and pondered what to do. I wondered if I could call Chris and ask him or if I should try calling Charlie again.

My fingers hovered indecisively over their names, and I clicked on each one before cancelling. Dr Finchley came in the door at my back and barked at me for not being on the reception desk. I couldn't be bothered explaining that I was on my break.

My brain was pounding in my skull, so I went back out to the desk, managed to trip over my own feet and landed on the floor just outside of the reception with my dress around my waist. Luckily, no one was around, and I managed to get into the reception area with my dignity mostly intact.

I was working in the back office, filing, when I heard a commotion outside in the waiting room. I ignored it for a bit but then heard my name and moved towards the reception desk in time to see Charlie punching Warren full in the mouth.

"Stay the fuck away from her. I mean it. If I catch you anywhere near her again, I'll fucking end you, you little fucking weasel."

Charlie was shaking in fury, and Warren swung for him, catching his cheek.

Charlie didn't flinch. In fact, he laughed. "Is that the best you can do, fuckface?" he spat, and Warren bristled in fury, trying to swing for him again, but before his fist connected, Chris and another cop walked through the door and grabbed Warren.

"Warren Graham, I am arresting you on suspicion of assault, bribery, and fraud. You do not have to say anything, and anything you say can and will be used against you in a court of law."

Chris smirked at me, and I winced at the darkness under his eyes as he stepped towards the reception desk.

"Hey," he muttered, and I stepped around Brenda who was watching the scene with her mouth open.

"Hey. I thought you were off today?" I asked him and he grinned widely.

"They were short staffed, so I went in to cover, but I'm not driving today obviously."

Celibet

Charlie stood and watched us, and I glanced towards him to see him glaring at Chris, then at me.

I shrugged.

"We'll need a statement from you, but one of the patients and Mrs. Meggs called us and reported a suspicious man hanging around the practice. You can pop down tomorrow after work, and I'll take your statement." He opened his mouth to say something else, but his radio crackled. He gave me a brief nod before he turned to answer it. When he was done, he spun, gave me a wave, and left the practice.

"Thanks Chris," I said loudly as he left, and Brenda stood up from the desk.

"I'm done today. You're on the desk until closing. Mind you lock up." Her brisk words told me she was going to call Warren's mum as soon as she was out of earshot, but I didn't care.

Charlie came back towards the desk and I glanced at his cheek. "You okay there, Rocky?" I asked him in an amused voice, and he gave me a wry grin.

"I'm fine, Bethy. Are you okay?" His voice was low and concerned, and I reached out, touching his cheek and gave him a watery smile.

"I am now. Rambo here saved the day."

He laughed and leaned into the desk, but before he could say another word, someone cleared their throat behind him. Mr. Roberts was standing there.

"Ah, Mr. Roberts. Take a seat. Dr Finchley will be right with you." I checked him in on the appointments list and looked to see who else was expected in; two more patients and then that was us for the night.

Charlie cleared his throat and I glanced up at him from under my lashes. "Charlie, why don't you take a seat and I'll come grab you when I'm locking up."

"Fine. Fine. I have some calls to make anyway." He moved away, and I couldn't stop myself watching his arse. His jeans were tight and fitted and showed the shape off. He'd always had a sexy arse, but if he'd caught me looking, he'd never let me live it down.

I quickly dropped my eyes to the keyboard and concentrated on finishing off my daily chores. I emailed the pharmacy again after Dr. Morgens made changes to a repeat prescription and updated them, and I was just typing out an email in response to a request for a fundraiser when Mr. Harris arrived for his appointment, followed by Mai Smith. Mai was one of my favourite patients and we were chatting about her new baby when Dr Finchley buzzed for Mr. Harris. Dr Morgens called Mai in and she gave me a cheery smile and a wave, and I finished composing my reply.

I was desperate for the day to be over. My headache was getting worse, and I was so glad I was off the next day. I'd taken a day's holiday because the Wanker and I had been supposed to be going up north to visit his friends.

"Shit." I apparently said it aloud because Charlie came over. I hadn't cancelled the fucking hotel and I'd already paid for it, but I hadn't booked travel because he'd supposed to have been driving us.

Celibet

"What's up, Bethy?" Charlie asked, and I glanced up at him to see his furrowed brow and mouth in a tight line. Great. He was fucking worried about me.

"Nothing. I just booked and paid for a hotel for that walloper and me, and now I'm stuck with a weekend break I can't get to. Uh, fuck my life," I whispered, putting my head down on the desk.

"Where is it?" Charlie asked, and I muttered against the desk.

"Where is what?"

"The way to Amarillo?"

I lifted my head and squinted at him in confusion as he burst out laughing.

"Where is the weekend away?"

"Oh, it's uh, in Glasgow. We were supposed to stay at the Radisson in Glasgow and meet up with some of his friends." The booking was in my name and I hadn't told him what hotel we were in, so he wouldn't be able to go without me.

"Okay," Charlie said in an amused whisper, and I could tell he was planning something. He was typing away on his phone as he walked away from the reception desk.

As the last patients left, Dr. Morgens came round and handed over the Dictaphone with a smile. I knew she would want it transcribed, but I was due to finish in ten minutes and I wouldn't have time. She smiled when I told her and told me to leave it for Julia who was covering me the next day. She gave me a smile and breezed past Charlie, who watched her go with interest.

It made me a little uneasy watching him, so I turned away and began wiping down my desk and making sure everything was turned off.

Suzy, the practice nurse, came out of her office, roaring with delight at the sight of Charlie, and flew over to give him a hug. "Come on, tell me everything? How was the movie?" she asked him enthusiastically, and he gave her a smile before catching my eye and winking at me.

I couldn't believe I hadn't even asked him the same question, but he had arrived back at four in the fucking morning and had caught me having sex with someone.

My cheeks heated again at the memory of him standing there, and I quickly shook it off, checking and locking all the doors, making sure the percolator was off as I grabbed my jacket and purse from the tearoom.

Suzy walked in after me and bounced around getting her coat and bag. "He's such a hoot. He just told me that Jessie Lewis has horrible breath and Carter Cummings is a limp dick." She grinned at me and walked out of the room as I quickly scanned and made sure everything was shut down. The room was empty, so I switched off the light and locked the door, hanging the keys in the reception.

The door was an automatic lock, and I called Charlie over. "Charlie, it's time to go."

He glanced up from his phone, gave me a warm smile and slouched towards me. I grabbed his hand and pulled him along because the train was in ten minutes, and if we missed it, the next one wasn't for another fifteen and it took longer. I wanted to get home. In fact, I was desperate to get home, so I pushed him out of the door.

Celibet

He pocketed his mobile and turned to face me, pulling me in for a surprise hug.

My body relaxed into it. Charlie had always been my safe place, and I knew he wouldn't hurt me. I was so relieved he was home that I wanted to cry because he was my best friend and I'd missed him dreadfully while he was gone.

"Thanks for coming today and for defending me," I muttered against his chest and his arms tightened.

"Anything for you, Beth. I'll always defend you." He took a breath like he wanted to say something more, but then just shook his head and dropped his arms. "Come on. Let's get to the train station. I want to get home and find out what happened while I was gone."

He pulled me along, and we made the train just in time. We couldn't talk whilst we were on it because it was packed to the brim with commuters, and Charlie was getting some looks. I didn't blame the girls for checking him out: with his movie star good looks, easy smile, and approachable nature, he was perfect for ogling. One girl recognised him from his time in Eastenders, and that was it. She talked his ear off about his character and told him she had been gutted when he'd left for Spain—his character, at least, had gone after a fight with his mum and siblings because he was gay. She also told him that him being gay was such a waste, and he met my eye with a smirk. He wasn't gay at all, but he was good at acting

He thanked her and moved away from her, coming to stand beside me, and murmured in my ear. "Thanks for the help, Bethy."

I giggled and he shook his head. "You handled it fine on your own."

We reached the station and left the train, heading for our flat, but he dragged me into the supermarket and picked up some essentials: bread, eggs, wine, and toilet paper.

"We are going to Scotland at six am tomorrow by train, so I don't want to buy too much."

Wait! What?

"I booked us a train and we leave at five in the morning. You okay with that?"

"Yeah, that sounds great. It won't be the first time we've shared a hotel room," I muttered, and he grinned at me as he scanned and paid for the things.

I flashed back to Zante when we'd been twenty-one and remembered the drunken kiss we'd shared before he fucked off with the girl from the next room, but I was over that. It was years ago now.

Chapter Fifteen

CHARLIE
Fight Club

Once I'd dealt with Warren, I followed Beth into the surgery and took a seat while she finished up her shift. When the two officers had walked in after me, I had to take a second look.

So that's what he looked like in clothes. He's the guy that was in Beth's bed at four am this morning.

He saw me eyeing him and gave me a nod before his gaze shifted back to Beth sat behind the desk. They shared a brief moment when their eyes met, and I felt the frown pull at my brow as I witnessed it. I pushed back the smallest amount of jealousy I seemed to be feeling when Beth told me to take a seat.

While Beth had been busy working, I pulled up the train app on my phone and booked two return seats for us. I'd missed my friend and she needed me and this way we could spend some time together, just us.

After literally trawling through my case that I still hadn't unpacked since I'd returned from Paris, we decided to go shopping for more clothes. Beth and I hit up Primark and bought ourselves some things we could take with us. That way, I didn't have to wash my clothes in time, and I knew there weren't enough clean ones in my wardrobe. This was easier.

Once we were loaded with bags of the basics, we had more essentials to get, like Jack Daniels for the room. After tackling the crowds in Asda and getting what we needed, we got back to the flat and ordered ourselves a Chinese before crashing out.

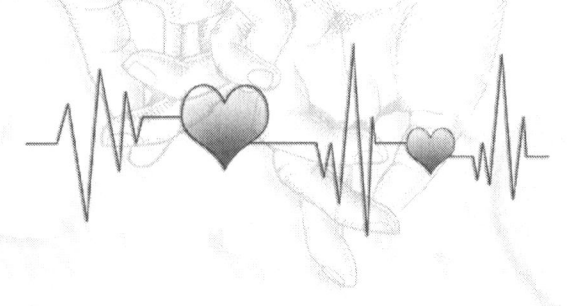

The next day, we were up bright and early, packed, and ready to leave. With the train station only being a short walk away from our place, we dragged our cases with us and sat down to wait for the train. In my rucksack, we had snacks and drinks for the trip as it was a few hours. Beth was all smiles again, and after that dickwad had showed up

Celibet

yesterday and given her hassle, I'd just wanted to see her smile again.

I grabbed us both a coffee from the café at the station while we waited, seeing as it was still early. We all knew Beth wasn't a morning person, and this was better than her taking someone's head off.

When the train rolled into the station, we found our seats and settled in for the journey.

Beth linked her arm with mine and rested her head against my shoulder.

"So come on, Bethy-babe. What's gone on? Why did Warren the Wanker dump you, and why is he harassing you? There's nowhere to run and nowhere to hide. All you can do is tell me the truth." I smirked, knowing that I'd cornered her. Yesterday, she'd run out to work. Today, and on this train, she didn't have a bloody choice.

I heard her sigh, and I smiled to myself as she shifted her head slightly and looked up at me from under those pretty lashes.

Her eye narrowed and her lips pouted, but I wasn't budging. I held her gaze instead and waited patiently.

"Fine." She sighed and rolled her eyes. "I think he cheated on me."

Anger surged through my body and I pushed myself to the edge of the chair, my knee bouncing erratically. "Well if I'd known that yesterday, I'd have beat the fucking shit out of him!"

"Charlie, calm down," Beth said as she tried to soothe me. Her hand rubbed my arm as she spoke. "There's nothing you can do now, so why don't you sit back, and I'll tell you the rest."

I looked back over my shoulder, and with just one flutter of those bastard lashes, I was done for.

She rested her head back on my shoulder and began from the beginning.

It was going to be a long fucking journey to Glasgow that's all I could say. I didn't know how anyone could treat Beth like that: she was one of the sweetest and nicest girls you could ever meet. She'd always been too good for that piece of fucking shit!

I looked down at her again and sighed. Beth had always been able to get me to do what she wanted, and right now this wasn't going to be any different. Warren on the other hand, would find out how fucking livid I was when I got back from this trip.

"So," she started, regardless of my sudden mood change, "I knew something was wrong when he left me stranded at work…"

Oh yeah… he's dead. I'm going to kill him.

Chapter Sixteen

BETH

Charlie fumed as he sat sullenly beside me, but I knew better than to interrupt him when he was this angry. The hostess with the trolley passed, and I grabbed a Jack and coke for Charlie and a rosé wine for myself.

Charlie grunted at me as I passed his drink but didn't speak, continuing to type furiously on his phone. I finished my wine, but my signal was shit and I didn't want to read, so I decided to go to sleep.

I curled up and lay my head on Charlie's shoulder, but it wasn't comfy, so I tapped him, he lifted his arm, letting me curl up on his chest. He plucked his hoodie up from the floor and wrapped it around me, giving me a soft kiss on the forehead as I snuggled into him and drifted off to sleep.

I woke up a few hours later and saw Charlie was sound asleep with his hands wrapped around me. I relaxed against him until I realised that I needed to pee, but he was holding me too tightly to move. I tried to ignore it, but I really needed the loo, and when I tried to wake him, he tightened his hold more, muttering something about boobs. I was almost about to burst when I managed to break free from his hold and hurried towards the bathroom.

I almost made it without incident until a six-foot guy stood up suddenly and stepped into my path, causing me to careen into him, fall backwards and land on my arse in the aisle in absolute mortification.

He glanced down at me, shrugged then turned and went into the bathroom. I wanted to get my stiletto out of my case and stab him in either the eye or the junk—both were appealing—but instead, I stood up and moved further down the train to the other bathroom, which—although smelled awful—was thankfully was free.

I quickly locked the door and began to pee, but the train lurched sideways. I managed to hold on, but a little pee got on my leggings.

"Fuck my fucking life," I hissed as I wiped at my piss-stained leggings with a wet wipe from my bag. I had other leggings, but they were in my case, and it was currently buried underneath a mountain of other cases, so I couldn't even change.

I managed to get back to my seat without incident but sitting down was impossible because Charlie now had a

Celibet

companion. A pretty brunette was in my seat, chatting to him, and when I approached, she glowered in my direction.

"So, are you and that girl together?" she asked as I hovered a few feet away, waiting to get back to my seat.

"Me and Beth? God no. She's my best friend, but no, we aren't together. I don't like her like that."

His words cut into me, and I swallowed the pain, ignoring the girl's triumphant smile as she watched me.

"So, do you want my phone number?" the girl asked, and Charlie turned to give her his full-on smirk, giving her a once over.

"Sure, that'd be good. What's your name again?"

"It's Zoe."

"Okay, type your number in here." He passed over his phone and she typed in her number, calling her mobile from his, and then she leaned over and gave him a kiss on the cheek before her friends called her back to them. She pushed past me, and I smirked at her because he likely wouldn't even text her back. He hated pushy girls and loathed it when girls hit on him. However, I watched in surprise as he sent her a message. He didn't even notice me standing there and didn't react as I slumped down on the seat.

So much for us spending time together.

I ignored him as they began texting and didn't say a word to him for the rest of the journey. A few times, he began to start conversations with me, but I gave him one-word answers until he gave up.

As the train pulled into Glasgow central station, Zoe came over and he ignored me completely as he spoke to her. She asked him if he wanted to meet up with her over the weekend and he fucking said yes.

I wanted to swing for him, so I stood, hitting him intentionally with my bag, and stormed towards the luggage rack, tugging my overnight case down and marching towards the train doors.

I didn't wait for him to catch up to me as I disembarked, but I had to wait for him to get out of the turnstiles in the station because he had our tickets. I turned back to see what was taking him so long and saw her wrapped around him on the platform.

He was kissing her, and for a moment, I felt a hot swoop of jealousy wash over me. Then, I remembered he wasn't mine and how he'd sworn after Zante that he'd never kiss me again, which had made me feel so attractive.

I tore my eyes away and wished we'd never booked this stupid train. I wished I were at home in London where I could escape to my room and not have to see him sucking face with a bimbo he met on the train.

They walked up to me holding hands, and Charlie held my ticket out towards me with a grin, but I just snatched it from his hand and spun towards the barrier, marching through, and leaving him to say goodbye to Zoe.

"Uh, what a stupid fucking name," I muttered to myself as I strolled away from him in entirely the wrong direction. "Get another syllable," I spat realising that there were two syllables in her name but who fucking cares, then continued walking until Charlie caught up to me.

Celibet

"Beth, Zoe says you're heading in the wrong direction. The Radisson is the other way."

"Well, if Zoe says it then it must be fucking true," I hissed at him, and he stepped back from me with wide eyes and a hurt expression on his face.

Fucking typical. He ignores me, kisses a fucking train floozy and then makes me feel bad for being angry about it. Uh.

I spun around and began walking in the opposite direction.

"Beth are you okay?" Charlie asked in a low voice, and I shot him a glare.

"Oh, I'm just fucking peachy," I exclaimed as I reached the escalator and went down it. He followed me wordlessly. As we emerged into the wet Glasgow afternoon, I could see the hotel was across the road from us, but there was a pub facing it and I marched into it and ordered shots at the bar.

Charlie stood beside me, texting on his mobile, and I wanted to take it off him and drop it into the pint he'd ordered. He just didn't fucking get it, and I was done with men. All fucking men. Even the heroic, sexy as sin, best friend type men. I was just fucking done with people who thought with their cocks instead of their fucking brains.

Chapter Seventeen

CHARLIE

"Are you going to be on that bloody thing all day?"

I dragged my eyes from my screen and turned my head to look at Beth. She stood beside me with her hand on her hip and a fierce look on her face.

"Jeez, Bethy. Chill would ya?" I knew what was eating at her. I wouldn't tell her that though. If the truth be known, I kind of scared myself when I noticed I'd been holding on that tightly to her on the train. When that girl Zoe came over and started flirting, I thought maybe it was the best thing to do. Beth didn't usually give a shit when I flirted with women.

Celibet

Her eyes narrowed as she glared at me. If I had a hard on right now, it would fucking wilt. I sighed at her, shook my head, and slid my phone into my front pocket of my jeans. "Better?"

"Shut up. I'm not talking to you."

The barman came over and asked us what we were having. Beth piped up asking for wine and Jägerbombs while I grabbed my pint.

"Is one of those for me?"

"Yep. You're paying." She plastered a false grin to her face, and before I paid, I ordered a jack and coke too. I handed the barman a twenty. Beth walked away with her wine and a Jäger and found us a table. Once the barman had brought over my extra drink, he passed me my change, I pocketed it and turned to walk away. I watched, amused, as she tried to get on the stool. She was only 5'3 and watching her having to lift a leg so she could hop up was funny.

Tiptoeing up behind her, I placed my glasses on an empty table and wrapped an arm around her waist, hoisting her up until her arse cheek was planted on the stool.

"I can manage."

"Well, I've helped you now." I said and smirked. "Tell me what's wrong?"

"Nothing. I'm fine." She picked up her Jäger and held it up to me. "You ready?"

I lifted mine and we clinked glasses before I knocked the entire thing back. I wasn't a fan of Jäger: it tasted like fucking cough medicine. You may as well have a shot of

Covonia and be done with it—at least then you could get rid of an annoying tickle at the same time.

"How do you drink this fucking shit?" I shook my head and chased the liquid with my friend, Jack, getting rid of the shitty taste in my mouth.

My phone vibrated again in my pocket, and I was in two minds whether I should answer it. "I know you're not fine. I know you better than that."

"Okay, Mr Big Shot, you tell me what's wrong… seeing as you know so much."

"Is this because of that Zoe bird on the train?"

"On the train? How about when you were trying to eat her fucking face on the platform? How about you arranging to meet her when you're supposed to be here with me?"

"Are you jealous?" I smirked, teasing her a little bit.

"Fuck you, Charlie. I should have just come here on my own." She drained her glass of her wine and slid off the stool before heading back to the bar.

Following her, I took her by the shoulders and bent my head to her ear. "Why don't we go check in. Then, we can come back if that's what you want?"

She snapped her head my way and huffed out loudly. She obviously didn't like that I was right. Her shoulders dropped, and leaving her glass on the bar, she shrugged my hands from her shoulders and turned away. She grabbed the handle of her case and started to leave through the pub before I'd even got my rucksack on my back.

"Fucking women."

Celibet

I managed to catch up to Beth when she stood at the reception desk of the hotel. She passed her credit card over for security, so I stood behind and waited for her to finish.

She held the plastic card in her hand and walked away saying nothing.

Fuck.

I trailed after her like some fucking pet, and once we reached our room, I dumped my case in the corner. I took a hold of her hand and dragged her to the bed, sat down and made her sit with me.

"Look, Beth, if I hurt you, I'm sorry. But we're here for two days. We can't be arguing the whole time."

"Who's arguing? It means fuck all to me that you completely ignored my presence on the train for the rest of the journey or the fact you left me standing on a platform on my own for some tart."

"Well, I don't think that's right. I tried to talk you, you ignored me, and I didn't shag her in the toilet, did I?"

"I'm surprised. But who the fuck goes up to a strange man who—may I add—has been sitting with a fucking woman the whole journey? She's a fucking tart, Charlie!"

I needed to make this right. I hated fighting with Beth. She was my best friend. I shouldn't have even kissed that girl, but the person who seemed to be on my mind constantly didn't seem to want me. When I'd held her on the train, all those feelings I'd felt that time in Zante had come flooding back. She'd made it quite clear back then that it was a mistake, a one-time thing, but it hadn't felt like that to me. What would be different this time? I'd watched her hang around with dicks since then, and Warren—oh my God, Warren. What the fuck she'd seen in him, I had no fucking idea. He was definitely the worst.

"I tell you what, how about I turn my phone off. Would that make you happy?"

Her blue eyes were wide with anticipation as she nodded.

"I promise this weekend is all about you."

The corners of her mouth turned up slightly as I pulled my phone and turned the thing off. I skimmed it to the other side of the bed and smiled at her. "Better now?"

She shrugged and her eyes turned downcast.

I lifted her chin and dipped my head before looking into her powdery blue eyes and raised an eyebrow. "Well?"

She nodded this time. I shifted from the bed and grabbed my bag. I opened the zip and pulled out a bottle of Jack and unscrewed the lid. "Want some?"

She snatched it from my hands, lifted it to her lips and shot some from the bottle.

"That's my girl. Now, why don't you get changed and we'll hit the bar downstairs."

Our faces were dangerously close, and as our eyes met, I could see the want swimming around in hers. I couldn't let anything happen. Not again.

Pulling back, I took a much-needed breath into my lungs

Beth's gaze fell on anything but me then moved away. "Great idea." She shifted from the bed and stood. "I think I pissed on my leggings on the train."

Celibet

Screwing my face up, I stared at her back as she waltzed into the bathroom and locked the door behind her.

Yep that's Beth: classy bird, but I'd have her no other way.

Chapter Eighteen

BETH

I stood in the bathroom shaking. I'd thought he was going to kiss me. I couldn't believe that I wanted him to, and when he'd turned away, a sliver of disappointment rolled over me.

I glanced at myself in the mirror and then remembered that I told him I'd pissed my leggings.

Way to go, Beth. Now he's going to think you're a total moron.

I didn't want to think any more about Charlie or how jealous I'd felt at seeing him with someone else, so I turned on the shower and stripped. My case was in the room, but I wanted to wash the grime of the journey off, and I needed a bit of time to compose myself before I got dressed up and went to a bar with him.

Celibet

As I scrubbed at my body, I thought about the past few weeks and I knew I had to come clean with Charlie about the fact that Warren had been stealing from me. Seven fucking grand. Amazon had refunded eight hundred quid, and I'd gotten paid today. My bonus was in there, because I'd never taken a sick day in the past year, so I was okay financially, but I still had to pay my dad back.

I washed my hair and heard the bathroom door open. Charlie walked in and started gelling his hair. Normally I didn't mind, but with all the traitorous feelings I had coursing around, it made me nervous to have him standing on the other side of the shower curtain.

I peeked around the curtain and saw his toned back, the muscles bunching and moving as he moved his hands and gelled his longer than normal hair into curls.

He had tight, dark blue jeans on, his feet bare, and for a second, as I stared at him, I wished he'd strip and come into the shower, but I shook it off and stepped back in, hitting myself on the soap dispenser on the wall. It stung like a bitch, but I managed to keep myself quiet. Leaning back, I rinsed my hair again, enjoying the feeling of the water massaging my scalp. I closed my eyes, letting the water roll down my body, and for a few minutes, there was complete silence. Then the bathroom door opened and closed.

Fuck, I'd forgotten he was in the bathroom for a second.

I switched off the water and grabbed a towel, wrapping it around my body and went out into the room. Charlie was facing away from me over by the window and didn't look around as I tossed my case up onto the bed and lifted out my black and red bodycon dress. It was totally fitted and showed off my curves, and it was so tight it didn't matter that it'd been pressed in my case for hours. I dressed quickly and went back into the bathroom to do my hair.

My hair always curled so I used a little product and scrunched it until it fell in loose, glossy waves down my back. I clipped it back and began to work on my makeup. When I was done and satisfied, I popped on some sultry red lipstick and squirted my favourite perfume.

I turned and went out into the room, but Charlie wasn't there. He didn't have his mobile on him because it was still sitting on the bed, but glancing around, I saw a note from him propped up in front of the pillow.

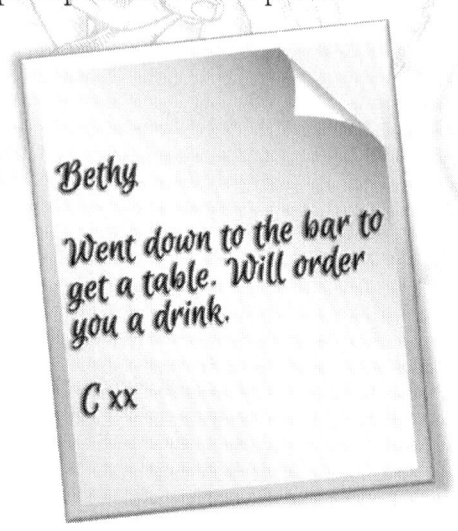

Bethy,

Went down to the bar to get a table. Will order you a drink.

C xx

Celibet

I wondered why he hadn't waited for me, but I was almost ready. I quickly pulled on my dress and pushed my feet into my black Louboutin's, fastening the straps.

I snatched up my dress handbag and shoved in my lipstick, eyebrow pencil and mascara. I also put my phone and my little black purse with my bank card in before quickly taking the room key from the table and going downstairs.

I needed food because I hadn't eaten all day, and the alcohol was sloshing around in my gut. Walked into the bar area, I saw Charlie sitting with his back to me, facing out the window.

I felt kind of bad for my bitchy behaviour earlier, but not so bad that I wanted to tell him to go out on a date with the train trollop.

"Hey," I muttered as I reached him.

He glanced up at me and gave me a once over. "You are gorgeous, Beth," he breathed, and my cheeks heated at the compliment. He wasn't usually shy about complimenting me, but something about this felt different.

He pointed to the chair across the table and I saw a Pornstar Martini sitting there waiting for me.

Leaning over, I gave him a brief hug before sitting down. He met my eyes for a moment and then lifted his drink, taking a long sip as he watched me.

He was wearing a dark grey, fitted shirt with the top buttons undone and my insides quivered.

Just as I opened my mouth to say thank you to him, Train Trollop and her shrieking friends appeared at our table. I narrowed my eyes at Charlie and didn't say a word as I sat and sipped on my drink, plotting his murder.

Would a pillow do? Or should I shove him in a bath with my hairdryer?

He didn't meet my eyes as he chatted easily with them, but he reached under the table and put his hand on my bare knee, giving me a gentle squeeze.

I finished my drink and wanted another, but I wasn't leaving my seat. The trollop's friends were giving me glacial looks, and I wasn't about to move and let them take my seat, so I ignored them and took out my mobile, texting my dad, Callie and reading the threatening messages from Warren.

I had notifications on my social media accounts, and I opened my Instagram to see the video of me drunkenly giving that douche a lap dance front and centre. My mobile slipped from my frozen fingers as I gasped, and Charlie turned to face me.

"Beth, what's wrong?" he asked in a low voice, but I didn't answer because the alcohol was about to make a reappearance. I shot up from my seat and flew out of the bar, running towards the bathroom with my hand over my mouth.

I made it just in time and vomited up all the alcohol I'd drank and then some. My stomach heaved, my eyes watered, and my face was a red blotchy mess as I surveyed myself in the mirror.

My eyes were full of tears, and I just wanted to run away. I didn't want to go back into the bar and see those fucking

Celibet

girls, and I didn't want to speak to Charlie either. He could have told them to get lost, but he didn't and part of me hated him for it.

I took the straps off my shoes and was about to walk out of the bathroom when I heard the door open, so I quickly darted inside the nearest loo, closing, and locking the door.

"So, who is she anyway?" one voice asked.

Another replied, "A nobody. She's his best friend according to him, but not for long. I'll push her out. I'm much prettier than her. I mean, she looks like a tramp in that dress…"

Her friend giggled and agreed with her, and I stood for a minute with my face burning. I was about to let it go, but it wasn't in my nature to allow someone I didn't know to make me feel like crap about myself, so I unlocked the door and stepped out to face them.

"Hey, you know what lasts longer than a trollop like you?" I asked in a high clear voice and she met my eyes in a mirror.

She glared at me for a minute and I stared right back, refusing to be intimidated.

"A fucking STD! And you know what else I know about Charlie? He doesn't keep trollops around for long, but I've been his friend for the last seven years, so go ahead and try and push me out. We'll soon see which one of us is around at the end!"

Her friend stepped around her and went to say something, but Trollop stopped her and came towards me.

She opened her mouth to say something when Charlie came into the bathroom. He didn't care that it was the ladies' room, and he ignored her completely, pulling me out of the bathroom and away from her. He had my handbag and he dragged me to the bank of elevators, pressing the button for the fourth floor, and took me into our room without speaking.

Once we were there, he paced around like a caged animal and didn't say a word. His pacing made me more nervous, and I wanted to cry because fucking Warren had released that video.

My mobile began to ring inside my bag, and I quickly dug it out, shaking as I took in Callie's name on the screen. Before I could answer it though, Charlie snatched it from my fingers and ended the call. He turned to me and winced when he saw my expression.

Before I could say or do anything, he slumped down on the bed beside me and pulled me into his arms as I burst out crying.

Chapter Nineteen

CHARLIE

She cuddled up to me, holding on tight, like I was going to leave her. There was no way that was going to happen.

I knew something had been wrong when the colour had drained out of her face, leaving her looking like she'd seen a ghost. When her phone crashed to the table and she ran out, it was obvious something was wrong. I knew she didn't like Zoe, and I had no fucking idea why I'd said to meet me in the bar. I could have kicked myself right then.

I hadn't been able to leave her there alone.

I grabbed her handbag and phone from the floor. The screen lit up with her locked screen and asked for the passcode. Zoe and her friends were cackling and shrieking behind me, but I was in no mood now.

"So where are we going next, Charlie?" Zoe hung off my arm with her drink in her hand and her cute body rubbing up against me.

"Can you just give me a minute?" I told her, hoping she'd get the message.

"I need to powder my nose anyway." She giggled and blew me a kiss before linking arms with one of her friends and walking away.

I entered Beth's passcode, and whatever she'd been watching began to play. What I didn't expect was to see Beth, my Beth, to be doing what looked like a strip for someone. As the video went on, my anger soared to another level and then I heard it, his fucking voice: Warren.

He was fucking videoing her.

That bastard was going to get the wrath of Charlie fucking James when I got back.

Turning off the video, I tensed my jaw, my teeth grinding as I found his number in her list of contacts, entering it into my phone. Warren the sleaze was going to get a call from me very soon.

I dropped her phone into her bag and headed for the toilets. As I stood outside, I could hear voices, and putting my ear to the door, I heard the word tramp.

Celibet

Then I heard a door bang and Beth's voice add to the conversation. I wasn't listening to this fucking shit, and I wasn't having some slut treating Beth like that. Beth came first—always.

Zoe's face was a picture as I stormed into the ladies and removed Beth myself. I'd had enough of bitchy women lately, thinking they could do what they wanted with no regard for others.

Beth's tears leaked onto my shirt, but I didn't care. I placed my hand softly on her head and stroked her hair hoping I was helping to comfort her. I wrapped her up a little tighter pulling her closer into my side.

"Charlie?" She looked up at me, her face soaked with tears. "Did you see it?"

"See what, babe?" I probably should have just said yes, but I didn't want her to think I'd been snooping.

"Please don't make me say it. I can't."

"Yes. I watched it. I want to fucking kill him."

Beth sat up and wiped her face then faced me. "There're things you don't know."

"What things?"

She rose to her knees and took her bag by the strap before she reached in and pulled her phone out. She unlocked the screen and scrolled until she found some messages she was looking for and handed it to me.

I read through each and every one of those messages where Warren had threatened her, and when I was done, I was so fucking angry, I wanted to jump a train right then and go back to London to find him. When I got my hands on him—well I had no idea what I'd do. I'd probably strangle the little cunt with my bare hands.

"Please say something."

"I don't know what to say."

"Please don't be angry with me." There was a wobble in her voice, and it made me feel like shit but still, I reared back, not able to understand why she'd think I was angry with her.

"Beth, I could never be angry with you. This is him not you." I sucked in a calming breath and tried to keep myself centred. "He shouldn't have done this, and I'm going to sort it." I twisted my body around and pushed my legs out in front of me, placing them either side of her body, caging her in.

Reaching up, I placed my hands on her cheeks and gently rubbed the tears away with my thumbs. Our gazes met, and my heart began to pound out of my chest.

No-one had ever made me feel like this.

As her chin wobbled and a ragged breath left her lips, I pulled her closer and put my lips to hers. I needed her to feel better; I just wanted her to see she wasn't the person those girls said she was—that she wasn't the person Warren made her out to be—but as soon as our lips touched, a spark ignited. A fire was lit, and I couldn't put it out until I'd felt that heat. Her lips were pressed against

mine and I realised what I'd done. This wasn't about me; this was about her.

I pulled back like her lips were made of hot lava and dropped my hands from her face.

Celibet

"Oh my God, Beth, I'm so sorry. I shouldn't have done that. You're not ready for that—not ready for my baggage." I stood and moved away from her to the other side of the room.

"Charlie, it's okay." Her hand rested on my back, but I didn't turn around.

I couldn't—not yet.

There'd been something bubbling up between us for so long, but we'd always ignored it. We were friends and that couldn't change. Seeing her in that dress tonight after I'd seen her in the shower in the reflection of the mirror, I'd been so fucking hard, and I'd struggled to control myself, hence why I'd ran out on her.

I needed to find a way to see her the way I used to and not let it come between us but, I wasn't sure how.

I turned around and faced her. If I were anything, I was a man, and I'd deal with my shit. "I'm sorry," I said again.

Chapter Twenty

BETH

My body still thrummed from the kiss, and I wished he hadn't pulled away, but how did I tell him that without blurring the lines of our friendship more?

When he said he was sorry again, I wasn't sure if he meant he was sorry that the kiss happened, sorry that it stopped or sorry that I wasn't ready.

I reached up, cupping his cheek, and he met my eyes with fire in his. My breath quickened, and I licked my lips as he glanced down at them and then back up to my eyes with longing evident on his face.

Just as I decided to step forwards, he stepped back and turned away from me, walking into the bathroom and

Celibet

closing the door. I heard the click of the lock, and I leaned against the wall trying to calm the racing of my heart.

I'd completely forgotten about Warren and the shitshow he'd created for a moment, and then it all came flooding back in glorious technicolour. My desire turned to fury, and I marched over to my bag and took out my phone, screenshotting the messages and the video and sending them in an email to the desk sergeant from the other night.

I kicked my heels off and sat on the bed, glowering at my phone, and then a message from an ex of Warren's pinged on my messenger as a request.

Hi Beth

You don't know me, but I was with Warren last year, and he told me he was only with you because you were loaded. He said you were a tight bitch with your cash and that he was going to try and get a hold of your trust fund details, so I'd check to make sure that he hasn't got them. I ended things with him that night.

I didn't know about you, I swear, but I saw that video of you on social media and figured that you finally dumped his ass.

Hope you don't mind me reaching out.

Greta

I didn't know what to say in response, so I just closed the message and leaned back on the bed for a moment. My heart pounded in my chest as I realised that he'd been cheating on me for our whole relationship. Thank God, I thought, that I'd refused to go bareback with him.

What a fucking douche. He deserved everything that was coming to him, but I needed to check my trust fund account. I quickly dialled the bank and went through the security. I checked the balance on my account and saw that it was fine.

I wondered if he'd dumped me because he hadn't been able to get access to it. I ended the call as Charlie came back out and sat down on the bed as far from me as he could get.

"I can't be with you right now, Bethy. I need to get some air okay?" he told me as he stood and walked towards the door. He grabbed his jacket and left the room without his wallet or his mobile before I could say a word to stop him.

I sat on the bed, still in my dress, and put the TV on, catching the end of Me Without You. It always made me cry, and I sat sobbing on the bed as the letter was read out. I didn't hear the door open, and Charlie came over and sat on the bed beside me, pulling me into his arms as the credits rolled.

"Sorry, Bethy, babe. I just needed a minute." He cracked open the bottle of Jack, took a sip and passed it to me, and for a while, we just sat passing the bottle back and forth without a word.

Celibet

"I was with Jessie Lewis in Paris," he told me as he took a sip and then passed me the bottle.

Jessie Lewis! Wow she was a fucking goddess. No wonder he pulled away from me. No way could I measure up to that.

"She cheated on me, so I can't…" he began and then broke off.

I tried to turn to see his face, but he held on to me tightly.

"You got screwed over by Warren and I caught my girlfriend in bed with another guy." He passed me the drink and I took a sip. Fuck he was right. I was so done with men!

"I'm just done with men…" I told him in a slurry voice, trying to think through my drunken thoughts.

"Wait, you going to bat for the other side babe?" he asked with a laugh, and I shook my head.

"No, women are too much trouble, too. I just want to stay celibate for a while."

"I agree. I can't be dealing with anymore girls thinking they are the shit and turning out to be fucking using me. I need a fucking break from the pressures of being with someone."

I pulled out of his arms and turned to face him as an exciting thought began to blossom. "How about we make a deal or a bet?"

He didn't answer me and stared at him as he nodded at me to continue.

"We both stay single for twelve weeks. No girls, no guys, no leprechauns! A 'celibet' if you will. And if you lose then you have to… uh… have to, erm, buy me a holiday to somewhere exotic, and put the picture you hate most about yourself online with the caption, Beth's Bitch."

I knew the picture and I knew he hated it. It was his year four photo. He was a chubby little guy with buck teeth and glasses. He loathed that photo. I'd only seen it because one of his boxes fell when he moved it and it fell out and his reaction was extreme to say the least.

He chased me around the apartment and yanked it out of my hands with a growl, but I didn't give up and I pushed him until he told me that he kept that photo with him to remind himself of where he came from and who he really was.

"And if you lose?" His eyes were narrowed. He looked at me in a way that made my heart squirm in my chest.

"Uh, if… if I lose, I have to take you to Australia for six weeks, all expenses paid..."

"And?"

He raised his eyebrow at me, and I knew I wasn't getting out of this as easily.

"I'll… I'll uh…."

"Spend a week with my mum in Dorset…."

"What? No way, Charlie. She hates me... why do you wanna do that to me? I thought you liked me?"

"I do like you, but this way we both have something to lose. I have my dignity and you have your pride. One week with my mum and you'll come away feeling like a total failure, so it's a win, win really..."

Celibet

He smirked at me and then leaned closer, sloshing a little of the jack. "So, twelve weeks?" he asked, and I nodded.

"Okay. Let's do it. How can we seal the bet?" He leaned closer and stopped millimetres from me. I could taste his breath as he leaned so close, and he licked my lips when he licked his own.

As soon as his tongue touched mine, I launched myself at him and kissed him fiercely. Our tongues tangled with each other's as we fought to dominate the kiss. His hands wrapped around my back and he dragged me closer, so I was on his lap. He slowed the kiss down and then broke away from me, breathing harshly and leaning his head on mine as we both struggled to get our racing hearts under control.

"Okay, a celibet!" He breathed against my face and I gave him a soft smile as we stared at each other.

This would be easy. It would be totally easy! I could do this.

I could still feel Charlie's erection against my thigh, and I gave him a nod and scuttled back from him to sit on the bed at his side again. My body was tingling all over, and I wanted more than anything to climb back on Charlie's lap and have him take me to places I'd never gone before with him, but I knew we couldn't do it.

We had a bet now, and I had to win. No way was I spending a week with his mum. She loathed me. She really did and she made it very clear that she didn't think I was anywhere near good enough to be Charlie's friend.

"Beth, what if we both win?" Charlie asked me in a low, hoarse whisper.

I glanced over at him. His cheeks were flushed, and his eyes still blazed, but it was his lips swollen and red that made me want to say screw it.

"Then we decide on an adventure together."

He nodded, and his stomach growled. I checked my phone and saw it was a little after six pm. No wonder he was starving. I was, too, but not for food.

Chapter Twenty-One

CHARLIE

A bet. A fucking bet.

How the hell could I think of staying celibate after that kiss? I could say no to everyone else, some normal woman, but what was it going to be like at home now? Beth would get out of the shower in just a skimpy fucking towel wrapped around her and barely covering her arse cheeks, and the snake that resided in my pants was going to want to play. In fact, this fucking bet was just going to make it so much harder… I meant keeping my hands to myself, I wasn't even thinking about my dick. Well, I told myself that.

My stomach growled just then, reminding me I hadn't eaten since earlier on the train, but it hadn't been up there most with the most important things that were now playing on my mind.

I needed to get out of this room though before I said, 'fuck it' and bent her over the bed. I had visions of stripping that fucking sexy as sin dress from her body and make her forget all about that dickhead. In fact, I was hoping I could make her forget her own fucking name as she writhed on my cock… If she remembered mine when she was screaming, who fucking cared.

"I need food. Let's go."

"Wait. I need to quickly re-do my makeup." She went over to the bathroom, "I can't go out looking like Alice Cooper," she shouted from the bathroom as I stood from the bed and re-adjusted my cock's position from where it was straining against my zip. At this rate, it would have track marks down the shaft.

I grabbed my phone and wallet and walked towards the door, stopping at the bathroom. I happened to glance to the side and saw her spreading gloss over her lips. "That's not fucking fair," I whispered more so to myself as I pulled on the door, walked out, and leaned against the wall.

All I could think of now was her glossed up lips moving up and down my dick… I really needed to calm myself. I sucked in a few deep breaths and blew them out slowly. By the time Beth joined me, my hard on had wilted to a semi. At least it was enough to be able to sit opposite her and eat.

We walked around Glasgow until we found a nice-looking Indian restaurant and went inside. The waiter

Celibet

found us a table straight away and took our drinks order. I got Beth a bottle, yes, a bottle, of house rosé, and me a beer.

The thing I'd always loved about Beth was she wasn't picky: she wasn't one of those girls—you know, the high maintenance ones—who needed to be wined and dined in expensive places. She'd quite happily spend her night in a pub dancing and grab a kebab on the way home.

My gaze found her again, and she smiled at me from across the table. A smirk tugged at my lips, and I folded my arms in front of me on the table. "So how does this bet even work?"

"I don't know. I was hoping you'd have an idea?"

The waiter returned with our drinks, halting our plan temporarily, and took our order. We skipped the starters, other than poppadom's, and ordered our main meal. I grabbed me a tikka masala curry with chips and Beth had a chicken korma with mushroom pilau rice, and we topped off the order with a cheese and garlic naan to share. The waiter smiled and left us alone.

"Do we actually go on dates or not? I mean, I'm not sure that if I went on a date, I'd be able to keep it strictly platonic…"

"Then you'd lose, buster. And I'd win." The grin that spread across her face was quite amusing. "And anyway, what's the point of a date if we're staying away from them?"

I lifted the bottle of beer up and placed it at my lips, tipping it up and drinking a good portion of the beer. "I guess it's just us for the next twelve weeks."

Beth lifted her glass and held it up. "To us, I guess."

My bottle clinked her glass. "May the best person win." We drank at the same time and grinned at each other…

Fuck this was going to be hard work.

Chapter Twenty-Two

BETH

I would win because for as long as I had known Charlie, he couldn't keep it in his pants. He loved the ladies and hated having to work hard to get a girl. If a girl was too much work, he usually backed off and left her to it.

We ate in silence, and I managed to finish the bottle of wine. I was more than a little tipsy as we made our way along a street where a bar was playing loud music.

"Come on, Charlie," I said loudly as I dragged him towards the door and past the security guards.

It was packed and there was a small dance floor.

"Drink first," Charlie yelled over the music as he linked his fingers with mine and tugged me along to the bar. He ordered another beer for himself and a glass of wine for me—rosé of course.

We sipped on our drinks and then Dirty by Christina came on, and I dragged him to the dance floor. My bag was over my shoulders and I began to dance with him. We'd always danced like no one was watching, and soon our bodies were moving against one another to the beat of the song.

I was facing away from him, moving my hips with his hand around my waist holding me to him.

His lips found my neck and he kissed, licked, and sucked on the tender skin there before he pressed a soft kiss under my ear, tugging me closer to him. My whole body began to respond. My pulse quickened and my breathing sped up, but I was trying to stay focused on our bet. It wasn't fair, him kissing me like that, because I wanted more of it—so much fucking more.

The song ended and Golddigger came on.

I spun around to face Charlie and he pulled me towards him, dropping his eyes from my burning gaze to our connected bodies.

"You sure about this bet, Bethy?" he asked me in a hoarse voice as we danced.

I glanced up to see the desire I was feeling reflected back on his face and opened my mouth to say no when I was shunted from behind. Charlie managed to keep me upright, but his eyes widened as he saw who was behind us: fucking Train Trollop and her posse had found us again, and this time she was glaring daggers at me.

Celibet

"Charlie, I waited on you to come back!" she called over the music accusingly.

I rolled my eyes and pulled myself out of Charlie's hold, going back to the bar to order some tequila. I noticed a group of people appearing by my side in time to see my drink lifted by the trollop. She tossed the contents of the glass over my head and red wine rolled down my face and hair, soaking my dress.

I wanted to swing for her and was about to step towards her when a bouncer came and carted her and her idiotic friends out of the bar, leaving me standing there, shaking in fury.

Charlie appeared by my side, and his eyes widened as he took in my soaked hair and ruined makeup.

"Jesus, Beth. What happened to you?" he asked innocently, and I wanted to scratch his eyes out.

"Uh nothing. It doesn't fucking matter!" I hissed at him.

His eyes widened at my cold tone and absolute fury at his stupidity in kissing a fucking girl on the fucking train.

I turned around and stormed away from him, leaving him at the bar as I marched outside to the now pouring rain of Glasgow city. He followed me, seemingly confused, but the adrenaline had worn off and I was feeling the alcohol I'd consumed.

"Beth, do you want to go back to the hotel?" he asked in a concerned whisper, and I nodded my head.

"Yeah. I'm drunk and I'm all wet."

My innocent answer made him chuckle and he leaned down to help me to my feet. "Come on, baby. Let's get you back to the hotel."

"Charlie, I'm all sticky," I slurred as he tried to help me walk, but I was staggering all over the place, so he heaved a sigh and then scooped me up into his arms.

I rested my head on his shoulder, the smell of his Boss aftershave invading my nostrils and turning me on. The rain pelted down, and a raindrop ran down his neck in front of my eyes.

I reacted on instinct.

My tongue darted out, and I licked the moisture from his neck.

His whole body shuddered in response. "Jesus, Bethy," he groaned, and his arms shook under my body. I licked at his neck again, and he leaned down capturing my lips in a soul-shattering kiss before he pulled back and shook his head.

"Beth, the bet," he muttered.

I gave him another soft kiss before I rested my head on his shoulder. "Love you, Charlie." I told him softly as I drifted off to sleep.

I woke up hours later in the hotel room to my stomach rolling. I ran into the bathroom, making it just in time as I projective vomited right down the pan. My body heaved and shuddered. I couldn't remember anything after leaving the pub. My dress was soaked, and I could smell alcohol

Celibet

on me, which set me off again. I leaned down and vomited until there was nothing left.

Stripping out of my dress, I climbed into the shower in my underwear, taking them off as the water began to make me feel a little better. I washed my hair and scrubbed my makeup from my face.

As I got out of the shower, I glanced into the room and saw Charlie fast asleep in the bed. His face was so beautiful, and I knew something was changing between us, but I was scared as I remembered the depth of emotion I'd felt when he kissed me.

His kisses had caused my stomach to erupt in butterflies and my body to clench with need, but it was the tenderness that made him dangerous. He was hot, fiery, and full on, but he could also be tender, sweet, and sensitive. He was the perfect package, and I knew any girl would be lucky to have him. I dreaded the day he found the one because I was beginning to see he was my 'one' and I knew when he found his forever girl, I wouldn't be able to bear it.

I quickly dried myself off and crawled back to bed after opening the bottle of water on my side of the bed and taking a few sips. I swallowed the two paracetamol that were sitting there, finished my water and leaned over, pressing a soft kiss to Charlie's temple as he slept.

His soft snores made me relax, and I snuggled down in the bed, falling asleep in the bath towel with wet hair and no shame.

Chapter Twenty-Three

CHARLIE

As I woke, I turned over and nearly choked on Beth's hair. It had somehow whipped me in the face at some point in the night and found its way into my mouth... When my eyes opened, though, and looked to the side of me, my brow furrowed to see Beth in a towel. I didn't remember her going to sleep like that.

Did we have sex?

NO. I know for a fact we didn't. I wasn't that drunk.

Beth, on the other hand, had been shitfaced. I never got a chance to find out how she got wet either.

I watched her sleep for a minute longer, feelings of lust creeping up, and I knew I needed out of this bed.

Celibet

Instead of running the risk of waking her, I decided to have a shower first before I made coffee. Once I was standing under the spray, I felt the tension from the last

twenty-four hours begin to ease but getting in the shower was probably the worst thing to do today, especially after waking up to Beth in just a towel. Not only that, the kiss from last night, the bet, her telling me she loved me…

My dick awakened. I needed to get rid of this tension somehow. I placed my hand against the wall and held my weight up, wrapping my fingers around my dick and moving it slowly up and down. I only had to think of Beth's lips sucking and moving along my neck last night, her naked body the other night… In fact, I'd come to realise that Beth seemed to be at the forefront of all my fantasies.

As the water ran over me, my hand slipped up and down freely and oh so easily. I moved faster, squeezing the head as I reached the top. My balls began to tighten, and my legs stiffened, and I knew it wouldn't be long. I pictured myself pounding into Beth's pussy, her taking everything I was giving her, her nails digging into my arse cheeks. I knew it wasn't going to take much more, and before I knew it, I was spurting my orgasm against the wall of the shower.

My heart pounded and my legs were like jelly. I gave myself a moment to calm down, and as soon as my heartbeat had begun to settle and return to a more regular rhythm, I washed up, rinsed off my body and stepped out, wrapping a towel around my waist.

I was absolutely starving, but by the time I was out of the shower and had put the kettle on, I realised we'd probably missed breakfast. My stomach growled on cue, and Beth was still asleep. I grabbed my phone from beside the bed and powered it back on. I had missed texts from that Zoe girl, so I messaged her and told her not to call me again.

We needed to do something today. Yesterday had been a washout for one reason or another, so I was going to make sure today was better. While I waited on the small kettle to boil, I searched through Google, looking for places for us to visit. There were a few in Glasgow, but best of all, I found just the place for Beth. It would mean booking a couple of train tickets, but I reckoned the trip to Pollok Park where Outlander had been filmed may just be worth it.

I pulled on a pair of black jeans and a white T-shirt and ran my fingers through my hair before going back to the bathroom, cleaning my teeth, and spraying some aftershave onto my neck.

Finally, I heard the click of the kettle, and I made us both a coffee. Once it was just the way she liked it I put both cups down and bounced on the bed at the side of her.

I leaned over her and whispered in her ear. "Bethy-baby, wakey, wakey, rise and shine."

"Ugh, I'm dead," she murmured quietly.

"No, you're not. Wake up."

"No. Please let me die."

"Where is the fun in that? Come on; up you get. I've made you coffee."

She opened one eye and squinted at me.

Celibet

"We've also missed breakfast, so we need to go to Wetherspoons for a fry up."

She groaned and rolled to her front, burying her face into the pillow. "I'm not well…"

"No, you're hungover. The best thing for a hangover: a fry up. Come on, Beth."

I went to the window and pulled back the curtains. The sun was shining, and it was a great day for a trip. I went back to the bed and smacked her arse.

"Ow."

"Get the fuck up. I've got a surprise for you today."

She swung her head towards me.

"Surprise?"

"Yeah surprise. Now come on. Up. I need breakfast, man."

I watched amused as she tried to sit up and keep the towel over her, so I made it easy for her: I turned around, giving her my back, and started to drink my own coffee. "Can you turn around?"

"Yes."

When I turned back, she had already sat up, the towel had gone, and the sheet had been put in its place to cover her modesty.

"You're so lucky we have this bet going on, Bethy-babe, because seeing you in just a towel did nothing for the stonker I was sporting when I woke up."

She shook her head and rolled her eyes.

"I had to have a soapy one in the shower." I winked at her and smirked again.

"Fucking men." Dragging the sheet with her, she gathered it at the back and held it tight, picked up her coffee and went into the bathroom. "I need paracetamol if you want me to function," she shouted as she closed the door and locked it.

Knowing she was going to be in there for at least the next twenty minutes, I grabbed my phone and wallet and the key card. I shouted that I wouldn't be long on the way past the bathroom and left.

I found the nearest shop and bought a couple of packs of paracetamol and a bottle of Pepsi for us both and went back to the hotel. By the time I got back to our room, she was just getting dressed.

"I'd dress comfortably if I were you."

She kicked off her skirt right in front of me and pulled on her jeans.

I sat on the bed and went through my emails while I waited for her to finish up. One from the director of the film we'd just finished shooting, congratulating us on a good shoot and saying he'd be in touch when it was being premiered.

My eyes rolled at the thought of seeing Jessie Lewis again, but I wasn't going to let that bitch put a dampener on my day.

Today was about cheering up Beth.

"I'm ready." She took her sunglasses from her bag before pulling it onto her shoulder and making sure I had the key card again, we left.

Celibet

As we entered the lobby and got nearer to the exit, she squinted at the sun that was blaring through the glass doors and put on her glasses.

"Now I'm ready.

I held out my arm for her and she linked hers through and we made our way to the nearest Wetherspoons. I needed sustenance.

Chapter Twenty-Four

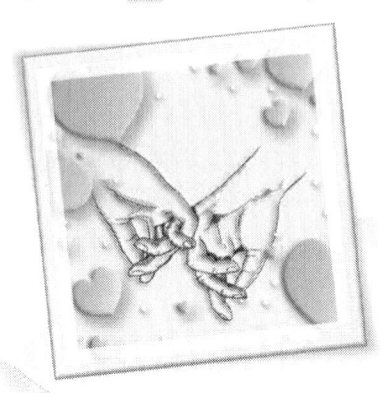

BETH

Hearing him say he'd rubbed one out in the shower made my stomach squirm, and I began to recall all of the kisses we'd shared the night before.

My heart hammered in my chest as I remembered making that stupid bet with him.

Fuck!

Why had we done that?

My body trembled as I remembered his kissing my neck in the pub, but then the memory of that idiot from the train resurfaced and my desire went out the window.

I quickly tamed my hair into a ponytail and put some light make up on, but my head was hammering in my skull.

Celibet

I heard Charlie return and walked out to find him holding two paracetamol and some Pepsi.

I dressed quickly and followed Charlie to the pub with a squiggly feeling in my stomach every time he looked at me or smiled at me. Something had changed with us. I knew we'd broken the unwritten rule of friendship, but I couldn't find it in myself to regret it, not really.

"What do you want for breakfast?" Charlie asked, and I scanned the menu. What did I want? A fry up or toast, bacon and potato cakes and mushrooms.

Uh. Too many choices.

"Just get me a fry up please with a latte and a water!" My stomach was still squiggly from the night before, and I wasn't sure I'd be able to tolerate much food.

He gave me a terse nod and went to order our food. I sat texting on my mobile, re-assuring Callie, Jay, and some other friends that I was okay. The video had been taken down by Instagram and Warren's account had been suspended.

I busied myself putting his texts and calls on do not disturb and saw that the last messages were all, **'you asked for it', 'I can't believe you went to the cops', and 'you've ruined my fucking life, you bitch'.**

I ignored his messages and squirmed with renewed longing as Charlie came back with my latte. I sipped on it as we waited for our food, but he looked a little uncomfortable sitting with me.

"What's up, Charlie?" I asked him, reaching over to cover his hand with mine, and he gave me a soft squeeze and then lifted his eyes to meet mine, a soft smile playing on his lips.

"Nothing, nothing! I'm just thinking back to last night. You got soaked, and I never did find out how, but I know now, and I'm so sorry!"

How did he know? I hadn't said a word, but I saw his mobile light up with another call and the name Zoe popped out.

"Ah, did she tell you she poured a massive glass of wine over me?" I quizzed him, and he shook his head.

"No, she said she poured a drink over you, not what it was! God, Bethy. I'm sorry!"

I linked our fingers and smiled over at him. It didn't matter today. It was only a drink, and I had been drunk enough already. If we'd gotten any drunker, we might not have made it past day one of our bet.

"It's fine. She probably did us a favour!"

He stared at me nonplussed for a second and then raised his eyebrow in a quizzical expression. "Huh, how did she do us a favour?" he asked in a low whisper, and I leaned across the table until we were almost nose to nose.

"We'll if we'd have gotten drunker, we may have decided to give up on our bet, so she saved us from a very awkward morning this morning."

His eyes darkened as I spoke, and his fingers contracted in mine.

"You think sleeping with me would make things awkward between us?" he probed, and I wondered

Celibet

whether to lie. I didn't mean awkward as in with regret, just different and unnerving.

"Yeah, don't you?" I muttered, and he tugged his hand from mine and took a long drink from his coke.

I pulled my hand back across the table as the silence between us grew. I tried to think of something to say to break the tension, but I had nothing. After a few more minutes of uneasy silence, the food arrived, and we ate without a word.

As we finished, he stood and left the table, going to the bathroom, and I sat and sipped on my water. I did feel better, but also worse at the same time. I hadn't meant we'd be awkward, but there was no way to fix us without making things more awkward.

As I waited for Charlie to come back, a guy came and sat down at our table uninvited and began talking to me. His name was Craig, a businessman apparently, but his attractiveness did nothing for me because he wasn't who I wanted, plus, there was no way was I going to lose this damn bet.

"Sorry, I have to go!" I interrupted him as I stood and grabbed my sunglasses and mobile. My legs shook as I walked towards the exit and a hand wrapped around my waist.

Charlie's aftershave invaded my nostrils, and we walked out of the pub, turning left, and going back into the train station. As we climbed the escalator, he turned me around to look at him and I met his eyes.

"No. I don't think that. Not for a second!"

We reached the top, and I almost fell, but Charlie caught me and walked me backwards, off the escalator. He moved me to the side and brought his lips to mine. His mouth moved roughly, and his tongue slipped into my mouth as I wrapped my hands around his back. I held him tightly against me until he pulled away and rested his forehead on mine.

His breathing was harsh, but so was mine.

"Awkwardness isn't an emotion I think I'd ever feel with you, babe."

His finger stroked my cheek causing more butterflies to erupt at both his words and his reaction to our kiss. He leaned over and gave me an even softer kiss, then pulled back, linking our fingers together and led us towards the centre of the station.

We boarded a train to somewhere called Kilmarnock, and he checked the stops religiously, dragging me off after only two. As we walked outside, we came out on this residential street with houses opposite us.

He tugged me left again, and we walked down the road until we came to the entrance to a park: Pollok Country Park.

He led the way inside, and we stopped at a board that told us where to go.

Pollok House, I wondered, or the Burrell Collection. We began walking, but we didn't talk because he was busy on his mobile, and honestly, I didn't know what to say to him.

Celibet

Those kisses hadn't been the first ones we'd shared sober, and I knew that whatever we'd changed wasn't going to go back to normal anytime soon.

He walked us by this odd-shaped building, that I saw was the Burrell Collection, and led me down by fields of highland cattle. And then I saw an old-looking house.

We kept walking down a hill and came out of a wooded area on the right to see a small canal on the right and a large country house on the left. Something about the house was familiar, but it wasn't until we climbed the steps and began exploring the gardens that it dawned on me.

"Oh, my God!" I exclaimed as I remembered where I'd seen this house and these gardens. "Outlander was filmed here!"

Charlie nodded and dazzled me with a bright smile. "Yeah, I thought you would like it, but no leaving me for a handsome Scot!" he joked as I barrelled into his arms.

Our hug was different, charged even, and when I pulled back and looked up at his face, I didn't think. I just stood on my toes and pressed a soft, opened-mouthed kiss to his lips which he returned before pulling back and stepping away from me.

"Come on. Let's go inside for lunch." His smile was off, but I knew him better than to push, so I let him lead the way back up the hill and into the front of Pollok House.

Chapter Twenty-Five

CHARLIE

Well, Pollok Park went well. I' gave myself a high five for that one.

I'd never seen such a beaming smile, and it stayed on her pretty face the whole time we were there. But she had to stop kissing me. Although I knew that one had been a heat of the moment way of expressing her thanks, it had done nothing for my physical state, nor had it helped the fact I was supposed to be working on being celibate for the next twelve weeks. I'd never wanted someone more than I wanted her right then.

She linked our arms on the train journey back to the hotel and sat way too close to me, but I wouldn't push her away. If I were really honest, I hoped neither of us won

Celibet

this stupid bet because as least then I could have her the way I wanted her.

"Why don't we grab a drink in the hotel bar when we get back."

She angled her head up so she was looking up at me. "Can do. I'm not getting drunk today."

"Okay. I'm just talking about a quiet drink. We could get some food."

"Is that all you do, eat?"

"Pretty much. You should see me when I'm on set. I never stop." I smiled down at her. Her eyes seemed cloudy with thought, and I knew exactly what was running through her mind: it was us. This new version of us. It wasn't awkward like she thought this morning over breakfast—there was just more to us. We'd crossed an invisible line, and neither of us really knew how to act.

I couldn't watch her strip off her clothes without feeling something. She couldn't give me a kiss without it setting off a spark, and worst of all, I couldn't see her talk to another man without fighting with my jealousy. At least with this bet going on between us, I wouldn't need to worry about her bringing some tool back to the flat and have me wanting to cause him actual harm.

I looked out of my window and watched the countryside whizz past us as I fought with my feelings.

"Are you okay?" Beth's voice was laced with concern and it cut into my thoughts. As I turned to look at her, I saw she had a worried look on her face.

"Course I am babe." I needed to put her mind at rest if nothing else.

The rest of the train trip was quiet. When we rolled into the station, I got off first and held my hand out for her so she could step off onto the platform.

We then made our way back to the hotel with arms linked.

I went straight to the bar when we got there. I needed a drink. I'd never had pent up tension—was that what it felt like? If it were, I'd rather not have it.

Beth walked up behind me, placing her hands on my sides, she told me she was nipping upstairs for a minute, so, I got us some drinks.

I found a table over the back and in the corner and went to sit down with a wine for Beth and a beer for me. Once she'd returned, we tried to talk about everything other than the elephant that seemed to be following us everywhere we went. It was hard, but we managed it, I thought.

We talked about the movie in depth. I did tell her that the zombie apocalypse really wasn't my thing if I had to choose, but that it had been a main role and it was good money. We avoided the subject of Jessie and the email I'd had yesterday about the premiere. I'd tell her about it when a date had been confirmed. We ordered food and more drinks, but it remained civilised. I finally realised, watching how happy she was, that 'my one', had been right under my nose all this time—I had just been just too blind to see it.

Beth then told me about all the bother at work with the doctors. I felt like I'd missed so much being away, and all I wanted to do was to turn back the clock and be there for

Celibet

her. She told me how much she'd needed me at home, especially when Warren had taken all that money from her.

Little Warren and I were going to be having words at some point when we got back to London.

When we were back in the room later, it was harder to keep up the pretence we'd found downstairs. I was fidgety; I couldn't keep still. I kept my phone in my hand just so as I didn't have to look at her. She went into the bathroom to get changed into some shorts and a vest to sleep in, and I stayed in my jeans for the time being, just stripping off my top.

I stood at the window and looked out into the night. The city lights blurred into one as I stared at them. Maybe once we were home, we could get back to normal. Bedrooms separated us there, and this, whatever it was, would fade away.

Her soft hand on my back had me spinning around breathless. She was much smaller than me, standing five foot three or four, so she had to look up at me. The last thing I needed was to have her looking at me like that. She pushed up to her tiptoes and placed a small peck on my cheek. "Thank you so much for today; it's been amazing."

"Anything for you."

A small smile tugged at her lips while our gazes met.

How was I supposed to deal with this? How could I walk away without just one more taste? I wasn't going to break the bet as much as I'd love to have said fuck it.

Our relationship had become serious suddenly. We used to just have fun, take the piss out of one another—everything had been a joke.

Cupping her cheek, my thumb grazed her soft, fair skin. Her chest rose and fell quicker than before, and I could feel her breath on my thumb as it turned more ragged.

Fuck this.

My head dipped, and I put my mouth on hers. She didn't hesitate to kiss me back. I licked against the seam of her lips and pushed my tongue just inside her mouth to meet hers. Sparks flew through me, and I knew I had to stop otherwise the bet would definitely be over because once I started, I wouldn't stop.

As I pulled away, her eyes were still closed it was like she was savouring every moment. "I probably shouldn't have done that, but I couldn't help it. I'm sorry."

"Don't be sorry, Charlie." She placed the tips of her fingers against her lips and closed her eyes again. "I'm going to go to bed and get some sleep. Night."

She turned away from me and went over to the bed, pulling back the duvet and crawling inside, facing away from me lying on her side.

"Night, Beth."

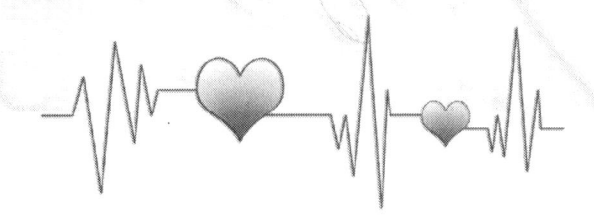

Celibet

It was a long night, oh so long. I thought daylight was never going to come around. And no matter how far we tried to keep our distance, I still woke up with her in my arms as I spooned her from behind.

I'd been awake for a while, but I was too scared to move because no matter how softly I tried to move away, my rock-hard dick would be straining against her back.

"Charlie," Beth's husky, sleep coated voice called to me. "Down, boy..."

"Sorry." I slipped from under the covers and went into the bathroom to change while Beth got up.

A little while later, we packed, went to the restaurant for breakfast and checked out. It was only a half hour wait for the train home. Once it rolled into the station, we got on and spent most of the ride home with our own thoughts other than when Beth put her head on my arm and went to sleep.

I put my earphones in and played some music.

At least this train journey home was uneventful.

Chapter Twenty-Six

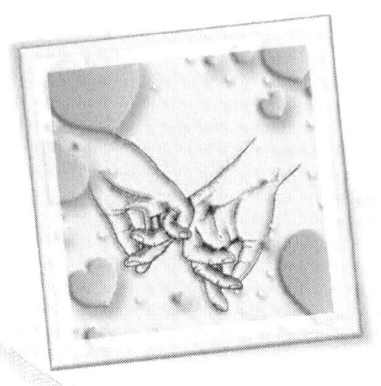

BETH

After we arrived back in London, Charlie disappeared into his room, and I didn't see him for the rest of the night. After work on Monday, I got away early because Marg was back at work and felt guilty about me closing up for her the previous week. She wouldn't take no for an answer, even though I was working the back shift again.

I caught an earlier train home, intending to ask Charlie if he wanted to grab some Chinese takeout.

I knocked on the door of his room but there was no answer. I stood for a few minutes listening intently, and I could only hear his harsh breathing.

When he didn't answer his name, I pushed open the door gently and saw him tugging on his cock through the

Celibet

door. He twisted and squeezed it as I stood transfixed in the doorway.

He hadn't seen me yet because his headphones were on and he was half sitting against the headboard, his eyes closed.

I knew I should shut the door and step away, but the sight of him held me transfixed and I watched as his movements got faster and jerkier.

Seconds later, he leaned his head back and moaned softly as he came all over his hand.

I backed away slowly, closing the door softly, and walked back into the living room.

My eyes caught my reflection in the mirror, and I could see the flush on my cheeks. My nipples were clearly visible through my silk blouse and my panties were soaked.

This stupid bet was going to end me.

I shot up from the sofa and spun around when I heard him moving in the hallway and walked into the kitchen flipping the switch of the kettle. I focused on setting up a cup for each of us with hands that shook with want and need and desire.

I wanted his cock inside me, but we'd made that stupid bet, and now I was hot, horny and frustrated.

"Beth?" I heard him call, and I cleared my throat giving myself a mental slap. I could act normal. I could act like I hadn't seen him stroking the snake…

Charlie came into the kitchen, giving me a soft kiss to my cheek as he did. He smelled like sweat, Boss aftershave and sex, and need coiled in my stomach.

"I'm heading out, babe. I've got an audition for a new E4 show. It's a good part, so keep everything crossed."

I couldn't quite meet his eyes as I wished him luck.

He leaned over and pressed another soft kiss to my cheek before he turned and left me trembling in the kitchen.

After a few moments, I heard the front door shut and I walked over to the dining table and collapsed down onto it.

My clit was throbbing, and I was still more turned on than I'd ever been with Warren.

My body had been electrified like a live wire ever since I'd woken up the previous morning with Charlie's rock-solid erection against my back.

I'd lay there for a while, wondering if he would move and fighting my instinct to turn around and say screw it.

His cock had pulsed against my back, and all I'd wanted was to climb aboard the Charlie Express.

I'd spent the rest of the day trying to keep my distance from him because my hormones had wanted me to ride the orgasm express all the way to the fireworks.

My mobile began to vibrate from the couch in the living room, bringing me back to the present, and I rushed into the living room, seeing a missed call from him.

I carried my mobile back to my room, too turned on to call him back right away. I tugged out the drawer under my bed and found my box of tricks, pulling out my trusty vibrator.

Celibet

My need spiralled as I slipped my pencil skirt down my legs, imagining it was Charlie doing it the whole time, and I stepped out of it and my knickers.

The feeling of the silk blouse against my skin turned me on as I lay on my bed and ran my vibrator up and down my seams before inserting it inside and pressing the button to make it vibrate harder.

I imagined it was Charlie thrusting into me and envisioned his hands all over me as I brought myself closer and closer to an orgasm.

It was a Rabbit, so it set it against my clit, and I toyed with my nipples, twisting, and squeezing before I spiralled apart. My body collapsed on the bed as my mobile rang again, but I was too breathless to answer it and I let it ring out.

My cheeks flamed when I checked a few moments later and saw it was Charlie again. After taking a few deep inhales, I quickly dialled him back and he was breathless when he answered.

"Beth, I forgot to tell you: I have a meeting with the director of Wandering Warrior after my audition, so I'll just book into a hotel tonight."

"Oh, okay. See you tomorrow I guess," I answered in a hoarse whisper.

"Yeah. See ya," he muttered in a distracted voice. I heard a female laugh before he quickly ended the call.

My desire was suddenly gone, and mortification took its place because I didn't know what was wrong with me. I'd never had those kinds of feelings about Charlie before, and hearing that girl laugh, I realised once again that Charlie and I were poles apart. He was so far out of my league that we weren't even in the same stratosphere. Plus, with the stupid bet in place there was nothing we could do even if we wanted to.

Dejectedly, I stripped off and went to the bathroom to clean Vinny the Vibrator in the sink.

I put it down and turned the shower up hot as I quickly washed. Once I was a little cleaner, I stepped out of the shower and groaned. I'd only gone and forgotten the fucking towel again.

My wet feet slipped and slid across the wooden floor as I went to the hall closet, freezing halfway there as I heard the front door opening and closing.

"Beth, you here?" Charlie called out excitedly, and before I could move or even react, the door to the hall opened and Charlie stepped out.

"You'll never guess—" Catching sight of me standing naked and dripping wet in the hall, his eyes darkened, and his mouth popped open as his gaze roamed all over me. He released a breath and ran his fingers through his hair as he licked his lips.

"I uh… I forgot my towel…" I told him stupidly, trying to break the tension that flooded the hall.

"Yeah… I can see that." He answered in a croaky whisper. For another moment, neither of us moved, and then he took one step towards me before he spun around and stormed back into the living room closing the door at his back.

Celibet

My whole body began to tremble as the tension left me, and I quickly rushed to the closet and pulled out a towel, wrapping it around my body tightly before I ran to my room and closed the door, collapsing against it and trying to slow my breathing.

After a few minutes, I heard the front door close and I knew Charlie had left. My mobile vibrated with a text message.

Charlie: Beth, I had to leave. It was either leave the flat or come and drag you to bed so I could lick every droplet of water from your body. I've also left my key. Leave it under the mat when you are going to work tomorrow please. C xx

My heart hammered in my chest as I quickly changed into my pj's and went back into the living room.

I ordered my takeout and sat waiting for it to arrive, pondering what to text back. Eventually, I just messaged back 'okay' because I didn't know what else to say. I wanted to apologise, but he told me he wouldn't be back, and to be honest, it was entirely his fault because I'd caught him jerking off when I returned from work.

The image of that popped up in my mind, and I jumped hard as there was a knock at the door. I opened it, surprised and irritated to see Wanker standing there.

"We need to talk!" His hiss and the glacial look in his eyes set my nerve endings alight and I shook my head.

"No, we fucking don't. Piss off Wanker!'" I hissed him and began shutting the door, but he shoved it open hard, hitting me on the shoulder and sending me clattering to the floor.

"Yes, we do!" He shouted as he advanced on me. He grabbed my hair and pulled my head up.

"You're hurting me!" My voice was calm as I stared him dead in the eyes, but fear uncurled in my gut. I didn't see the slap coming, but the sting made my eyes water.

I glowered up at him in irritation, trying to hide the fear I was feeling, and he slapped me again.

"You shouldn't have gone to the cops!"

His cold voice and the complete certainty with which I spoke made it quite clear that I was in trouble. My mobile was in my room charging, and I just needed to get away from him so I could call for help, but his grip on my hair was unrelenting.

I tried to think about the self-defence class that Callie and I had taken, and suddenly I knew what to do. Without thinking it through any more than that, I quickly lifted my hand with as much force as I could muster and brought the full force of my arm up between his legs. He dropped my head and I scampered back from him as he howled in pain and fell to the floor.

I didn't wait to see him land; I shot up from the floor and pelted for my room, making it inside and locking the

Celibet

door just in time. He hammered on the door, and although I knew it was strong, I began to panic.

What if he got through?

I grabbed my bookcase and threw all the books to the floor as I shoved it sideways. There was a part of the wall that curved, and I managed to wedge it in there and against my wardrobe on the other side.

My whole body shook as I rushed towards my bed because I could hear a series of loud bangs on my bedroom door.

I called the cops and told them what happened and texted Charlie at the same time.

Come please! Warren's here and he's trying to get into my room. I need you! Please hurry, Charlie. I'm really scared!

The call handler told me the cops were on their way, and I sat for the next twenty minutes with my phone in my hand staring at it, but Charlie didn't text back.

I heard the commotion as Warren was arrested, but I couldn't move. It wasn't until I heard Bessie calling for me that I managed to crawl across the floor and put the bookcase upright.

I opened the door, and she swept me into her arms, tugging me out of the flat and across to hers where two cops were sitting and waiting to take my statement.

My fingers held tightly onto my phone, and I sat with Bessie and the cops for over an hour giving my statement. Charlie still hadn't answered, and as the cops left, my tears started. I was more hurt that he hadn't replied or called me than I was about the whole Warren thing.

Bessie set me up in her guest room and made me a coffee and some dinner. She talked endlessly with me about her daughter and grandkids but didn't ask where Charlie was, or if he'd be home and I didn't want to talk about it because truthfully, I didn't know where he was or if he'd come back for me.

I escaped into the bathroom as my emotions began to overwhelm me, and I caught sight of my face in the mirror. My cheek was darkened with a bruise and my lip was split, but other than that I was relatively unharmed.

I stood over the sink and began sobbing, but it didn't last long, and I sucked in a few deep breaths before going out and asking Bessie if it was okay if I went to bed.

I just wanted to be alone.

"You just go right to bed, Beth. You're safe now!"

I smiled at her, or at least I tried to, but it hurt so bad that I gave up.

Clambering into the soft bed, I pulled the covers up, expecting to be awake for hours, but as soon as my head hit the pillow I was out like a light.

Chapter Twenty-Seven

CHARLIE

By the time I got back to my room, I was exhausted. I'd got through my audition and I knew I had a good chance of getting the part. The director didn't take his eyes off me and when it was over, he smiled and clapped nodding his head. He leaned towards someone else and nodded again, so I was taking that as good news.

After my audition, I came from the set and went to grab my phone from my pocket to check on Beth. Things had seemed a bit weird between us earlier before I'd left; I wasn't too sure why. I know after knocking one off on my bed helped me to relax anyway. Since we'd got back from Scotland, it'd been a daily thing. Picturing Beth naked in my head always worked. I needed the real thing, though, and it didn't matter how many times I tried to imagine it was her, palming my dick it wasn't the same, at all.

I patted my pockets and realised that I hadn't lifted it, fucking great. I'd need to have my meeting and ring her once I was back at the hotel because we really needed to talk. If she was serious about this bet, then I couldn't see her naked again. It was fucking killing me, seeing her, but not being able to act on the desire that coiled in my gut at the sight of her. As I grabbed my jacket from the sofa, I started to walk towards the door when someone blocked my path.

"So, Charlie... rumour has it you played next to Jessie Lewis." A petite redhead was sidling up against me.

I raised my eyebrows. "Does it now. Well, that rumour would be true."

"Wow. What was she like? I bet that was amazing."

I didn't think she wanted me to burst the bubble she had Jessie in, so I went to move away. "Amazing..." I exaggerated and changed the tone of my voice.

"So... how about we get out of here and grab a drink?"

Chuckling inwardly, I remembered the time I'd have jumped at the chance. Now though, Beth was the only one I want to take for a drink. Sad, I knew. She's put a spell on me, I think.

"I'm sorry... I'm sorry what's your name?"

"Sophie."

"Look, Sophie, I'm sure you're lovely, but I have a meeting with the director that I need to get to." Smiling, I placed my hands on each of her shoulders and moved her aside so I could leave.

"Another time then?"

Celibet

"Sophie. Don't waste your time on an actor. Get yourself someone who has a normal job." I left her standing there with those words of wisdom.

With my key card in hard, I let myself into my room and walked straight in with just one aim: to find my goddamn phone. I needed to hear her voice.

Once located, I grabbed it from the side of the sink in the bathroom and unlocked the screen. I found messages and missed calls all from Beth.

I read the message she'd sent, and my stomach bottomed out.

What the fuck!

I clicked the green receiver icon and listened to the incessant ringing on the other end. My stomach was like a coiled ball of string, and it was getting tighter every second that she didn't answer. There was only one thing I could do: I had to get back home. Beth needed me.

Once I'd shoved the toiletries back in my case, I headed downstairs and told the receptionist I had an emergency, needed to check out and that I'd need a taxi, too. She rang the taxi company first then took my payment for my room before I went outside into the night air to wait.

I was too scared to think of what he could have done to her. If he'd hurt her—if he'd laid one fucking finger on her—the bastard was dead. I'd kill the fucker. The ball in the pit of my stomach was getting bigger. I tried to swallow past the lump in my throat, but I couldn't.

The taxi idled at the curb, and I threw my case in the boot while I got in the back and told him where I needed to go. It felt like the journey had taken forever by the time we finally reached the flat. I practically threw the twenty at him and got out of the car, grabbing my case out of the boot, and once I was through the door, I took the stairs two at a time.

I lifted the corner of the doormat for the key I asked her to leave but it wasn't there. 'Bollocks."

Making a fist, I banged on the door, hoping she was even here. If she weren't, I'd be totally screwed. I didn't have her friend Callie's number, and that was the only other place she could have been. I banged again before I shouted her numerous times.

Fuck, fuck, fuck!

I turned around and placed my back at the door. Just then, our neighbour, Bessie, came out of her flat.

"Bessie. Thank God. Have you seen Beth?"

"I have, son. Come in. She's sleeping, though, so be quiet."

"What the hell happened?"

She led me through to her living room and closed the door. "That ex-boyfriend of hers came banging on the door, from what I can gather from her statement to the police anyway…"

"Statement? What the f… hell did I miss?"

"Come on. I'll take you through."

Letting her lead the way, I followed her through to what I assumed was her guest room and opened the door. Beth was curled up on top of the bed in the foetal position. She seemed so small and innocent. I rushed to sit on the edge

Celibet

of the bed and stroked her hair until she was murmuring and awakening.

"Beth. Bethy-baby. It's me, Charlie."

"I'll give you a few minutes."

I nodded and smiled gratefully at Bessie.

She roused a little, and I heard my name in a low and weakened tone.

"Charlie."

I stroked her head some more and leaned over her. "Beth, wake up babe. I'm so sorry I left my phone…"

She rolled to her back and opened her eyes. They were red and puffy. By the looks of it she'd cried herself to sleep. Now I felt like a bigger fucking jerk.

She turned onto her side and faced me. "Where were you Charlie? I needed you."

"I didn't realise until I'd finished the audition that I'd left my phone in the hotel room." Her hand slipped from her face and it was like there was a big arrow pointing to the obvious.

"What the fuck is that?"

There was a bruise on her cheekbone. I shoved my body up from the bed and pushed my hands into my hair tugging on the ends of it.

She twisted herself around and sat up on the edge.

"Beth I'm so fucking sorry." I dropped down onto my knees and sat in front of her. I reached up and smoothed my thumb over the bruise that was forming a dark shadow on her face.

"It's okay. I was so scared. He was manic. I've never seen him like that."

"You're safe now. I'm home, and I'm not leaving you again." I got up from the floor and pressed a kiss to her forehead. "Wait here."

I went through to Bessie in the front room. "Bess, thank you so much for looking after her. I can't thank you enough. I'm going to take her home."

"You're welcome, son. Look after her."

"You can bet on it."

I pressed a kiss to her cheek and went back to the bedroom. Beth had laid back down. I picked up her phone and her door keys and put them in my pocket. Leaning my knees against the mattress, I scooped her up in my arms and held her against my chest.

"Charlie what are you doing?"

"I'm taking you back to our place." I thanked Bessie again and she saw us out. Beth circled my neck with her arms and held on tight, her head falling into the crevice of my head and shoulder and rested her cheek on me.

I managed to get the door open and went right through to my bedroom placing her on the opposite side of the bed. "Wait there a sec."

I went back and grabbed my case, shoving it inside the door, and put the dead lock on. When I got back to the bedroom, I stripped the clothes from her, found one of my T-shirts and placed the neck over her head letting it fall down her body. She slipped beneath the duvet while I stripped down to my shorts and got inside with her.

With my arm outstretched, I pulled her towards me. "Come here, Beth." She snuggled up to me and placed her

Celibet

cheek against my chest, drifting off to sleep while I thought of every which way that I could kill Warren.

Chapter Twenty-Eight

BETH

I woke up to the sound of my alarm.

Fuck.

I'd been asleep for a solid twelve hours. I also wondered if I'd dreamed that Charlie came into Bessie's and brought me home, but no, I was definitely in his room and in his bed.

His arm was across my stomach and my pj's were gone, replaced by one of his T-shirts. It smelled like him, which made my stomach squiggle with butterflies.

He was curled up, facing away from me, and his toned back was on display, I know he'd told me what happened, but Charlie never left his phone anywhere. Not ever. It was like surgically part of his arm.

Celibet

Was it because of me? Was he mad at me? Did he regret what had changed between us?

My thoughts were a jumbled mess, so I decided to just go to work to distract myself. I tiptoed back to my room, quickly dressed, and used makeup to hide the bruise on my face, but I couldn't really hide my split and swollen top lip.

I used a little lip balm instead of my usual lipstick. I picked up my Kurt Geiger boots and my Donna Karen bag. I was dressed in a grey pencil skirt with a vest top and a see-through black blouse. I had a little time left, so I sat on my bed and curled my hair. It made me feel better to see that I looked good, and I used diamond studded clips to pin my hair back from my face.

One final check, a squirt of my perfume and I shoved my mobile and my keys into my bag and left the flat. I made the train and realised I'd forgotten to switch over my purse from my other bag, but I'd set up Apple Pay on my phone, so I'd be okay.

My mobile began to ring. I winced when I saw it was my dad calling me. He was going to go absolutely ballistic when I told him what had happened.

"Hi, Dad. How are you?"

He began telling me all about how Mrs. Ambrose down the road, was cheating on her husband and how the neighbours all knew, but the poor sap had no idea.

I waited for an opportunity to tell him about what had happened, but one never came up and before I knew it, I was at the door of the surgery and hanging up on my dad.

I walked inside and saw Brenda on the desk. She glowered after me, which surprised me as I moved through to the break room to put my bag and jacket away. I didn't know what her problem was, but I was too tired to try to figure it out.

I was early enough that I could have a coffee and a croissant from the plate that was sitting with a little note saying help yourself, so I sipped on my coffee, wincing as my lip stung and had to break my croissant into little pieces because I couldn't open my mouth enough to bite it.

I took my time and went out into the floor seeing Mrs. Graham standing there. As soon as she saw me, she came barrelling towards me and began shrieking at me.

Her words all blended into one, and eventually, I held my hand up and said in a forceful tone, "That's enough!"

She froze completely and stared at me in shock as I turned and began to walk away from her, but before I made it through to the reception area, she was shouting at me again.

Dr. Morgens came out of her office, which was the one closest to the reception, and moved towards Betty the Bitch and me.

"What's going on here?" she asked, and Betty promptly burst into noisy tears, trying to tell Dr. Morgens how I was abusing her son and that he was still in custody because I was lying about him.

Liz turned to me, and I saw her eyes narrow when she saw my lip and swollen cheek.

"Beth, go to my office now please and wait for me there."

Celibet

Her tone was firm, and I spun around and walked into the office. As I was about to shut the door, she began talking and I left it ajar so I could hear what was being said.

"I'm sorry, Mrs. Graham, but I cannot allow you to continue to abuse my staff. If you continue to do this then I'll have to ask you to find a new practice."

"She's ruined my son's life! She's accused him of theft and assault, and it's all lies!"

"I understand if that's the case why that would be upsetting, but you cannot come in here and continually abuse one of our staff members. It just isn't acceptable and if she's lying then I suggest you find another way to deal with it."

I walked away and left them to it as I sat down on one of the patient's chairs. My body was still sore from the night before, and I was pretty sure Charlie was going to be pissed that I'd come to work without even waking him.

I should probably have text him, but I couldn't do it now because my mobile was in the break room.

Dr. Morgens came in and closed the door over. Her eyes appraised my face as she came slowly towards me. "So, Bethany, I'd like to hear your side of the story before I make any decisions." Her cool voice and calm manner helped me to relax, and I stared down at my hands as I told her about the previous night in my flat.

"Warren, my ex, came over, burst into my flat and assaulted me. He was furious because I wouldn't let him steal from me anymore."

Her eyebrow raised as her eyes scanned my face and narrowed in on my split lip. "I take it the lip was Warren?"

she asked, and I nodded slowly. "Are you sure that you want to be here?" she probed, and I met her eyes.

"Yeah. I'm happy here and it helps to distract me."

"Okay. You can work in the back office, but if she comes in again and abuses you, I need you to come and get me as soon as you can."

I stood and mumbled my thanks as I went back out into the office. Marg was on the desk and Brenda was typing patient letters as I busied myself with filing, but Brenda kept throwing me stink eyes and I was beginning to get irritated with it.

Just as I was about to call her out on it, Charlie came barrelling into the surgery. I heard him ask Marg for me.

"Hey, is Bethany here?" His voice was panicked, and it sent a shudder down my spine.

"Yeah, she's in the back, love!"

I walked out of the reception area and around to the front to get to Charlie.

"Charlie," I called out in a hoarse whisper, and he moved across the room and pulled me into his arms.

"Bethy, why did you come into work? And why didn't you wake me?" he asked in a low voice, and I looked up to meet his eyes, making a split-second decision.

"Come with me." I led us both into the locum doctor's office because it wasn't being used and towards the chairs, sitting beside him.

"Why didn't you wake me?" Charlie pressed, and I reached over and took his hand in mine.

Celibet

"Charlie, I just need normality today, and I wasn't sure you even cared. I mean I know you came back to get me, but was it because you wanted to or because you felt guilty?" My words were harsh, and I knew they were uncalled for when I saw him wince as he digested them.

"Of course, I care! I... uh... Beth, you know how much I... uh... care about you." He stuttered the words out, and I met his gaze, taking in his dark blue eyes and earnest look.

It seemed like he was going to say something else but changed his mind mid-way through, and it set me on edge.

"Do you though? I needed you Charlie, and I couldn't get a hold of you!" My voice was beginning to rise, and my hands shook, so I sucked in a deep breath and stood up. "Look I can't do this. Not here at my work. Can we please just talk tonight when I get home?"

"I told you I forgot my phone..."

He opened his mouth to say something else, but I held my hand up and he held my gaze before he stood up. His face fell as he looked at me, and I nodded once before turning and showing him out of the office.

I knew I was being cold with him, but it was the only way I knew how to cope with the hurt and fear I was feeling. I watched him leave the practice and went straight back to work, working until closing time and then closing and locking the practice up.

I booked a cab and decided to go and visit Bar C's and see Callie. I wasn't ready to go home yet, and I needed some Dutch courage before I went back to see Charlie.

If I was being honest, I was so confused over how I was feeling about him that I just needed some girl time and a couple of drinks with my other best friend.

When I arrived in the bar, I sent a message to him.

Charlie, I'm at Bar C. Going to have a few drinks with Callie. Be back later. B

I went inside and found a spot on the bar, waiting on Callie to come out from the back room. She appeared and yelped when she saw me, rushing towards me and pulling me in for a tight hug.

"Why didn't you tell me you were coming in?" she yelled as she grabbed me a large rosé wine. She led me to a table, and we sat down as I filled her in on everything Warren related.

I was about to tell her about my conflicted Charlie emotions when she was called away to deal with a call in the back room.

I checked my phone for the first time since I'd gotten to the bar and saw two missed calls and three messages from Charlie.

Oh fuck.

He was going to be so pissed that I hadn't answered, but he'd just replied with**, 'okay'**. His next message was sent at half eight.

Charlie: I'm going to bed early. Got a callback tomorrow at seven. See you tomorrow night. C xx

Chapter Twenty-Nine

CHARLIE

As soon as I opened my eyes and saw Beth wasn't in bed, I panicked. I shot out of bed and searched the flat. It wasn't like the place was huge and we got loads of rooms she could be hiding in. Once I'd looked in the lounge, the kitchen, her bedroom, and the bathroom, I knew she'd gone to work.

I pulled some clothes on and ran to the train station like my heels were on fire, jumping on the train as soon as it rolled in.

Her face looked so bad when she came out of the staff door. I wanted to pull her into my arms and just hold her and promise her that I'd never let anyone hurt her again. But I couldn't.

Celibet

She kept me at arm's length; the closest we got was when she took my hand, but she then accused me of not caring about her.

Fuck no.

I didn't just care about her. In fact, I wasn't sure if I was falling for her. Not just 'let's see how it goes', but a 'I'm falling in love with you,' way. Not that I'd tell her—at least not yet.

When I left the surgery, I walked into the nearest pub and grabbed a pint. I needed something to calm me and this was the only way. I found a table in the corner at the back and sat down. I was so angry about all this. I pulled out my phone and started scrolling through Facebook and I saw Warren's name. That wanker was at the top of my shitlist. My blood began to boil. My fist balled just thinking about how much I wanted to go over there and beat the shit out of him for how he'd hurt Beth.

This wasn't getting me anywhere. I emptied the contents of my glass and left. I made it into the station just as my train rolled in and jumped on.

So much for an early night.

I'd been lying there since just after eight-thirty. Beth still hadn't returned, so I told her I was going to bed for an early night as I had to be up early for a call-back from the director for the audition I attended yesterday. I tossed and turned, and I couldn't sleep for shit. I tried counting sheep, lying with my eyes shut thinking that would work.

Nope. I needed to talk to Beth, but she'd made it quite clear that she didn't want to talk to me.

It was an accident. I didn't intentionally leave my phone in my room. I didn't ignore her call for help; I wasn't even hooking up with someone, so for her to treat me like I've done something wrong fucking hurt.

When I heard the front close and the deadlock being put on, I glanced across at the clock and saw it was just after ten. I could have gone to her, but she wouldn't have listened; there was no point. The click of her bedroom door closing softly echoed throughout the quiet flat, and I rolled to my side.

At least I knew she was home safe.

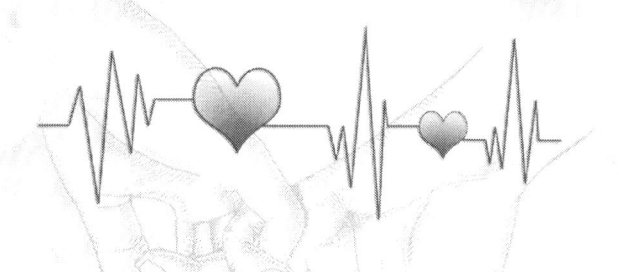

I was up at five next morning. I knew Beth would be wanting a shower before work, so I got up early and jumped in first. Wrapping a towel around my waist, I went to the kitchen and made a coffee, leaving one on the side for Beth. Just because we weren't talking right now didn't mean I'd turned into a selfish prick overnight. We should never have crossed that imaginary line; we shouldn't have made that stupid fucking bet. Life has changed so much in just the blink of an eye, and it was so much harder than ever before.

Celibet

With my coffee in hand, I went back to my room and closed the door. As mine shut, I heard Beth's open.

So, this was how it was going to be now?
That was fine.

My phone rang, and I immediately picked it up. I pushed aside all the shit I was dealing with right now and prepared myself for my call with the director. I needed this job. It was a good script. Anyone who was anyone wanted to play a sword-wielding warrior at some time in their lives, I was sure of it.

I heard the front door softly close. I kept telling myself that Beth didn't say bye because I was on the phone, but my heart still sank.

As soon as the director said, 'you're hired', and told me that my audition was the best he'd seen in a while, I felt like getting on the bed and jumping up and down like when I was a kid. This wasn't a movie, it was a TV drama series, filmed here in the UK, but it would be on the south coast and I couldn't wait to get started. Filming wasn't going to be starting for a couple of months yet, but he wanted me to help cast a co-star. That should be fun.

I jumped off the bed and went in search of Beth. I wanted her to be the first one to know, but as I walked out into the stillness of the flat, I remembered she'd already left for work… I guess I'd just have to tell her when she came back later. Hopefully, she'd be ready to talk to me because I knew I was ready. There're only so many times I could apologise for something that I hadn't actually done.

I knew she wouldn't answer, but I needed to get it off my chest, so I sent her a message:

Hey Bethy-babe. Guess who's just been offered the lead in Wandering Warrior? Had to tell you, couldn't wait until tonight. Hope you have a good day. Love C x

I wasn't expecting an answer, so I put my phone in my pocket and made coffee, stretched out on the couch, and flicked through Netflix until I found something decent to watch. When I came across Prison Break, I knew it was time for a re-watch. I had plans to lie here until Beth came back from work.

Let's see her avoid me then.

Chapter Thirty

BETH

My phone woke me up from a drunken sleep at twenty-past-five in the morning. Marg was calling in sick because her dog was dying, and she was distraught about poor Benji.

She called to ask me to cover her shift, and I of course, said yes. I was still a little drunk, but I moved about the flat quietly, feeling more than grateful when I saw Charlie had made me a coffee.

I wanted to go see him, but I didn't have time because today was the eight am day, and if I weren't there to open the practice, Dr Finchley would have a coronary.

My heart hammered in my chest as I left, and I knew I owed him an apology for accusing him of not caring about me. I knew he did, but I was still hurting over him not being there when I needed him the most.

I chucked my mobile in my bag as I walked through a very wet London morning towards the train station. I needed to eat and to grab something for my lunch, but I only had ten minutes to get to the train station, and if I didn't make it then I'd need to get a taxi and that would cost a fortune, plus it would take forever.

My mobile chimed with a message in my bag, but I ignored it as I rushed towards the train station. It was too wet to read it. I couldn't even see my hand in front of my face as I stood on the platform waiting on my train to come.

My fingers shook with the cold, and I checked my reflection to see my waterproof mascara was not in fact waterproof at all and I looked like something from a horror movie.

My hands shook as I set about repairing my face, and then I remembered the message that I hadn't checked yet. It was from Charlie and I wondered what it would say. I stared at it for a moment before opening it, but in the end, I couldn't resist seeing what he said and almost whooped in delight for him. I managed to control myself, and only gave a small squeal of delight as I saw that he'd been successful in his audition.

My fingers were sausage-like as I replied.

Three times I deleted and retype my message because I was worried that he'd take it the wrong way.

The first message was just:

Congrats, Charlie. I knew you could do it.

But after Glasgow that seemed too cold, so I tried again and wrote:

Wow congrats, Charlie. I'm so proud of you. I knew you could do it. Celebratory drinks tonight?

But then I wondered if drinks were a good idea, so I changed it to:

Wow congrats, Charlie. I'm so proud of you, babe. I knew you could do it. Celebratory dinner out tonight? B xx

I wanted to try and clear the air with him, but I was worried that he'd hate me because of how mean I'd been to him. I had to apologise, so I decided to do it over text and hoped he'd forgive me. This new normal between us was anything but normal, and it was much harder to navigate our friendship or relationship or whatever it was now because I'd always been hyper aware that I had feelings for him, and I hadn't known if he felt the same. Glasgow and our kisses seemed like a lifetime ago already.

Hey, I just wanted to say I'm sorry for being a dick to you yesterday. I was still a little freaked by what happened, and I shouldn't have taken it out on you. You're not my keeper or my boyfriend. You're my flatmate and you were busy and that's okay. Still friends?

It seemed wholly inadequate to describe Charlie as 'just my flatmate' when he had the potential to be so much more, but I needed to get us back onto an even keel, and if this was how to do it then so be it.

He hadn't replied by the time I'd gotten to work, and I then got so busy that I didn't get to check my mobile until almost home time. My whole body was aching by the time it was almost six pm, and I was desperate to get home and go for a bubble bath. I took my mobile out from under the desk about to text Charlie and ask him to run me a nice bath when I saw it was dead and I groaned to myself and smacked my head on the desk. Guess that's what happens when you end up drinking tequila with one of your besties in a bar and forget to charge your mobile before work.

I quickly called him from the work phone to tell him my mobile was dead, but it went onto voicemail. I left him the office number and told him I'd be home in an hour and a half.

As I locked up, I thought longingly of the bath that was waiting for me at home, and I dragged my tired ass to the train station. The rain hadn't stopped all day, and the line was flooded, so the train was cancelled.

I quickly used the pay phone in the station and booked a cab home. I was a soaked mess by the time I got there. I wanted to cry because my head was hurting, I was starving, and I was also cold.

I arrived back to an empty flat and was just about to start looking for Charlie when Bessie from next door knocked on our door.

"Hey, Beth. Charlie asked me to tell you he's been called down to the hotel for a screen test with a few females for the part in the show. He said he won't be long and to order takeout for you both."

I gave her a nod and closed the door over, deciding to go for a bath to relax as I waited on Charlie to get home.

I put some music on and began singing along. It'd been so long since I'd sung that my voice was a bit rusty, but soon enough I was singing in a clear voice along with Beyoncé. I washed my hair and shaved, plucked and otherwise dehaired my body.

I didn't hear the flat door open, or Charlie calling out that he was home. Nor did I hear that he had company as I sat singing 'Listen' as I plucked my eyes in the mirror.

When the bathroom door opened and a very pretty, but strange, girl showed up in my mirror, I almost took my eye out with the tweezers.

I slipped on the tiles as I turned around and managed to scratch my cheek as I fell, landing on the floor in an undignified heap as she quickly turned and walked back through the flat calling on Charlie.

Hearing her call his name made my stomach roll unpleasantly, and when he appeared in the door of the bathroom, I didn't know what to say to him, so I said nothing and went to my room, closing the door on his handsome face. He came to my door a few times and knocked, but I ignored him. I didn't want to argue, and I didn't want to listen to his excuses.

I could hear them talking and giggling, but I refused to go out there. I was humiliated enough, and I didn't want to see him with someone else.

It hurt enough to imagine, never mind seeing it. I lay in my bed and tried to ignore how hungry I was, eventually drifting off to sleep and dreaming of drowning Charlie in a pit of screaming girls.

I managed to sleep until five. I was covering for Marg for the next few days, so I had to be at work by quarter to eight, and I had to get up, but I was absolutely starving and exhausted.

I quickly dressed and tiptoed into the lounge, freezing by the kitchen door as I went to make myself a coffee. Upon seeing a leather jacket and pretty lace up boots by the sofa, I changed my mind because the sight of them hurt me in a way I couldn't describe. I left the flat with tears in my eyes and a sharp pain in my heart.

Chapter Thirty-One

CHARLIE

My back creaked as I moved to sit up. Being stuck in one position all night wasn't a good position for a man of my size. I was six foot four and wasn't exactly puny with it either.

I twisted my body around and sat perched on the edge of the sofa.

Why the fuck did I give her my bed.

As I stood and stretched my hands above my head, my back cracked, and my head smarted a little bit. I knew then that I needed stronger coffee than what we had. Plus, Mia, my new co-star, told me that she only drank Starbucks. The flat was still quiet, so I pulled on my boots and, knowing it'd been warm the last few weeks, I didn't bother with a jacket. Once I'd grabbed my phone wallet and door keys, I headed out.

I felt a little guilty. I'd had a plan for yesterday. After about three hours, though, it had gone tits up. The director had rung me and said he needed me to help him with auditions. I knew he'd wanted me to have the last say on my co-star, but I hadn't been expecting that to be yesterday. But of course, I was excited to see who'd he got.

Mia Jones. A pretty little brunette, standing around five-five with the perfect figure was cast as my co-star after three hours of auditions. To be honest, she was the best out of the five. If I were the Charlie from a few months back, I would have taken her out, and tried to have sex with her. If it weren't for everything that'd gone on between Beth and me, what happened with Jessie in France on its own was enough for me to get rid of that thought. I gave Mia my bed since she was totally smashed and I went back to sleep on the sofa, although I do remember her asking me to join her. I feel like a complete wanker missing mine and Beth's date, but this was my new co-star.

I arrived at Starbucks and ordered two medium Americanos to go and started the walk back home. When I got back, I saw a cup that was left on the side and knew right away it was Beth's. My eyes scoured the room and saw the scene that was playing out around me. Beth would think the worst. Mia's boots were near the couch and her jacket was slung over the back. With neither of us in sight, the shit just became a whole lot more complicated.

"Fuck!" I said to myself out loud.

Celibet

"Morning. Do you always talk to yourself?" Mia smirked as I turned around and saw her standing at the door of the front room.

"Always. It's what us actors do." I blew out a sigh and grabbed her coffee taking it to her. "I couldn't remember what you had, so I got you Americano, is that okay?"

"Of course. I need it this morning." She smiled and sat down. "So, that girl who came back last night, who is she?"

Who is she? That's a damn good question. I surveyed the question in her eyes, and I knew I had to tell her the truth.

"Mia look." I took a seat next to her. "Beth is my best friend, but she's becoming more than that. I can't explain it to you because I can't explain it to myself. Months ago, there was no amount of alcohol that would have stopped me from sleeping with you, but honestly, I'm really looking forward to working alongside you."

"Oh, Charlie. You're so sweet"—she chuckled— "but I didn't want to sleep with you. When I asked you if you were coming to bed, I asked because it's your bed."

"So, you didn't want to sleep with me?"

She shook her head, smiling while I was left feeling more than a little rejected. Well, that has never happened.

"No, Charlie. And since we're being honest with each other, you don't have the right appendage for me..."

I felt a frown tug at my brow, and in my hungover state something wasn't registering.

"I probably would have fancied your flat mate more..."

When I still hadn't got it, she went on.

"I'm gay, Charlie." She could obviously see I was finding it hard to solve two plus two and laughed.

"Oh. I didn't even get that vibe. Huh…"

She laughed again. "Oh, Charlie. I can't wait to tell Liz, my partner. She's going to piss herself laughing."

I could see Mia and I becoming great friends, and Beth, well, Beth was going to love her when she finds out.

Once Mia had left in a taxi, I jumped in the shower and grabbed some breakfast. I'd heard nothing from Beth. I knew she was still angry, so instead of doing nothing, I decided I'd make it up to her for the last few days. They hadn't been the best for either of us.

I made sure I had everything and went to the supermarket.

I picked her up some flowers and a couple of bottles of her favourite wine. I would order us a takeaway before she had finished work so it would be here for when she got back. I had it all planned. Now to clean up the place.

The Chinese food came at five-thirty, and I plated it up ready for when she walked through the door at quarter to six.

Maybe I should have texted her and told her to come straight home from work, but then I'd have had to tell her what I had planned…

When six o'clock came and went, I was hoping that it was just her train that got delayed.

Chapter Thirty-Two

BETH

Work was hard, and I didn't hear from Charlie all day. I was still covering for poor Marg. She was still distraught. I almost text Charlie to tell him I was doing a really long day, but I couldn't get over the hurt I was feeling, so I didn't bother sending the message.

Six arrived and I locked up. I was too tired to get a train, so I booked an Uber to take me home. I was exhausted, dejected and honestly so done with all the drama.

The cops had called. Warren had been issued a restraining order. He wasn't allowed to talk to me, text me or come anywhere near me. I was so relieved, but I couldn't even build up any enthusiasm because of Charlie. The thought of him sleeping with that girl made my stomach curl and my heart thump in pain, but I didn't want to deal with it, so I was trying to block it out of my mind.

The cabby chatted all the way to the flat, and by the time we arrived, I was absolutely over speaking. I just wanted to go in, eat and go to bed.

I was hoping not to see Charlie, but when I walked in, he was sitting on the sofa with a frown on his face. When he saw me, he stood and marched from the room, leaving me looking around at the scene in front of me.

The dining table was set and there were Chinese takeout in the cartons on it, with a bouquet of flowers and a bottle of wine sitting in an ice bucket. There were candles lit, but they were almost down to the wick, so I walked over and blew them out as Charlie walked back in with his jacket in hand.

I turned to meet his eyes and saw a cold look on his face, but I wanted to know if he'd done this for me, or for the girl from the night before.

"I'm going out!" he spat out as he walked towards the door without looking at me.

"Charlie, wait!"

He froze then shook his head and walked out, closing the door with a snap at his back.

"Fuck!" I muttered as I glanced down at the food with my stomach growling, but I needed to catch him. I had to stop him from leaving, so I turned and ran out and bumped right into him as he stood in the landing.

I went stumbling back and tripped over my heeled feet, twisting my ankle, and howled in pain.

"Ouch, fuck, ouch!" I hissed out.

Celibet

Charlie spun around and looked at me holding onto my ankle and wincing as white-hot pain shot through me. My ankle throbbed and burned as tears formed in my eyes.

For a moment, it was as if he was torn and was about to leave, but then I cried out as I tried to move my ankle and his cool exterior melted.

"You okay there, Beth?" he asked without moving, and I glowered up at him.

"Oh yeah, I'm fucking peachy." Fuck it hurt, and the pain was making me a bitch, but I couldn't help it.

He grimaced as he crouched down and slipped my shoe gently from my ankle. His eyes met mine and he cupped my cheek, wiping the tears from my eyes.

"I'm going to lift you, okay?" he asked, and I nodded, grimacing as another wave of pain rolled over me.

"Beth, wrap your arms around my neck and hold on."

My eyes met his and his gaze was steady on mine. Butterflies erupted in my stomach, and my lips were dry. My tongue darted out and moistened them as he stared at me.

His eyes darted down to them and then he shoved his arms under my butt and around my back. He stood up and staggered to the side before righting himself and carrying me back to the flat.

The door had closed, and I didn't have my keys. My heart rate sped, and I began to panic, but Charlie pressed a soft kiss to my forehead holding his lips there for a beat.

My heart rate to soared and my breathing sped up.

He pulled back a little and muttered against my forehead. "Grab my keys, babe. They're in my back pocket."

It took a few minutes of moving around and my hand roaming down his sculpted back, but it was as I moved over the crease of his jeans that his eyes blazed out of control.

"If you don't want me to combust, stop groping me and get the keys, please, or I'm going to forget all about that stupid fucking bet and kiss the fuck outta you."

My hand clenched on his ass and he growled, a low sound in his throat that caused my lady parts to squirm, but I ignored the desire coursing through me and slipped my hand into his pocket to pluck the keys out.

My fingers shook as a wave of pain rolled over me, and I winced promptly dropping the keys. Charlie sighed, and my face went beet red because not only had I locked us out, but I'd also dropped the keys that would let us in.

"I'm going to need to put you down, babe, so I can get the keys," he began and he moved me against the wall, lowering me to the ground when a loud voice from the stairwell made us both jump.

"I knew it! I fucking knew that something was going on with you two!"

Charlie hissed a menacing sound out of his mouth as he registered who it was speaking, and my whole body trembled in alarm. He wasn't supposed to be anywhere near me, at all.

Celibet

Once I was on the ground Wanker came over and punched him hard, while he was still helping me.

Charlie made sure I was steady and then spun around, shoving Warren hard away from me. "Get the fuck out of here before I fucking kill you!" Charlie's lip was split, and he turned and spat blood on the floor. Warren tried to go for him again and Charlie did some crazy move that ended with Warren sliding along the floor on his backside.

"I'm warning you now! This ends here. You get her money back to her tonight or I swear to fucking God, I'll end your fucking career and go after everything you have!"

Warren glowered up at Charlie and then glanced towards me. "What the fuck ever. She was never any good in the sack anyway, so you're fucking welcome to her fat ass…"

Charlie roared and Warren scrambled up, scuttling away down the stairs as my eyes filled with tears. I glanced down, and all I could see were rolls of fat and flab. My confidence hit rock bottom as Charlie came back towards me, scooped up the key and opened the door, helping me back inside the flat.

He walked with me to the couch and I sat down, lifting my leg and I winced as sharp shooting pains shot through my leg. For a moment, Charlie stood indecisively before spinning around and walking into the kitchen, bringing back a packet of frozen peas and a dishcloth.

He grabbed a cushion from the couch and pulled the coffee table closer to me, lifting my leg and gently setting it down on the sofa before wrapping the peas and placing them on my ankle.

We didn't speak at all until he'd set my ankle up and then he walked around the table and dropped to the floor beside me. He was facing me, and his eyes burned into mine as he began to speak in a hoarse whisper.

"Beth, I didn't mean to miss your calls the other night. I left my mobile in my hotel room and I came back as soon as I saw you'd been trying to get in touch."

I opened my mouth to say it was okay and that I was sorry, too, when he lifted his finger and placed it on my lips.

"No, listen to me please?" he asked, and I nodded.

"I didn't sleep with Mia. I know you probably thought that this morning, but I swear I didn't. She's gorgeous and funny and I can see us being great friends, but she's also gay and her girlfriend thinks I'm hilarious because I missed the memo on that."

My body sagged as relief washed over me, but he wasn't finished. He slipped his hand into mine as he spoke again.

"Since Glasgow, I haven't been able to stop thinking about you. I haven't slept right or anything and things were so fucked up when we got home, but I need you to know that the only person I want is you…" He paused and sucked in a breath as I stared at him in complete shock, but he didn't let me speak as he continued.

"Now I know we have that stupid fucking bet, and I will stick to it, but I propose an amendment. How about at the end we give us a try? We date each other and see how it goes because I want you…"

Celibet

Warren's words sounded loudly in my ears, and I glanced away biting my lip. Charlie was amazing and he was perfect, but fucking Warren had ruined my confidence, and I knew Charlie would end up needing more.

"No. I'm not good enough or pretty enough for you… you need…" I began, but Charlie didn't let me finish. He rammed his lips to mine and my body exploded with need as he took everything that I was willing to give in the kiss. His hands wound around my neck and his tongue darted around my mouth, licking at my lips and toying with my tongue. It was heaven and hell because I wanted him so badly, but according to Warren, I was useless in the sack.

I lost my enthusiasm for the kiss because I was so worried that I'd disappoint him, and I pulled back. Charlie held on to my neck, though, and pressed some soft kisses to my lips that almost made me melt, but I still held back because I was too fat and not enough for him and it was killing me.

Chapter Thirty-Three

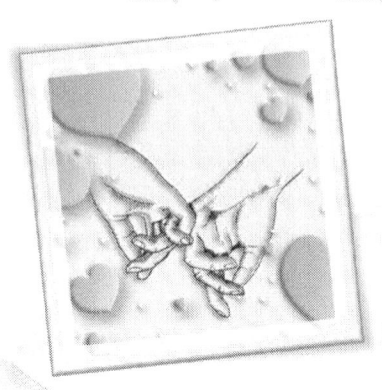

CHARLIE

My lip stung like a bitch after that piece of shit blinded sided me with a right hook, but I didn't fucking care because I had Beth in my arms. When she pulled away from me, I knew it was because of what Warren had said but there was no way I was going to let him get inside her head. He'd done enough damage to her, and if he were to come around again, I'd be waiting to teach him a lesson.

"Please don't pull away from me, Bethy." I gave her my most sincere stare. I needed her to see how much I wanted her. "Get Warren out of your head. He's full of shit and wouldn't know a gorgeous woman if she kicked him in the dick."

"I can't, Charlie. I'm not enough for you. I know what you need. I've known you long enough to see the kind of woman you go for. They're elegant and classy. Me, I'm just

Celibet

frumpy and below par in the looks department, so why, Charlie? Why would you want me?"

"Stop," I said a lot firmer than I meant to. "I'm not listening to that shit. It's all lies. Do you not remember the hard on I woke up with in Glasgow? As soon as I saw those missed calls and texts, I came straight back here. I've never done that for anyone." I licked over the small cut on my lip and tried to ignore the sting before I pressed my lips back on hers. I knew this was going to be a work in progress, but that was okay because I'd make sure that she knew how beautiful she was by the time this stupid fucking bet was over.

My lips moved softly against hers until she gave in to my charms and kissed me back. Her hands cupped my neck before she twisted her fingers into my hair and tugged lightly on the ends as I'd pushed up to my knees and cupped her face. She opened her mouth and our tongues met. The spark I felt last time was there again. only this time it was bigger, and I felt it all the way to my dick. I willed for it to go away, but I knew it wouldn't; I'd have to live with it. I pressed harder, firmer until we were lost in each other.

Beth pulled away first, and a small smile tugged at the corners of her mouth. As I looked into her eyes, I knew what I'd been missing all this time.

"Wait there…"

"I'm not exactly going anywhere." She chuckled as I got up from the floor to grab her glass.

"Have a drink."

She put her lips to the rim and tipped it back before handing it back to me. I sat at the other end of the couch and took the bag of peas from her ankle.

"How's it looking?"

"It's badly bruised, I think. You may have just sprained it, but if it's not better by the morning then you'll need to go to the hospital to get it looked at."

She smiled gratefully and twisted her neck to look behind her. "What about the food? It's been wasted. I'm sorry Charlie, it was such a nice gesture, too."

"It doesn't matter. You're more important."

"I'm starving though."

"Why don't I go out and fetch some more."

"But that's more money you've spent that you didn't need to."

I placed my finger against her lips, "Shh. You let me worry about that."

I pressed another kiss to her lips and grabbed my jacket. "You've got your wine, keep that foot raised and unless you're desperate to pee, you're not to move." My eyes narrowed as her mouth tugged into a smirk.

"You can always get it re-delivered if you don't trust me…"

"I haven't got enough cash to pay on delivery, so I need to pop to the cash point."

"I have cash I think…Oh, no I don't, I gave the taxi driver my last note."

Bending down towards her I kissed her again, smiling as I pulled away and left the flat.

Celibet

Plucking my phone from my pocket, I rang the Chinese around the corner and ordered again, telling them I'd be there soon to pick it up. I made my way towards the town and used the cash machine first. On arriving at the takeaway place, I gave the woman my name as I walked in and took a seat. I had to wait about thirty minutes, but it was cool. She placed the white bag of food on the counter and I grabbed it with a thanks and a smile and started my walk back to the flat.

As I walked through the main door at the bottom of the building, I could hear shouting. It sounded like someone was having a domestic. Great. My foot had barely touched the bottom step when I thought I heard Beth's voice… taking the steps two at a time, I ran up them until I was turning the corner and couldn't believe what I was seeing.

Warren had Beth pinned against the wall.

Rushing towards them, I dropped the bag that was in my hands and grabbed Warren by the scruff of the neck, turning him around and punching him square in the face. I hit him again until he fell to the floor.

Scrunching his T-shirt in my hands, I wrenched him towards me until I was right in his face, I spat, "Stay the fuck away from her, Warren. I fucking mean it. The next time you show your fucking face, you'll have no bastard teeth and you'll be having your meals through a fucking drip." Shoving him back to the ground I gave him a boot for good measure. "I will fucking finish you after this. That's not a threat: it's a fucking promise. Expect a visit from the police."

I collected the bag from the floor and wrapped Beth in my arms, kissing the top of her head and slamming the door behind me.

Chapter Thirty-Four

BETH

Charlie was gone all of twenty-five minutes when the door went again. I didn't answer at first, but then I saw Charlie's key sitting on the table. I stood up gingerly on my ankle.

It took me a couple of minutes to get to the door, and each step caused a wave of pain to wash over me. I paused at the door and sucked in a breath before I opened it, and I squeaked in alarm when Warren grabbed me and swung me out into the hallway slamming me against the wall.

"Beth, I'm going to fucking end you for ruining my life. I've lost my fucking job and it's all your fault." He hit the wall behind me, and I jerked a little, but then my blood started pumping and my fury overtook my sense.

"Are you fucking serious?" I yelled at him. "You stole my fucking money, put me into debt and assaulted me and you are still fucking trying to blame me! What a crock of shit, Warren!"

He slapped me hard across the cheek and my head hit off the wall, but I wasn't going to let him hit me again.

"It is your fucking fault. Maybe if you weren't so fucking tight with your money then I wouldn't have had to steal it. You're a cold bitch. I bet you let Charlie live with you rent free."

His voice echoed along the landing, and I goaded him. I couldn't resist getting a dig in about Charlie, so I leaned to him and yelled in his face. "What I do with Charlie is absolutely none of your fucking business!!"

He howled with rage and pinned me to the wall by my neck. He shouted in my face and his eyes were wild. He was positively unhinged as he pushed harder, and I struggled to breathe.

"You are a fucking bitch…"

My ears started to ring as I gasped for air, and then suddenly Charlie was there. He punched Warren hard on the side of his head and Warren's fingers loosened from around my neck. I was able to draw a breath in as Charlie punched Warren again and threw him away from me, standing over his hastily retreating figure.

Warren looked surprised to see him, and I wondered if he'd been waiting outside the building, had seen Charlie go and assumed it was safe to come in.

As Warren left with Charlie's threat hanging in the air, Charlie came over and pulled me into his arms. I hadn't

Celibet

even realised I was shaking until I began shivering against Charlie's hold.

"Sssshh, I got you babe," Charlie muttered in a low voice as he led me inside and set me back down on the couch.

He unwrapped the parcelled food, and for a while we were silent as we ate, but I still had Warren's words ringing in my ears. I went to bed early and left Charlie to do the washing up.

I'd drunk a few more glasses of wine with dinner, so the ache in my foot wasn't too bad and as I cleaned myself up in the bathroom, I checked my reflection in the mirror.

My curves, which I usually loved, seemed too much, and my stomach wouldn't ever be as flat as Charlie's last few girlfriends. Gazing over myself with a critical eye, I decided I was nothing special. I was pretty, sure, but so were other girls. I couldn't see the appeal, and although he'd said he wanted me—and when he'd kissed me, I'd been able to feel how much he wanted me—but was it just because I was convenient or was it something more?

My confidence was in my boots as I moved through the flat heading to bed, but I met Charlie in the hall and his eyes widened at the sight of my bare legs and low-cut vest top.

"Beth," he began in a croaky whisper, and I stopped moving, turning to face him.

"Spend the night with me. Come sleep in my bed, or I'll come sleep in yours, but either way…"

My eyes scanned his face, and I knew that I would disappoint him. I would turn him from the amazing, sweet guy he was into a raging psychopath, just like I'd done with Warren. It seemed to be the pattern that was going on with my life.

"Not tonight, Charlie," I told him carefully, and then I made up a lie that sounded plausible because it was partly true. "I can't because if I end up in your bed, we'll break our bet. Remember, celibate for twelve weeks."

He stared at me and then came slowly towards me in his sleep trousers and nothing else. My mouth watered at the sight of him.

"Is that the only reason?" he probed as he reached me, and his eyes scanned my face. I knew I couldn't lie to him, so I shrugged, and he leaned down pressing a soft kiss to my lips. As we broke apart, breathlessly, he spoke again.

"Beth, you are so sexy and amazing, and I swear, I'll rip his nuts off for making you feel like you aren't enough for me. You're all I fucking see."

My heart soared and he kissed me again, more firmly, wrapping his hands around my back and holding on to me, moving us back until I was against the wall.

He pushed his rock-solid dick to my stomach and then lifted my legs up.

"Wrap your legs around me," he commanded in a heated whisper, and I acted without thinking.

"Do you feel that?" he asked as he slid his cock between my thighs. He rubbed it along my seams, and I was soaked as his lips moved down my neck and nipped at my collar bone. I didn't answer, and his hand smacked my arse and I moaned out loud.

Celibet

"Do you fucking feel that?" he probed in a louder voice as he pushed harder against me.

I whimpered. "Yes, I feel it…"

"This is all for you, and one day soon, my dick will be fucking it's way inside you and claiming you because you **are** enough for me. Your body turns me on like nobody else's ever has before and all I want to do right now is take you to bed and make you forget that little prick ever existed…"

He broke off, breathing harshly as he pushed against me again, capturing my lips in a hard, punishing kiss that made his lip bleed a little.

"You are fucking mine, and I'll show you how amazing you are, but you have to let me in, Bethy-babe…"

I almost came as he ground into me again and his tongue invaded my mouth. For a moment, there was silence and then he groaned, untangled my legs from his waist and set me gently on the floor.

He ran his fingers through his hair and stepped away from me, muttering in a hoarse whisper, "Beth go to bed. Go right now because I'm about a second from saying screw it and taking you right here and now…" His breathing increased and his eyes burned brightly, staring at me as I backed away and went into my room, intending to finish the job he'd started. I locked the door and moved towards my drawers pulling out my vibrator and laying down on the bed.

I turned it on and rolled it over my nipples and then down to my shorts, moving them aside. I ran it up and down before pushing it inside and turning it up.

The buzz got louder, but I didn't care because my orgasm was so close. I imagined it was Charlie's dick inside me, and within a minute, stars popped behind my eyes and my body began to convulse as I came hard and fast.

I lay for a few minutes breathing before I turned the vibrator off and tossed it back in my drawer. I'd clean it in the morning. And with that, I rolled over and went to sleep, not caring that my vibrator was loud or that Charlie had probably heard me as I chased the orgasm express.

Chapter Thirty-Five

CHARLIE

Fuck *me, I felt like a fucking teenager again.*

As soon as I demanded that she go to bed, I did the same. I closed the door stripped out of my clothes down to my shorts and lay down. My dick was harder than fucking steel. Well, it was more like Thor's fucking hammer.

That's when I heard the light buzzing. I could picture Beth lying in the middle of her bed, writhing as she held that vibrator against her pussy. My hand slid under the waistband of my shorts and my fingers wrapped around my shaft. I started to move my hand slowly up and down, but it wasn't enough. My balls were tight, and I had to get rid of this before I could sleep. The louder Beth's vibrator buzzed, the faster I got. I pictured her head thrown back, my lips at her pale neck as I pounded into her. I knew it wouldn't be long before I came. The buzzing got louder still, and I could hear Beth's soft whimpers through the wall and that was all I needed. Squeezing harder as I grabbed the head in my fist, I wanted her beneath me, not alone with a fucking inanimate object. Beth's muffled cries travelled through the thin walls, and it wasn't long after I was grunting low in the back of my throat and shooting my orgasm all over my hand. My body shook with aftershocks, and I lay there for a couple of minutes while my body came down off its high.

Opening my door softly, I grabbed a towel from the cupboard and went into the bathroom, jumping into the shower, making it as cold as I could stand. It was the only way I was going to get through these next few weeks: plenty of hand jobs and cold showers. Fucking roll on when this bet was over.

I meant what I said to Beth last night. I wanted her to be with me after all this. If it had proved one thing to me, it was that I didn't need some skank to get me off—a quick one-night stand. I needed the one thing that had been right under my nose for the last seven years.

Once I'd showered and goosebumps coated my skin because the water was so cold, I turned off the tap and stepped out. I pulled on some clean boxer shorts when I got back into my room and got back into my bed again. I felt myself shivering so I dragged the sheets up and covered my body.

Celibet

It was quiet in Beth's room, so I rolled to my side, slipped my hand beneath my head, and quietly drifted off to sleep to dreams of her.

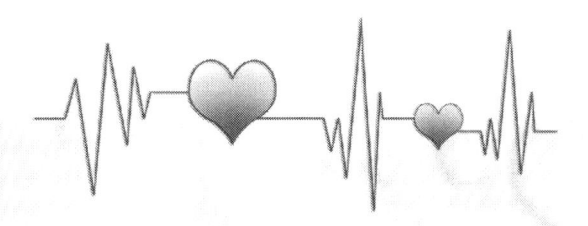

I was awake early the next morning. I knew Beth had work, and I wanted to see her before she left. I heard her going in the shower that sat next to my room. That was my cue to get up. I went through to the kitchen and made us both coffee and put some bread into the toaster. I slathered the butter on to the first lot and placed it onto a plate and then put another two slices in before doing the same again.

Taking the toast and the coffee over to the table where we were supposed to have dinner last night, I removed the burnt down candles and sat down waiting for Beth to join me.

I'd just put my lips to my cup and taken my sips of coffee as Beth joined me.

"Good morning sunshine."

She gave me a smile and I looked her over. Her dress sat just above her knee and she wore a back blazer. Her hair was piled up on top of her head in a top knot with light makeup, not taking the natural beauty from her face.

It felt like I was seeing her for the first time, and she took my breath away.

"What's this?" Her gaze flicked around and the room before landing on me.

"Breakfast is served."

She limped over, bringing back the memory of that wanker attacking her again last night, darkening my carefree mood. I knew she couldn't go to the police though because I'd hit him, and I'd get myself arrested.

"I haven't got the time, Charlie. My ankle is killing me, and if I'm going to make the train then I have to leave."

"No."

Her eyebrow cocked, and she looked quite amused.

I stood from the chair and went over to her, cupping her face in my hands and pressing my lips gently to hers. Her wide eyes looked up at me and a soft smile began to form.

I took her by the shoulders and looked into her eyes. "Breakfast first, then I'll grab you a cab.

"Charlie, I can't ask you to do that…"

"Well, it's a good job I offered then." I grinned in victory and led her to the table. She sat and took a slice of toast from the plate before taking a sip of her coffee, and we ate in a comfortable silence stealing glances at each other from across the table.

My lip smarted when it sat against my cup as I drank, but I'd survive as long as I wasn't needed on set. Luckily, filming hadn't started yet. I couldn't very well film looking like this.

Celibet

As soon as Beth was finished, I rang her a cab and took the twenty from my wallet and gave it to her.

"No, I'm not having it; I can pay myself."

I shrugged and dropped it into her bag. "Tough shit."

She clambered from the table and straightened her dress while I picked up her bag for her. As I passed it over, I cupped the back of her head with my free hand and put my lips to her forehead. "Get one of the doctors to look at your ankle."

"Will do." A ragged sigh left her lips as she looked up at me. I couldn't resist myself, so I pressed a kiss to those, too.

"See you later."

My gaze was stuck on her arse as it swayed, and she walked through the door, pulling it closed behind her.

I made another coffee before I cleaned up the place ready for when Beth came back later.

It was about an hour later when the door knocked with a bang. It sounded official to me... With a frown, I opened the door and unsurprisingly, it was official. A police officer and that Chris bloke stood there before me.

"Can I help you gentlemen?"

"Charlie James."

I nodded at the officer and Chris took over.

"Can we come in?"

"If you must, yeah." I opened the door wider and let them in. I followed them into the living room and invited them to sit.

"Charlie, do you know Warren Graham?" Chris clasped his hands and leaned on his knees with his elbows as he pushed forward.

"I've had the unfortunate pleasure, yes…" My eyes narrowed as I wondered where this was going.

"Mr Graham is accusing you and Beth of assaulting him."

"You fucking what?" I thundered as I shoved myself abruptly out of the chair. "Does this look like I assaulted him?" I pointed to my lip. It was lucky the little weasel had caught me with his pussy punch. "I came back to see him pinning her to the wall just inside the flat. Oh, and that was the second time that day, I'd just like to add. I pulled him off her and he hit me."

"He has bruises, Charlie."

"It was self-defence." I shrugged as I sat back down. "I mean, it's not like you haven't got a long list of charges against him is it? He's trying to get himself out of the depth of shit he's already in."

"Is there anyone that can corroborate your side of things? I will be speaking to your neighbour anyway."

"There was no one else around. But yeah, you speak to Bessie because she saw what had happened earlier in the day." My blood was fucking boiling. My knee was bouncing erratically as my anger amped up. I couldn't believe he'd have the fucking balls to do this. "Shouldn't he be locked up by now anyway?" I growled in Chris's direction. "If you'd locked him up for the fraud, or the last time he'd hurt her, you wouldn't be sat here now." I accused.

Chris sighed as he glared. "Okay. Well, we'll be speaking to Beth today. Is she at work?"

"Yep." I popped the 'p'. I was pissed off to the max, and I just wanted to hit something.

"Well thanks for your time, Charlie. We'll keep you informed. We may need you for further questioning."

"Whatever. So, I'm not under arrest?" I wanted to tell them to do their fucking job, lock him up and throw away the fucking key.

"Not as yet, no. But no leaving town, yeah."

"Yes officer. Oh, and by the way, Beth has yet another bruise on her face and she twisted her ankle. There will be a doctor's report because I told Beth to see one when she got to work."

With a nod, they left. Like fuck was I seeing them out. The door closed, and I heard the bang on Bessie's door opposite.

I plucked my phone from my pocket and sent a message to Beth to give her a heads up.

Guess who I've just had a visit from. Expect the boys in blue to come and see ya. Warren the fucking cunt has put a complaint in. Xx

I left that there and let myself seethe until I'd heard back from Beth. It was one thing after another recently, and I was fucking sick of it.

Chapter Thirty-Six

BETH

My ankle was throbbing painfully as I made my way down the stairs, but the pain was secondary to my thoughts because my body was tingling from Charlie's kisses.

I was so glad he'd given me the cash for a cab, but I'd be transferring it back to him straight away. I didn't like being beholden to anyone, and I wouldn't let anyone support me, not even Charlie.

I climbed into the cab, relieved as my ankle was hurting worse than ever, and no matter how much I tried to ignore it, the ache was almost overwhelming.

I quickly paid and hobbled to the surgery. Liz was first in and she watched me walk for a bit then dragged my ass into her office.

Celibet

"Beth, what happened to your ankle?" she asked as she told me to sit on a chair.

I didn't have socks on, and my pumps were squeezing my swollen foot which was bruised all the way around.

"Lift your foot and rest it on the chair," Liz commanded, and I complied. She poked and prodded at my foot and chewed on her lip. "What happened?" she asked again, and her eyes scanned my face, widening at the marks on my neck.

I met her steady gaze and mumbled my answer. "My ex assaulted me, and I fell over…" I told her, answering backwards. I knew my ankle was Charlie's fault, well kind of his fault. I ran into him, but I couldn't tell her that. Not when she was looking at me in shock.

"Did you report it to the police?" she asked, and I shook my head because I couldn't. Charlie had hit him and threatened him, and I couldn't throw him under the bus like that.

"No. My flatmate defended me, and I was worried that he'd get into trouble." I was honest with her and she gave me a perplexed look as my answer registered.

"Your ankle is swollen and bruised, and you need to get it x-rayed. Come on. I'll take you to urgent care. Suzy can mind the desk until we get back." She bustled out of the room and asked Suzy who was only too happy to oblige.

The next hour was brutal, and my ankle ached as I was examined and checked over.

Charlie had also text to say the cops would probably be by for Warren's complaint, and I rolled my eyes, dropping my mobile back into my bag.

I'd broken my third metatarsal bone in my foot and was given a boot to wear for a few weeks. They also gave me strong painkillers and the number for the domestic violence helpline.

Back at the surgery, I was set up in the back office and was typing up dictated hospital letters when Chris and another cop arrived at the surgery. They asked for me and Brenda gleefully told them I was in the back. I could hear her smirk in her voice as I stood and moved towards the reception area.

"Ms. Matthews," the cop I didn't know said as I approached them. "Can we have a word?"

Chris smiled gently at me, and I muttered yes and moved away to meet them. I lifted the keys from the wall and led them into the same office Charlie and I had sat in a few days previous.

Having Chris in the same space as Charlie had been, was making me uncomfortable and I tugged at my collar, forgetting for a minute the bruise Warren had left on my neck.

Chris widened his eyes and his colleague Officer Hamlin openly stared at me.

"So, Ms Matthews, Warren Graham has made a complaint against you and your roommate, Charlie James. We need your statement to continue with our investigation."

I gave them a stern look and began speaking. I told them all about the restraining order and how Warren was obsessed with me. I explained that he'd come by unannounced, assaulting me, and that Charlie had scared him away. I then explained that he'd come back and assaulted Charlie and then run away after Charlie defended himself and me.

Officer Hamlin stood and left to answer his radio, and I told Chris about all the trouble I was having with Warren. He already knew part of the story, but I knew he believed me when he leaned over and gave me a gentle kiss on the forehead.

"We'll deal with him, Beth. I think the court will be very interested to know that not only is he not adhering to his bail conditions, but he's also assaulting you."

He gave me a once over and nodded as the other office came back inside and motioned to Chris to leave.

"See ya, Beth. Tell Callie I said hi." I gave him a wide smile and watched both cops out of the door, before deflating for a moment and taking a deep, cleansing breath.

I was back at my desk, ignoring the questioning looks Brenda was throwing my way when my message alert sounded on my mobile.

Chris: Beth, I hope you're okay. We're charging Warren and keeping him in custody until his court hearing, let's hope he's getting put away. Mrs. Geralds backed up your version of events and said she witnessed hearing the whole thing. Stay safe, Chris

I smiled and sent a message to Charlie but didn't tell him that Chris had told me in case he wasn't supposed to. Charlie didn't text back for the rest of my shift, and as I locked up for the night, my mobile began to ring with Charlie's number.

"Hello," I answered, but the signal was dreadful, and the call dropped out.

I tried to call him back, but it went onto answerphone, so I decided to see him at home and made my way to the train station.

I missed my usual train and ended up getting home at almost eight. My foot was throbbing painfully because I hadn't managed to get a seat on the packed train and had to stand for almost an hour.

Once I was inside the building, I sat down on the bottom step and let a whimper of pain out. As I was sitting there, Chris came into the flat. He took one look at me and shook his head.

"Your ankle hurting?" he asked, and I wanted to say, 'well done Captain obvious', but I was hoping he'd help me to the flat.

"Yeah, it hurts like a motherfucker," I told him, and he gave me a smile that didn't quite reach his eyes.

"You want a hand up to your flat?" His question made me sigh in relief and I gave him a warm smile.

"Please?" I answered, and he leaned down and scooped me up into his arms.

"Don't tell Callie about this. It'll ruin my rep," he joked as he began to slowly climb the stairs.

Celibet

As he made our way along our landing, he froze outside Bessie's door and turned to knock on it.

I glanced up at him in confusion and he stared straight ahead.

"Can Beth stay here for a bit?" he asked without preamble as she answered, and I saw her glance over his shoulder with wide eyes before she nodded. He marched inside and dropped me on the sofa.

"Stay here, Beth, and don't move." He turned to Bessie and spoke in a firm voice. "Lock the door after me, and don't let anyone but me in!" he told her in his commanding cop's voice that had fear curdling in my stomach. He turned and left, closing the door after him.

Bessie met my eyes and rushed over, locking it.

For a while, there was silence. Bessie didn't speak, and I was too scared to ask what they'd seen. We both sat and she held my hand until Chris knocked at the door and told us it was him. Bessie rushed to let him in, and Chris instantly came over with another cop in uniform.

"Beth, I need to ask you a few questions. Is that okay?"

I gave him a nod and he met the other cop's eyes.

"Do you know where Charlie James is?"

His question threw me. I opened my mouth and thought back to the call, but I didn't know where he was, and my stomach contracted as worry settled over me. "No. He tried to call me earlier, but the call didn't work."

"Can you try and call him again?" he pressed.

I dug my phone out of my bag and rang Charlie's mobile. My fingers shook as I ended the call. "Voicemail," I told them in a scared whisper.

"Okay. Chris can tell you what's happened while I put out an APB on Warren Graham," the new cop said, and he turned and let himself out of the flat.

"Chris, what's going on?" I asked around the lump in my throat.

He met my eyes and then glanced down guiltily before meeting holding me with a steady gaze. "Your apartment is covered in blood. There are trails of it all over, but there's a pool in the living room, and we are concerned that it's Charlie's blood."

My ears started to ring, and my breathing sped up as I heard his words bouncing around in my head. It couldn't be Charlie's blood. It just couldn't. But then why couldn't I get a hold of him? Where the fuck was he?

My whole body began to shake as the prospect of losing my best friend settled over me. My eyes spilled over, and I picked up my mobile sending Charlie a text that I could barely see.

Call me. Please call me straight away. I need you! I need to know you're okay so call me ASAP!!! Xx

Chapter Thirty-Seven

CHARLIE

After the police left, I couldn't do anything but sit there and fume, and with Beth at work, my thoughts and the events of the last few days played on repeat in my mind. I had this nervous energy, and I really needed to do something. Rather than going to see Beth at work and upsetting her day more than it was already going to be, I put Netflix on. I settled back in to watch Prison Break where I'd left off the other day. Watching Michael Schofield plan yet another break out in series three probably wasn't the best thing to watch. Maybe I should have turned my attention to some crime drama so I could have planned Warren's death and gotten away with it. The only thing I could do was hope the police did their job and send him down.

Resting my head on the arm of the couch, I clicked play, folded my arms across my chest and got myself comfortable.

About half an hour into the second episode, my eyelids began to droop, and rather than fighting the urge to sleep, I just let myself drift off. It was better than if I'd punched a wall or a door and wrecked shit in the flat.

I woke a while later to a ringing phone. God knows how long I'd been asleep.

Trying to open one eye, I squinted and tapped around until I had my hand on my phone. Not looking at the screen, I just swiped across the icon and lifted it to my ear.

"Hello," I croaked out.

"Ah, Charlie. It's Peter London."

I bolted up and cleared my throat before I spoke again. Peter was the producer of Wandering Warrior. "Peter. Hi. Is everything okay?"

"Yes of course or at least it would be if you can get to Hertfordshire today?"

"Today? You mean now?"

"If you could. I'd like to do some trial set shots with you and Mia."

"I'll be there. Leave it with me."

I pondered for a moment if I could pull this off. I didn't have a car and if I took the train, I wouldn't get there until tonight. The next best thing would be Mia, so I pulled up her phone number.

After a couple of rings, she answered.

"Ah, Mr James. What can I do for you?"

"Have you heard from Peter?"

Celibet

"I have. I'm just preparing to leave the house."

"Swing around and pick me up, would ya?"

"I could, but I'd have to ask Liz. She's driving."

"Well, tell her I'm a really cool guy and she'll say yes."

"She already knows that." She chuckled as she spoke to who I assumed was Liz. "We'll be there in half an hour."

Mia sounded the horn outside the flat, and I locked up and left right away. Once in the car, Mia introduced me to her partner, Liz. She was a cute red head with what seemed like a fiery attitude.

"So, Charlie. I hear you were hitting on my girlfriend. Do that shit again, I'll cut your dick off, ya hear me?"

"N... not so much hitting on her, no..."

She laughed out loud at my stupid stuttering and we drove off the car park. The rest of the journey was loud singing from the girls and me taking in the sights of the countryside. I knew one thing though: I needed a goddamn car.

We'd been filming some shots when my phone rang. I pulled it out and lifted it to my ear as I walked up the hill of these godforsaken fields. I said hello and I could hear Beth's voice, but the call broke up with the shitty signal.

"Hello," I shouted again but nothing. I walked around, hoping to grab some decent signal... nothing. The call dropped and the beeps sounded in my ear. Pulling the phone away, I looked at the screen, but it was blank. I frowned because from what I could hear, she'd sounded desperate. I hoped to God there was nothing urgent. There was no way I could get back right away.

Mia sidled up against me. "Everything okay?"

"I'm not sure. Beth just rang me, but the signal dropped." I looked down at her and just smiled then shrugged. "Nothing I can do from here. I'll ring her when we're back on the road. Come on."

She linked arms with mine and we went back to the scene.

Chapter Thirty-Eight

BETH

I spent the rest of the night in a state of numb acceptance, waiting on word from the cops. Bessie made me eat and drink, but I barely touched my food.

My heart thumped painfully, and I couldn't get Charlie out of my head. I couldn't go back into my flat because it was being treated as an active crime scene.

My phone started to ring at a little after nine and I picked it up. My heart raced, and my fingers shook as I took in the name.

Chris was beside me as I quickly swiped at the call.

"Charlie?" I answered in a low whisper and heard Charlie's breezy voice on the other end of the line.

"Hey, Bethy-babe, are you okay? What's with the text?"

"Where have you been?" I asked around the lump in my throat, and he sighed.

"Is this how things will be with us? I'm not in when you get home, and you get all upset?"

"Charlie, please! Just tell me. Did Warren have you? Are you hurt?"

"What? Why would Warren have me? What are you talking about?"

Chris and Bessie were both watching me as I shivered on the sofa.

"Beth are you okay? What's happened? Why would you think Warren would have me? What's he done now?"

Hearing the concern in his voice was too much for me, and I burst into noisy sobs. Chris came over and plucked my mobile from my hand.

I heard him and Charlie chatting, and as Bessie hugged me tightly, Chris handed my phone back to me.

"Charlie's fine. He was on location today and is on his way back now. He didn't know anything about what's happened. He's going to need to give an official statement, but that can wait until tomorrow."

My body was completely overwhelmed by what had happened and from the relief I felt at knowing Charlie was safe and unharmed.

As the news sunk in, I sagged back on the sofa and Bessie went to make a cuppa. She moved about in the kitchen, and Chris and I sat watching a movie on the TV for a while. I began to drift off to sleep as Bessie came back into the sitting room with a tray laden with cups, biscuits, and cakes.

Celibet

She poured herself a cup, but Chris didn't finish his, and I was too tired to even drink mine. I just wanted Charlie to come home. Bessie went to get me a blanket. Chris, waited until she was gone, leaned close to me, and watched me intently for a minute.

"Beth, I'm gonna take off now. Derek is outside the door and will be staying there until Warren is apprehended."

He moved closer and gave me a soft kiss on the forehead, moving towards the door, but before he could leave, there was a commotion outside and he quickly locked the door, ushering Bessie and me into the back room where I'd slept in the last time I'd stayed.

"Stay in here and don't open the door for anyone, but me."

He spun around and bolted from the room, leaving Bessie and I alone, but when he didn't come back after a minute, I began to get worried. My whole body tensed as a series of knocks sounded on the door, and I heard Chris call out that it was okay to open the door.

My hand was shaking, and Bessie stood behind the door with a heavy ceramic statue of an elephant as I peeled the door open slowly.

My reaction to Charlie standing there was to howl in surprise and throw myself into his arms, capturing his lips in a firm kiss.

"I thought you were dead," I cried against his mouth, and he chuckled.

"I'm not that easy to kill."

I smacked his arm as he pressed another gentle kiss to my lips. "Sorry. It's okay. I'm okay. I'm here, and you're safe."

He opened his mouth as though he wanted to say something else, then closed it and smiled over my shoulder at Bessie who was watching us with a smile. Chris was also smiling at us from behind Charlie's back, but I didn't care. I buried my head against his chest and just breathed him in for a moment. **He really was okay.**

For a moment, he just held me and then Chris turned and left. Bessie offered us the room for the night.

"That's okay, Bessie. Thank you. Forensics have been and determined it's animal blood, so we are safe to go back in now."

Charlie glanced down at my foot as my boot clunked when I walked, and I saw him wince.

"Fuck, I'm so sorry, Bethy. That was my fault."

I just shrugged at him as we made our way across to our flat, and my eyes widened as I saw the blood on the sofa and along the walls. It was everywhere, and I wasn't sure it would come out.

The carnage got worse as we made our way out into the hall. Charlie's room was a mess, but my room was totally wrecked.

My gorgeous, four poster bed that had been a gift from my parents was destroyed, and my clothes all sat on the floor, pulled from their drawers or the wardrobe and caked in blood. My shoes were broken, and my underwear looked as though it had been cut up into pieces.

Celibet

My laptop was smashed, and my iPad had a cracked screen. Everything I owned, including my makeup, jewellery and bags were ruined. I had nothing left.

I turned to Charlie and saw him fighting to control his temper. His eyes darted around the room, and when he took in all of my possessions, his hands clenched into fists and his jaw ticked in what looked like fury.

I had nothing to wear to work, but I had put a wash on that morning, and my dark grey, wool dress and cashmere sweater were in the machine, along with my Victoria Secret bra and pants.

I spun around and marched back into the living room, walking into the kitchen. It was completely untouched, and I found some pj's and underwear, plus my favourite jeans, two tops and a work dress all hanging to dry.

Charlie came into the kitchen at my back. He was holding something in his clenched fist. For a moment, he didn't speak, and then he opened his hand and showed me my mum's locket.

It was the last gift she'd ever given me, and it had been in Charlie's room from the night I'd spent there recently. He'd put it in his bedside drawer as we'd gone to bed and it was completely fine.

My eyes filled with tears, and I leaned up and pressed a kiss to his lips.

"God, I wish we weren't doing this stupid bet now…" I told him, and he smirked at me and then nodded at my foot.

"I think sex is out for you anyway, babe. Pack a bag. We're going to a hotel tonight."

He leaned down and brushed my tears from my eyes as he gave me another whisper soft kiss.

"Love you, Bethy-babe," he muttered, and my whole body shuddered in response because while he'd told me he loved me before, he'd never said the words to me since way before he'd gone to Paris, and I didn't know if he meant 'love you old chum' or 'love you, love you'.

I hoped it was the second one because if I were honest with myself, the only time I'd ever really felt love, felt a true connection with a man, was with him. Other than my dad, he was my person, and I loved him, too. I wasn't ready to say the words to him yet because I didn't say the words. At all. Ever. The last thing I'd said to my mum was I love you, and the next morning a brain aneurysm had taken her from us, so, ever since then, I hadn't told anyone I loved them, ever and I'd never, not once, said it to Wanker because I didn't. I never had.

Chapter Thirty-Nine

CHARLIE

Once filming was over, I was eager to get home. I had to make sure Beth was okay. Between the text and the call that dropped, I was a little concerned. We were only in Hertfordshire for a little over five hours, but then we had an hour's drive back to the city.

Mia kept asking if I was alright, and I was, I just must've been quieter than I realised.

When she pulled up outside our place, I thanked Liz for taking me and offered her some petrol money—not that she took it. I gave them both a kiss on the cheek and winked.

As I got out of the car, I saw a police car parked outside the main entrance door.

Okay.

I wasn't sure why my stomach had churned, or why there was this lump in my throat, but all of a sudden, I felt sick. It was probably because of the call earlier, but with all the shit that had happened to Beth recently…

With my hand on the door handle I flashed my fob over the sensor and the door unlocked. I tugged it open, lifting my hand in a wave to the girls, and proceeded to run up the stairs. As I turned the corner, there was an officer outside our flat, standing guard with his arms folded against his chest.

"What the fuck is going on? Why are you here? Where the fuck is Beth?" I roared as I took in the streaks of blood that were on the door. The copper raised his hands in front of him to calm me down when Bessie's door opened.

Chris appeared from around the back of the door. He turned to look over his shoulder and whispered something before shutting it behind him.

"Charlie." He looked me over and sighed with what looked like relief, placing his hands on his hips.

The door opened again, and before I knew it Beth had thrown herself at me. Her head crashed against my chest as she took a hold of my neck. My arms tightened around her back and I held her. Her body sagged into mine, and I dipped my head and sank my nose into her hair. I didn't give a fuck who was around to see it either. I looked down and saw the boot that was on her foot and guilt washed over me.

Chris turned away, smirking, and lifted his ringing phone to his ear while I held her for a bit longer. Bessie

Celibet

broke the silence to tell us we could stay in her spare room just as Chris re-joined us.

He confirmed it wasn't human blood, and that it was animal's blood.

What the actual fuck had gone on here today?

After we went into the flat and saw the shit that had been left for us, I was almost shaking in anger and I thought to myself that Chris had better lock Warren up in case I find him because the next lot of blood won't be from an animal: it'll be fucking Warren's.

As I watched Beth go through her torn and cut up belongings, along with her smashed up laptop and iPad, I was brimming with rage.

I scooped her up into my arms and she looked up at me, her eyes full of desire.

"God, I wish we weren't doing this stupid bet now…"

I nodded down at the floor and smirked. "I think sex is out for you anyway, babe. Pack a bag. We're going to a hotel tonight. Love you, Bethy-babe," her body tensed, and her breath quickened. She held on to me a little tighter, and I just enjoyed the warmth of our embrace. Saying that to her was like a weight had lifted from my shoulders, and it felt good.

I booked us into a Premier Inn just for the next two nights. If Beth was going into work tomorrow, I'd go back to the flat and start the clean-up.

Once I'd got us checked in and up to our room, she clunked over to the bed and slumped down. Her shoulders slouched, and her head hung. Closing the door, I dropped the bags and sighed before I walked over, hooking my knuckle beneath her chin and tipped her head back. I pressed my lips to hers, and she kissed me back, her bottom lip trembling against mine.

I pulled back an inch.

"Hey. I'm okay." She nodded and I told her to hang on a second. I opened my bag and dragged out one of my T-shirts and threw it at the side of her.

I slid the zip of her dress down and asked her to lift her butt a little pulling it from beneath her. Slipping her cardigan from her shoulders, she shrugged out of it, and I tugged her dress up and over her head, throwing it to the floor out of the way. Once she was in just her bra and knickers, I kissed her shoulder. My dick was rock hard, but it wasn't important tonight. Guiding my T-shirt over her head, it fell to her legs, and I stripped down to my boxers before I pulled back the sheet and lifted her leg onto the bed.

"I need to take off my boot."

"Okay. Lie back for me."

She rested her head on the pillows and watched me as I back drew back each of the Velcro straps, carefully removing it from her foot. I placed it at the side of the bed and moved around to the other side, sliding in beside her.

She lifted her head so I could put my arm around her, and she snuggled into my side resting her cheek on my chest.

"So, what did the doctor say about your foot?" I was trying to think of anything to talk about other than what had happened today.

Celibet

"I've broken my third metatarsal. I'm gonna be stuck in this thing for a few weeks."

"That's my fault for rugby tackling you."

"I don't blame you, Charlie." She lifted her chin and her blue eyes bore into mine. "I blame that wanker. I blame him for everything. Why did he do this to me? He dumped me. He stole from me and all because I wouldn't give him my trust fund. He hit me and made my life fucking hell… I just don't get it." Water filled her eyes, and I put my lips to her forehead. I felt the shudder that shook through her body. I leaned back and watched as tears ran down her cheeks. I pressed my thumbs to her face and swiped as gently as I could beneath her eyes then held her in my arms as she cried.

Chapter Forty

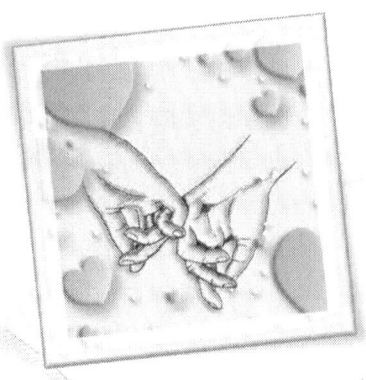

BETH

Once I'd cried myself out, I fell asleep and woke up to my alarm. My heart hammered wildly in my chest when I realised Charlie wasn't there. I scanned the room for him and pushed myself up into a sitting position. The bathroom light was on, but the door was ajar, and I couldn't hear him.

I needed to use the bathroom, so I hobbled there without putting my boot on, but I stopped when I saw Charlie standing in the shower.

His hand was around his cock, and water ran in rivulets down his toned body and abs. I licked my lips as desire uncurled in my stomach. He twisted, squeezed, and moved his hand up and down, grunting softly as he did. My eyes

Celibet

drifted back up his body. He was biting his lip, his cheeks flushed.

As I scanned his face, his eyes opened and he caught me watching him, but he didn't stop. He groaned just enough to set off butterflies in my stomach and his arm moved faster.

My eyes scanned downwards, and I watched in fascination, feeling moisture pool between my legs as he stroked his length. After another few seconds, he threw back his head on a moan as moisture shot out of his cock, coating his hand and the wall beside him.

As he spurted, I stood on my good foot, breathing heavily, and he gave his hand a wipe with a facecloth, cleaning the wall as he did. He turned away from me, and I watched his firm arse move as he turned the water of the shower back on.

"God, Beth," he breathed in a croaky whisper, "seeing you standing there watching me does crazy things to me."

I hopped into the bathroom and reached over, running my hand over his ass and up his back as he stood under the cool jets of the shower. He spun around, leaning down, and capturing my lips in a scorching kiss that almost knocked me on my arse. Shower water sprayed over us as we kissed, and then he pulled back, glancing down at my now soaked T-shirt. My nipples were erect, and he licked his lips as he ran wet hands over my shoulders and down, circling my nipples with his thumbs.

Fire raced through me at his touch, and my body—already more than turned on at the sight of him jerking off—responded to his touch.

"Beth," he breathed, and I glanced up to see him shaking his head and lowering his eyes to my lips. "No offence, but can you leave please?"

My breath huffed out and, I hopped back from him, hurt, and confused. He must have seen my pained expression because he spoke again in a hoarse whisper.

"We can't do anything, and fuck," he paused, running his hand through his wet hair in a way that caused the muscles in his abdomen to move. I couldn't take my eyes away from him. He said something else, but I was distracted by his incredible body, and didn't hear him.

He flicked some water over me.

"Huh, what?" I asked and he chuckled.

"Beth, I want to get out of this shower and strip that soaking wet T-shirt from your body, running my lips all over you and tasting you, so I'm begging you to leave, because my restraint is about to snap."

My eyes darted back up to his, and he smirked at me and moving towards me, but I knew we couldn't. I hopped towards the sink as Charlie stepped out onto the tiled floor onto a mat, grabbing a towel from the shelf beside the bath. He wrapped it around his body and before I could move, he was standing in front of me, breathing hard.

"You are so beautiful," he muttered as his fingers moved a strand of my hair from my forehead, and he pressed a soft kiss to my lips, before plunging his tongue in and pulling my body flush against his. Electricity raced through me at our connection, and he took everything I was willing to give him and then some before he stepped

Celibet

back and winked at me, as I stood there, a shaking, horny mess.

He left the bathroom whistling, and I leaned back against the sink, knocking over his aftershave and my meagre toiletry bag as I did.

The contents spilled everywhere, and I slowly turned around, putting my things back in my bag and splashing cold water over my face as I tried to calm my racing heart.

As I dried my face, Charlie appeared at the door and called in that he was going for coffees, leaving me so hot for him that I barely managed to wash myself because I was too busy envisioning his hands all over me.

Half an hour later, I was in my wool dress, sitting on the bed trying to do my makeup when he arrived back with coffee and a few bags of goodies. He dropped the bags onto the bed beside me and came over giving me another soft kiss before he set my coffee down at my side.

"I went to Tesco and got you some stuff." His cheeks heated as he took a sip out of his coffee, and I turned on the bed to peek into the bags.

My fingers shook as I opened them and saw he'd gotten me new pjs, socks, panties, and a work dress in deep red. In the other bag were two black dress tops, a grey pencil skirt and a black one. There was also a dress jacket in the bag.

"Charlie, you didn't have to..." I began, but I broke off as emotion overwhelmed me. He simply shrugged and came over, wrapping his hand around my neck and giving me another kiss.

"I know I didn't," he told me as he kissed me again, "but you deserve it. You didn't deserve what happened to you yesterday, but I figured I could help you get started on replacing your clothes. The girl in Tesco helped me…" He broke off and pulled away as his mobile rang. I glanced at the time, finishing getting dressed because it was time for me to leave.

Charlie answered the phone, and I quickly finished my makeup and slipped my foot back into my boot, doing the straps. I grabbed my bag and jacket and moved towards him, wrapping my hands around him from behind and pressing a kiss to his shoulder before stepping back. I scooped up my coffee and checked to make sure I had my mobile with me as I readied myself to leave with him still on the phone.

Chapter Forty-One

CHARLIE

I watched Beth leave the room with a desperate hunger as I answered my phone. Trust that to fucking ring. All I really wanted to do was throw her back on to the bed and lock the door. I wouldn't have done anything last night, though, she had been way too upset. I'm not that much of an insensitive bastard.

Her soft kiss to my shoulder shouldn't have me feeling the way I did. It had been innocent, but there had been a certain feeling to it—in the way she'd lingered her lips against my skin. I did take note of how Beth had never told me she loved me, but after everything that had happened with Warren it wasn't surprising. I'd wait for that day and cherish it with my world when she did.

"Charles, are you still there?"

Fuck, I'd forgot my mum was still talking to me when I'd zoned out thinking about Beth.

"Yes, Mum, and it's Charlie. I hate Charles. I've always hated it."

"Just like you've always hated what I wanted for you…"

"Mum, please don't start. I have stuff to do today."

"Don't start?"

My eyes rolled to the top of my head, and I sank onto the bed.

"What could possibly be so important that you can't spare your mother a minute?"

I blew out a tired sigh. "We had the flat broken into, Beth got hurt and today I need to go and clean the flat up."

"Pfft, that would never have happened if you weren't living in the city. If you'd followed our path…"

"Oh yeah, that's right, doctors or lawyers don't get broken into do they. Of course not. Have you not watched Death Wish with Bruce Willis?" I chuckled to myself, knowing Mother would never watch that kind of film.

"Charles Lewis James!"

Oh, fuck I was in trouble now. "I have no idea what you're talking about. So, you're still sharing a flat with her then?"

"If you mean Bethany, then yes, Mother. She's my best friend, but lately things have changed…"

"Really?" Mum's tone rose. I could imagine her eyes widening with glee and hoping that I was going to say I was moving out.

Celibet

"Yeah, since I came back from Paris from shooting that movie, we're have been much closer... I can see us becoming a couple."

"What? Oh, for goodness sake, Charles. You can do so much better than her...."

"What? Mum.... No can't hear, ya. Signals going, sorry..."

I hit the reject button and cut the call. I couldn't be doing with her screeching my down my ear anymore. I was so sick of her constant badgering—sick of her saying my job wasn't good enough, where I live wasn't good enough and Beth, she'd never really approved of Beth. She had this stupid idea that Beth led me astray. My mum wasn't really a religious woman, but she was certain that Beth had put some kind of spell on me. Crazy woman! Most people would love to be doing what I'm doing: acting, living in the city with their best friend... I thought I had it fucking great. I was living my life the way I wanted to. How many people could honestly say that?

I threw my phone to the bed and ran my hands through my hair. I knew I had to get moving, but right then, I couldn't be arsed. My thoughts went back to this morning when Beth had watched me giving myself a soapy hand job in the shower. If it hadn't had been for her fucking ankle, I'd have pulled her in the bath with me and fucked her senseless instead. I'd shot my load as our eyes met, hunger and desire spilling from us both.

Once I was dressed, I shouted back that I was going to get us coffees.

When I'd walked through the entrance doors of Tesco, I'd seen the clothing department to the left of me and an idea hit me. I'd wandered through and grabbed her a couple dresses that caught my eye and that I thought she'd like and some other essentials. I wasn't great on what style most women would like, but Beth, I thought I knew her pretty well and unlike most guys, I knew her sizes, too. Not that I'm some kind of perv and go rifling through her underwear drawers, but when you're washing your smalls together, you tend to take notice.

I could feel my eyes beginning to close, and I knew if I laid here any longer, I'd be asleep again. I didn't have the best sleep anyway because I was worried about Beth.

I bolted up off the bed and went into the bathroom, running the cold tap until it was freezing cold and cupping my hands beneath it before splashing water on my face. Blinking through the water in my eyes, I dried it off and turned the tap off.

I grabbed my shit together and left the hotel to go back to the flat to start the clean-up, stopping back off at the supermarket to grab extra cleaning products.

Sliding my key into the lock of the flat, I was apprehensive to say the least, but I opened the door because I knew I had to. I didn't want Beth to come here because she'd get upset all over again. If I could prevent that, I would.

Armed with my bag of cleaning products, I sucked in a breath and walked in. Dumping my stuff on the kitchen counter, I went into the living room It was like mass

Celibet

murder had been committed. I had no idea how I'd get the blood off the furniture or the walls—it looked like we needed to redecorate.

My phone rang in my pocket.

"Hey babe."

"Hey," the way she'd answered I could imagine the soft smile that played on her lips. "Don't forget this weekend is my mum's birthday, and I'm supposed to be going to Dad's country house."

"I remembered." I so fucking hadn't but, that made things easier. She'd told me she wasn't going to go, but I had soon changed her mind, telling her she needed to. I'd make it happen.

I ran the hot tap and began to fill the washing up bowl, squirting a little fairy liquid into it. I grabbed the scrubbing brush and went into the front room. Dipping the brush into the water, I got on my hands and knees and started on the carpet. I scrubbed that hard my arm ached, but when I sat back and looked at the patch I'd cleaned, it didn't look any better.

I clambered up to my feet and went into Beth's room. Grabbing a black bin liner, I gathered everything together before throwing it inside. I sighed as I sat on the bed. If I couldn't get rid of all this mess, Beth would be gutted.

Maybe we'd be better off moving and finding somewhere else to live.

I heard the sound of my phone and I went into the front to find it. An email had come through from my old producer about the premiere of the movie we shot in Paris.

Great! That's what I need after everything the last few weeks: a night of Jessie Lewis and her fucking ego.

Chapter Forty-Two

BETH

I spoke to Charlie on my break at work. He knew it was my mum's birthday weekend and that I was supposed to be going home to spend it with my dad, but with all the carnage at the flat I wasn't sure I was up for going.

We'd talked on the phone earlier and I'd told him I was thinking of cancelling my weekend away.

"You're going. It'll do you good to get away from London for a bit, and you're off next week, so you should totally go," he countered and my heart sank because I was worried he'd wanted me out of the way, but I knew it was just my anxiety talking.

As I locked up, a car pulled into the lot and idled by the curb. My anxiety levels shot through the roof at the thought of Warren, but when the door opened, my mouth popped open because Charlie was sitting in the driver's seat smirking at me.

"Hop in, babe. We're going to your Dad's country house. He's already there with your aunt and cousins, and he's so excited that we're going. I got a car specially for it."

I glowered at Charlie and he pouted at me.

"Come on, baby," he muttered, and my insides danced a jig at hearing him call me baby. He'd always called me babe, but baby was different.

I moved towards the door and he smiled widely at me, stealing my breath, and making my panties soaked all at once.

I hovered at the door and glared at him. "Fine, but if Julia hits on you, you're on your own."

Julia was my cousin, and she was awful. Every time she saw Charlie, or in fact any guy, she hit on them, and almost every time he would succumb to her charms.

"Oh my God, you can't leave me with her." He chuckled at me as I climbed into the car.

"Well, you know if she's there, she going to try and get in your pants."

She'd hit on Warren loads over the years, and a few times I'd wondered if they'd actually slept together. They'd always assured me it was harmless fun, but I wasn't so sure.

"Hey, where'd you go?" Charlie asked, and I shook off the thoughts that were circling in my head. Charlie wasn't Wanker, so he'd never do that to me.

For the rest of the journey, Charlie played his god-awful rock music with his hand on my knee. He rubbed in

Celibet

rhythmic circles as I sat and looked out the window. My dad's house in Kensington was about an hour and a half from where we were, so Charlie drove us there via McDonalds.

When we arrived, the driveway was lit with lights, and I could see my aunt Tess and Julia inside.

My dad came out to meet us, giving Charlie a hug and raising his eyebrows as he helped me from the car.

We went inside, and Tess began to quiz Charlie. She didn't like him and made it clear, but Charlie took it all in his stride. Julia asked where Warren was and smirked when I told her we'd broken up.

I wanted to punch her, but Charlie linked his fingers with mine as my dad showed us to our rooms.

My room was all creams and magnolias with a wooden bedframe, a bay window and fireplace. It was my favourite room in dads house, and everywhere I looked, I saw my mum's touches.

It was in the throw pillows and the curtains, in the cream and grey rug and the wooden chair that was by the en suite bathroom.

Charlie was shown to another room down the hall, opposite Julia's, and he was back in my room as soon as my dad was gone.

"Oh my God, I forgot what a fucking nightmare she is. She was all over me. She actually tried to kiss me."

My amusement soured as I stared at him, and he watched me stiffen with indignance and anger. He moved towards me and pulled me into his arms, holding me tightly as he brushed his lips against my head.

"Hey, it's okay! I shook her off. The only person who's lips I want to taste is currently in my arms." He broke off, breathing hard and pressed soft kisses along my jaw until he reached my lips. Tugging even closer, he captured my lips in a kiss that made my insides quiver and my body shake.

Our kiss began to deepen when there was the sound of a throat clearing behind us.

He sprang away from me, and I turned to see my dad standing there, a stern expression on his face.

"Charlie, I think we talked about this," he muttered in a low and deadly voice and Charlie sheepishly stepped back from me.

My dad gave me a sharp look as Charlie left the room and said in a low voice, "Sorry, sir."

My dad didn't even look at him. His eyes were trained on my face, and I could see the disappointment on his face.

"Beth, you know I'm not one to lecture you, but you've just got out of a relationship."

He came towards me and stopped as he reached me, clasping my hands. He stood looking down at me. I knew he didn't understand why I was able to move on so fast, but Charlie wasn't Warren.

He was so much more.

He always had been.

For a few seconds, we stood and stared at each other before he spoke again.

"Just don't jump in feet first. Charlie has so much more potential to hurt you. I see the way you look at him, and

Celibet

you never looked at Warren like that." He gave me a gentle hug, holding me tightly as he did.

"Thanks, Daddy," I told him as I breathed in the comforting smell of my childhood.

"Your mum always loved him, so I can see why you're falling in love with him, too, but I worry about you."

My whole body froze as my dad's words permeated my skull, and I remembered a conversation I'd had with my mum about three months before she passed. We'd been out for coffee and we're sitting chatting as Charlie and Damien had come into the coffee shop.

Mum's eyes widened as Charlie came straight over and pressed a soft kiss to my cheek. He was out for an audition and was looking totally gorgeous. His hair was curled, and his smile was breath-taking as he smiled at me, grabbing his coffee, and leaving.

My mum waited until he was gone and then turned to face me with a smirk. "That boy is crazy about you!"

Her words made me start because I was trying to keep my feelings for Charlie a secret, so I brushed it off and told her I was with Warren. Her gaze darkened as I mentioned Warren because my mum and I didn't have secrets and she knew exactly what Warren had asked me.

She had not been happy to say the least and advised me against it, and now I was so glad I'd listened to her.

I didn't say a word to my dad about my feelings for Charlie, but I whispered as a wave of sadness overwhelmed me, "I miss her, Dad."

He hugged me tightly, giving me a kiss on the forehead as he said in response, "I know. I do too, but let's go downstairs before Julia tries to eat Charlie alive. Tess has cooked up a storm today, so I hope you're hungry."

We walked down the wooden stairs, and I paused as I watched Charlie brush off Julia and laugh as Tess said something I couldn't make out. His smile widened as he caught sight of us, and I instantly walked over and wrapped my arms around his waist, pressing a kiss to his chest as everyone in the kitchen froze and watched our interactions.

Chapter Forty-Three

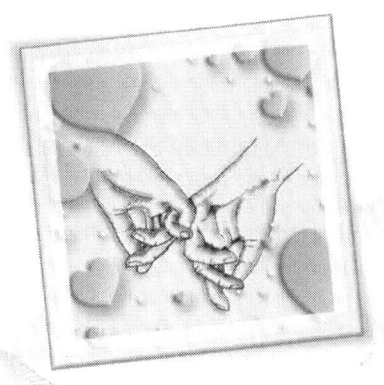

CHARLIE

Once I was done at the flat, I was achy and sweaty, and I felt dirty. Other than some more clothes for both Beth and I, I left everything there and grabbed the bags I'd packed for us both before heading for the train.

When I got back to the hotel, I jumped straight in the shower and stood under the flow of water, turning the dial to as hot as I could stand it and eventually felt my body relax. I washed the grime from my body and stepped out. Wrapping a towel around my hips, I towel-dried my hair and packed the two cases. Once I was done, I pushed my hand through my still damp hair and finger combed my hair. I didn't need a comb since I'd been blessed with curls, and even when I tidied it up, it still looked a mess. I knew Beth loved my curls. Years ago, when we'd first met, it was the one thing she had commented on.

I slipped my wallet into my clean jeans, made sure chargers were put in the bags and I plucked my phone from the back pocket of my other jeans.

Next stop was a car. I was hiring one for the weekend, then when I arrived back from Kent, I would be buying a new one. I couldn't get around without a car anymore, especially when my next location shoot would be down on the south coast.

I hired a metallic blue sporty Focus ST and it drove like a dream. I couldn't wait for Beth to see it. I returned to the hotel to grab our bags, piled them in the boot and checked out.

I wanted to surprise Beth and seeing as she didn't know I was doing any of this, I decided to meet her from work.

I pulled up to the surgery, just as Beth was locking up telling her to hop in and where we were going.

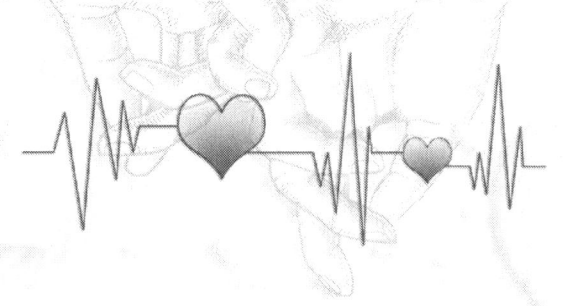

When we arrived at Beth's dad's country house, everyone was outside. If I didn't feel so comfortable around her family, I'd probably think this was what it was like to be in front of the firing squad. I helped Beth from

the car with that big bloody boot on her foot, and I grabbed the bags.

Celibet

Once her dad had shown us to our rooms, I sneaked back to Beth's and stole a kiss.

When I reached the downstairs, Julia came straight over to me and linked my arm with hers. I pulled it from her clutches and went into the kitchen to Tess. I felt safe with Tess.

"Hey Charlie."

"Hey yourself." I smiled and leaned against the kitchen cupboard as she began putting some garlic bread on a plate and turned off the burner to the massive pot of chilli, she'd been cooking for us all.

"We weren't expecting you this time. Can you keep a secret, though?" She leaned over towards me...

I nodded and she pushed up to my ear.

"I didn't like Warren. I'm glad he's not here."

"Warren won't be here ever again; you don't have to worry about that."

She smiled wide and began taking food through to the dining table. "Come and help me?"

"Of course." I picked up the pile of plates and took those through to the table then I grabbed the garlic bread.

As I looked through the gap of the door, I heard Beth's voice.

I went into the sitting room and stood in front of the fireplace. My eyes didn't stray from Beth, but her dad's eyes didn't shift from me. Julia wandered over and stood by me, staring up at me and fluttering her eyelashes. Tess walked past muttering something under her breath, but I didn't quite catch it, mainly because I'd zoned out at the beautiful blonde who was making her way down the stairs.

As I smiled, she walked over, wrapped her arms around my back and my breath stuttered when she placed a kiss to my chest.

In that moment I didn't care that everyone had seen. I didn't give two shits if they had picked up on how much I loved her because I did love her, and if it were up to me, I'd shout it from the rooftops.

After way too much food and some drink, too, Beth had snuggled up to me on the sofa, her head rested on my shoulder and every so often Julia would look over and give Beth the stink eye. I had to bite back a chuckle more than once.

It wasn't long after that Beth had dozed off against me. Beth's dad didn't miss a trick. I couldn't blame him.

"Someone's tired."

I glanced down at her and gave a small smile. "Yeah, it's been an eventful few day."

"Eventful?"

Shit.

I wasn't sure if she'd told her dad anything of what had happened. I directed a tight-lipped grin and nodded.

"I think you and I need to have a chat tomorrow, son."

"Yeah…" I sighed. "I'm going to take Beth up to her room."

Supporting her head, I shifted gently from beneath her and lifted her up into my arms.

As I slowly took the stairs, I heard Tess speak.

Celibet

"Don't be too hard on him. He's one of the good ones."

I carried on up the stairs and with it being all wooden, their voices travelled, and I heard him answer.

"That's what I'm worried about."

Supporting her body against the wall, I managed to get the door open and lie her on the bed.

"Beth, baby. Get into bed." Hovering over her, I glanced at the door, and when I was certain there was no one around, I softly pressed my lips to hers. Her eyes flickered open and she smiled.

"You were waiting for that weren't ya?" I whispered, amused.

"Like sleeping beauty waiting for her handsome prince." Her eyelashes fluttered and my lips touched hers again only this time, I added a little more pressure. I had to stop myself from plunging my tongue into her mouth and kissing her like I really wanted to, but this right here was enough.

"Goodnight, baby."

"Night, Charlie."

I knew I had to leave her. I got up from the bed and began moving towards the door.

"Charlie."

I stopped and spun around. Our eyes met, unsaid words lingering in the air. My heart sped up and my breathing quickened. I felt like I'd run a marathon.

"Nothing. Goodnight."

My heart sank. I covered it up and pushed my hope back that she could feel half of what I felt for her. I smiled and walked through the door heading for my room.

I lay there awake for hours. I heard everyone go to bed—they weren't exactly quiet. I tucked my hands under my head and stared above me, watching the shadows dance across the ceiling. The knob on my door turned, and very slowly the door opened. I glanced across at the clock at the side of me and it read two am. Frowning, I hoped to God it wasn't Julia. I closed my eyes and pretended to be asleep. I felt the presence at the side of the bed, and I hoped my breathing wouldn't give me away as still being awake.

"Charlie. Are you awake?"

It was only when I heard the sweet sound of Beth's voice that I opened my eyes.

"Move over."

"What are you doing? Your dad will kill me if he finds you in here."

"I needed you. I had a bad dream."

Scooting over, I lifted the sheets and she crawled inside.

Lying on her side, she curled her body into mine and I wrapped her up in my arms, ignoring my hardening dick, and thought that maybe if I thought about Julia it'd soon wilt like a fucking dying flower.

I kissed the top of Beth's head and shortly after I was drifting off.

Chapter Forty-Four

BETH

***Oh** fuck.*

I woke up on my side with my arm over Charlie's chest and my leg around his waist. My foot was throbbing, but it was a dull ache, and I was going to attempt to move when Charlie tightened his hold on me.

His fingers began stroking my back, and I glanced up from my spot on his chest to see him awake and watching me. With every move of his fingers, desire uncurled in my body, and I became hyper aware of his touch and the increase in his heartbeat and breathing.

His chest was bare, and I moved so I could press a soft kiss to it. I could hear his harsh breathing, and his fingers slipped inside my top, running along the curve of my spine, holding me close to him and making me want him even more.

"Beth," he groaned in a low whisper as I ran my fingers up his chest and touched his neck. His eyes met mine and I could see the desire inside them, burning into me as his hand splayed across my back and moved my body closer so I could feel his erection pressing into me.

He tugged me up and captured my lips in a firm kiss, pushing his erection into me before he'd flipped us over and I was lying on the bed and he was hovering above me. Our kisses became more frantic, and his hands began to wander up my top and around to my ribs. He ran his fingers over my nipples and pinched as he moved against me.

My breathing was unnaturally loud, and I wanted more. My hand wandered and I ran my fingers along the shaft of his penis before wrapping them around it, giving him a squeeze. I moved my hand down, then back up, as he leaned his head against mine, hissing out a breath between his teeth when my finger slipped inside his boxers and stroked the head of his cock.

He roughly brought his lips back to mine, plunging his tongue into my mouth and pushing against my clit, making me wetter and eliciting a soft moan from the back of my throat.

"Fuck, Beth, I want you so much…"

I was just about to cave when the room door opened, and the light turned on. My cousin stood in the doorway,

Celibet

glowering into the room at us. Her gaze narrowed as she saw my body underneath Charlie's.

"It's your mum's birthday and you are seriously about to have fucking sex. What the hell is wrong with you?"

Her words caused my libido to crash and burn and my eyes to fill with tears. Anguish rolled over me in a wave and I dropped my arms from Charlie's back as the dream I had slammed over me again.

"And with him! I mean I've already been there, and it was nothing to write home about…"

My breath left me in a huff as Charlie stiffened and rolled away from me. She chuckled at the carnage she'd just caused and turned, leaving the room as I faced Charlie.

"Is that true?" I asked him, and I saw the answer written on his face. He didn't need to say a word because I already knew. "When?" My throat closed over, and I couldn't even get the rest of my words out.

"Christmas last year." His answer caused a clang of pain to echo through me and a tear rolled from my eye. I couldn't believe I'd almost let myself get carried away by him, by us, but this, this was too much, even for me.

I crawled towards the edge of the bed and Charlie's hand closed over my wrist. I couldn't look at him. My eyes stung with tears and my throat burned as I tried to leave with my dignity intact.

"Beth… wait, please?" His voice was soft, and I could hear the pain behind his words. I couldn't turn around to look at him because the tears had started to roll down my cheeks.

"Look at me," he begged, and I turned to face him. His eyes widened as he saw my expression in the dim light of the room, and he reached up and ran his fingers under my eyes, wiping away the tears that broke free.

"I am so, so sorry. I was wasted and hurt, and I didn't think... Please don't hate me for this! It was a mistake and I never intended for you to get hurt like this..."

I shook my head, and my foot began to throb painfully, causing me to wince and another tear to fall.

"Beth, please. Stay with me."

"I can't Charlie. I need a minute."

He nodded and swallowed, wiping at tear from his cheek as he watched me tug my hand from his and back away from the bed. I returned to my room, crawling underneath the covers, letting the devastation I was feeling wash over me.

He knew how I'd felt about her. I'd told him that she always went after my boyfriends and those closest to me. How he could sleep with her knowing she hated me so much, gutted me and I couldn't look at him without feeling that devastation wash over me again and again.

I drifted back off to sleep with tears still rolling down my cheeks and a fracture in my heart.

The next day, I barely spent any time alone with Charlie because Lawrence and Spence came. They were Julia's brothers, but unlike her they were wonderful. Lawrie was a lawyer in London and Spence was a doctor in Liverpool.

I avoided Charlie at all costs and made sure I was beside my dad and Spence at dinner. He tried to get me alone to speak to me, but I avoided him like the plague and didn't let myself get drawn into conversation with him.

When I woke up on Sunday, after sleeping in until noon, he was gone, and I didn't know where. For the next few days, I moped at my dad's and used my trust fund card to buy myself some clothes and things.

When I hadn't heard from Charlie by Friday morning, I was more than a little worried, but I couldn't bring myself to text him because every time I tried to type out a message it hurt. It really fucking hurt, and I didn't know what to say or do to even start a conversation with him again.

Chapter Forty-Five

CHARLIE

Have you ever wished that the ground would open up and swallow you whole? Or maybe wish that what just happened was just a dream and that you'd wake up and everything would be right in the world, or in your bed?

I wished everything was right in my bed… everything had been right in my bed until that fucking Julia opened the door. Fuck my life! I was sure every man and his dog were against us being together.

"Beth… wait." I called again as she left the room. I tried to explain. I could have just said that it shouldn't have mattered because she'd been with Warren at the time. I mean, surely to God it shouldn't have hurt her… but I knew it had.

Celibet

I saw the smug grin that appeared on Julia's face. She'd enjoyed that way too much.

Why would a cousin do that?

I'd get my own back on Julia before I left. I wasn't sure what had hurt Beth the most: that I shagged Julia in a drunken stupor or that she had been reminded that today was her mum's birthday.

I pushed to the edge of the bed and went to the door, hoping I could catch Beth up. Surely, she couldn't limp that fast on a broken foot. Beth was nowhere to be seen, though, as I peered down the hallway. I sighed and turned to go back in.

Then I heard it. That annoying screechy voice.

Gritting my teeth, I turned the other way and saw Julia leaning against the wall.

"Happy with yourself?"

"She had to find out sooner or later…"

"And it had to be you who told her. And on her mum's first birthday after her death." I lifted my hands and gave a slow clap. "Well done. Who do you think she'll hate more, you or me?"

Her head bounced from side to side as she pretended to ponder on my words. "Right now, you."

I nodded again. "Yeah you're right, but I'll come out on top, eventually." My head lowered until I was in her face. "The pity of it all is, I only shagged you because I wanted Beth. I supposed you were the next best thing, but know this, you'll never be Beth and me and you will **NEVER** happen again. Not in this lifetime or any other lifetime." I sneered in a low and lethal tone, smiling at her before returning to go into my room and slamming the door in her face.

After lying on the bed and feeling sorry for myself for a bit, I went to Beth's room and knocked on her door. "Beth. Please talk to me. Let me explain…" I was greeted with silence. Instead of knocking again, I headed downstairs for breakfast. Everyone was down there already.

Beth sat over by her dad eating bacon, Tess was drinking coffee and Julia looked like she was sucking on lemons. Now that did give me some satisfaction. Vindictive bitch. Some people just loved the drama.

Not long after breakfast, Beth's other cousins turned up. Tess's sons. Finally, some male company. My speech must have worked, though, because Julia didn't come near me again all day. I did see her giving Beth dirty looks, though.

Beth didn't talk to me all day, and I didn't get a chance to try talking to her because she made sure I didn't get one.

Tess came over to me and narrowed her eyes. "What's going on with you and Beth? Have you had an argument?"

Bending down, I kissed Tess's cheek. "I always liked you, Tess. You're a straight shooter." I sighed. I probably shouldn't have said anything but, fuck it. "It's just something that happened last Christmas, but maybe Julia can tell you all about it; she was quick enough to spill the beans to Beth."

"Do I even want to know?"

Celibet

"Probably not, but like I said, ask your daughter." I grinned and walked away, grabbing a beer, and downing most of it in one pull.

When it was time for bed, I came to a decision. It was obvious I was in the way. Beth didn't want me here; her dad didn't want us to be together and that had pretty much sealed my decision.

I got into bed and tried to get some sleep. I had an early start in the morning.

When my eyes closed, all I could see was Beth. I could hear her breathing beneath me as I touched her—could see the desire that was swimming in the blue of her eyes. I felt like I was stranded in the middle of the ocean as I got lost in them.

I tried to shut her out, but I couldn't, so instead, I went to sleep with the comfort of her in my head. It was like she was in my bed. I could still smell the scent of hair all over my pillow. That at least gave me some consolation.

I was up early next morning as planned. I threw yesterday's clothes in my bag and dressed in clean clothes, zipping up my case. I made it downstairs as quietly as I could. It was only five am I knew nobody would be up yet: they'd all had too much to drink last night.

I thought about leaving Beth a note. I even thought about going into her room and giving her a kiss goodbye, but it was no good. She hated me.

Creeping past her room, I made sure to avoid the squeaky floorboards on the stairs and made my way down to the bottom before softly opening the front door.

Once my case was in the boot, I left.

I stopped off at the drive thru costa and grabbed a coffee before making my way back to London. I wasn't going to make that hour and half drive without caffeine.

I took a sip, turned up the volume of Def Leppard and hit the road.

It felt like it had been ages since I was here last, yet it had only been two days ago. I pulled into the car park and took my case out before locking the car up. I'd got it for another couple of days before I had to take it back.

I went upstairs and into the flat, facing the carnage that I'd closed the door on the other day.

Going into the bedroom, I threw my case on the bed, changed into my old clothes, and got to work. I had an idea of what I wanted to do. If Beth hated me now, I was hoping that she wouldn't when she got back.

I scrubbed the furniture with washing up liquid, and slowly the blood started to come out. I ordered paint, a new rug, and some throws for the settee.

Next was Beth's room. I bought her a new iPad and ordered a new dressing table for her. I saw her four-poster bed was broken, too, but I wasn't sure what to do about that. I'd have to wait and see what she wanted first.

Once I had everything, including paint, I started my recon. I pushed everything to the other end of the room and painted the walls. The telly had a crack in it and wouldn't even switch on, so I ordered a new one of those. By the time I was done, there had been an almighty dent made in my bank balance, but I didn't care because this was for Beth.

Celibet

Beth Matthews was my world, and if last weekend had taught me anything, it was that I knew that in my heart I'd do anything for her. Beth was the keeper of my heart.

Chapter Forty-Six

BETH

Friday, my dad, and I went for a walk after Tess had left. Her and Julia had stayed the entire week, and Julia had continued to make sly comments about Charlie.

I'd wanted to punch her, but it wasn't fair on my dad. He adored Julia and although he liked Charlie, he hadn't approved of his career choice. He'd said as much around the table at lunch.

I checked my phone again, and there were still no messages. I wanted to text him, but what did I say.

I'm sorry I got butthurt over something you did before we were together. I'm sorry I didn't talk it out with you.

Celibet

As we walked to Mum's grave and the rose bush dad had planted, I was lost in thought.

"Beth," my dad said as he walked beside me, and I slowly turned to face him, chewing on my lip.

"What happened with Charlie?"

He'd asked a few times over the week, but I hadn't felt like telling him with Tess there. Lawrence and Spence had only stayed until Monday, but Julia had been like a bad smell and hadn't left until that morning.

I hated it. I just wanted her gone.

"Beth!" My dad chided me, and I gave myself a shake to stop my falling down the rabbit hole.

"He... uh... he slept with Julia."

I didn't keep secrets from my dad, so I told him the truth.

"He did, huh?"

"Yeah, at Christmas."

I was only giving short answers, and for a bit there was silence as we walked further into the graveyard.

Then my dad stopped and turned to me. "Beth, you know I haven't been completely supportive of Charlie in the past but he's a good guy and even I can see that he'd do anything for you, so I don't think you should judge him based on that. You were with Warren and he didn't really do anything wrong!"

I saw the truth in what he was saying, but it still hurt that he hadn't told me. We were best friends. We told each other everything. Then I remembered that just before New Year, he'd asked to speak to me. We'd been having a party in our flat, Warren's idea, but before we'd gotten a chance to chat, Warren had interrupted us and dragged me away. I'd then gone on holiday to the Canaries for a few weeks and hadn't see Charlie because he'd been filming his final EastEnders scenes.

My dad had started to walk ahead, and I caught up to him just as we reached my mum's grave. He leaned down and was sorting something on the grave when movement caught my eye.

I turned to the side and saw Charlie standing with a bunch of roses and a box of chocolates.

"Bethy-babe," he breathed as I rushed over and hurled myself into his arms. He held me tightly and pressed whisper-soft kisses to my head as he dropped the flowers and chocolates at my feet.

"I'm so sorry. I should have told you. I tried to, but then the longer it went the harder it got."

I looked up at his face and lifted my lips to brush the edge of his.

"I love you, Beth," he told me as he pressed soft kisses to my mouth and wrapped me firmly in his embrace, and I knew he meant that he was in love with me. I wanted to say it back, but I couldn't, not yet. I would, though, because I was sure I was totally, irrevocably, and completely in love with him. I was sure I always had been, but I'd been too afraid to say it.

"Ahem," my dad muttered, and we both turned to face him. I expected to see a disapproving look on his face, but instead he was smiling at me.

Celibet

"Charlie," he nodded at him and then winked at me as he began to walk away. My head was swimming, and I turned to face Charlie, suddenly suspicious of my dad's sudden decision to walk up to visit my mom coupled with Charlie's appearance.

"Did you call my dad?" I asked him, and he dropped his eyes as colour heated his cheeks.

"Yeah, I uh..." He broke off and leaned down to kiss me softly. "Yeah. I did. This was too important, and I didn't want to mess up again."

His lips moulded with mine when he finished, and I knew I wanted to say it to him. I wanted to tell him, but I didn't think my mum's grave was the right place.

"Come on, Charlie. Let's go home!"

"Our home, right?" he probed, and I nodded up at him. His whole body relaxed, he bent down to scoop up the flowers and the chocolates before wrapping his arm around my back and walking with me back to the parking lot.

I glanced around and saw my dad's silver Merc was missing, meaning we'd have to walk back.

"Fuck," I hissed, and Charlie glanced sideways at me with a raised eyebrow.

"My dad's gone back home. Did you walk here?"

Charlie started to laugh as he led me to a light grey Audi that was parked near the gate. He unlocked and put the flowers and chocolates into the back seat.

"No. I thought it was time I got a car."

I turned back to see the smile on his face, and he quickly kissed me again, before walking around the car opening my door. He was so excited, and I'd missed it. I'd missed him getting a car. I was standing chiding myself as he pressed another soft kiss to my lips before saying, "Come on, baby. Let's get you home!"

We drove back to my dad's where I loaded up Charlie's car with my new clothes and shoes. I'd also bought some new makeup, so the car was packed full as my dad saw us off.

He said something to Charlie as I finished putting my new handbags into the boot, and I watched as Charlie smiled and nodded at him.

My dad saw me watching them and came towards me, pulling me in for a tight hug, whispering in my ear, "He's a good guy, Beth. I think he can make you happy, but you must let him in. You have my blessing if that helps." He pressed a soft kiss to my cheek and walked me around the car, helping me into my seat before he leaned in and spoke in a firm voice. "Now don't be a stranger, either of you!"

My mouth dropped open because not once in the seven years I'd been with Warren had my dad said he was welcome with us. He usually didn't say a word, and I knew Charlie going to him for help had made him soften towards him.

We both waved as we drove home, and Charlie linked our hands on my legs. He only let go to park because his car was an automatic.

The drive passed quickly and all too soon we hit London. We arrived just as the roads were quietening and made it back to our flat by quarter to five.

Celibet

As we made our way up the stairs, both laden with bags, I was dreading going in. My heart thumped erratically in my ears as we walked along the landing to the flat, but when Charlie opened the door, my mouth dropped open.

He led the way inside and there was nothing: no blood, no mess. We had a new rug and a new tv and the flat smelled clean and fresh.

We dropped our bags and I moved through the flat. My bed was gone, and my room was no longer a mess. New wardrobes and drawers were built, and a new TV was up on the wall with a rug on the floor.

"I uh, I didn't know what bed to get," he told me in an embarrassed whisper, colour heating his cheeks.

My eyes watered and I turned to Charlie, who was watching my reaction with a worried expression.

"Did you do all this?" I asked him uncertainly because surely, he had gotten help, but he nodded in response, and I stepped closer to him.

"Why? Why didn't you wait for me? I could have helped?" My voice was low and throaty as emotion threatened to overwhelm me, and when I met his eyes, I saw the love he felt for me shining through.

"Because I love you, Beth, and I was so scared I'd lost you. I needed something to distract me from the pain, so I fixed our home."

My response was immediate. I wrapped my arms around his neck and pulled his head down so I could kiss him. My kiss said everything. It said, 'I'm sorry for hurting you, I'm so in love with you and thank you'.

"I love you, too, Charlie," I told him, and he smiled widely before scooping me up and carrying me into his bedroom.

Our lips didn't part, but as he lay me down in his bed, his mobile started to ring. He pulled back from me with a groan.

"Fucking, fuckety fuck!" he muttered as he checked the call. He gave my fingers a gentle squeeze before he spun and left the room, leaving me alone in his bedroom, surrounded by his scent and his belongings and I'd never felt more at home.

Chapter Forty-Seven

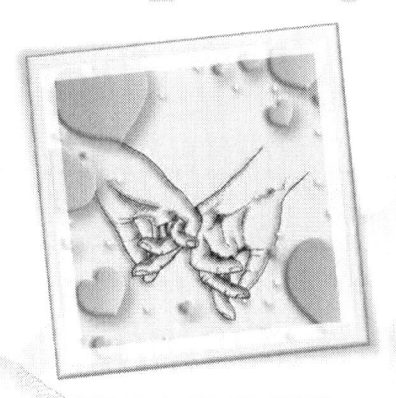

CHARLIE

I couldn't believe what I was hearing. She said she loved me; she actually said the words.

I checked the caller I.D. I held one finger up indicating I needed a minute to take the call and spun away from the beauty who lay on my bed, lifting the phone to my ear.

"Hello."

"Charlie. Is your passport up to date?"

"Hello to you, too, Peter."

"Oh, yeah hello. Well?"

"Yes, Peter my passport is valid. Why?"

"I need you in Spain." My heart sank. I loved my job, but I'd just got Beth. I wanted to spend some quality time with her, just us. No drama. No one getting in the way.

"Just for a week," Peter started again. "The show is starting there, so we need you on location in the Costa Del Sol."

"I have to be back for the premiere of my last movie. If I'm not here in four weeks' time…"

Peter cut me off. "It's just a week Charlie. If I didn't need you there, I promise you I wouldn't ask, and I'd send a body double."

I sighed. It was my job after all. "When do I leave?"

"Two weeks. I'll get my assistant to send you the flight details, tickets, and the hotel you'll be staying in. All expenses paid of course. I'll meet you out there. If we get done earlier than the week, then we get home sooner."

"Okay, Peter. I'll see you in a couple of weeks."

He cut the call and I placed my phone back into my pocket.

I stood at my bedroom door and stared at Beth. Her head was on my pillow and her eyes were closed, her eyelashes fanned the skin below, and her soft pink lips had a slight pout.

I gently crawled beside her and shifted the hair that had fallen over her forehead, kissing her cheek. I moved across to her lips and placed a small kiss to those. The poor thing seemed exhausted.

"Charlie."

"I'm here baby."

Her eyes fluttered open and captivated mine.

"You okay?"

Celibet

I propped my head up on my hand and she rolled towards me. Her hand settled on my chest and I covered it with mine lifting it to my lips.

"That call. It was the producer for the new TV series. I have to go away in a couple of weeks."

Her eyes told a thousand tales, but she forced a smile anyway.

"Okay. Where do you have to go?"

"Spain." I kissed across her knuckles, hoping to soothe the blow.

"Spain? I thought it was being set in Devon or somewhere."

"Actually Cornwall, but it's for the opening scene. He said if he didn't need me, he wouldn't be asking."

Pushing up onto her elbow, she pressed her lips to mine before pulling back slightly. "Charlie it's your job. I understand that."

Wrapping an arm around her back, I tugged her against me. Her breasts brushed against my chest as she pulled me back down towards her. My tongue plunged into her mouth as I licked and nibbled at her lips. All I could think about was the fact that this time last week I hadn't even been sure if we were still together. I knew what I'd had to do though. If I was ever going to get Beth to love me, I'd had to speak to her dad. I'd needed him on my side.

"Charlie, I need you so bad."

All thoughts of last week and her dad slid from my mind and I concentrated on Beth.

My dick throbbed as it strained against the fly of my jeans. I wanted to make her mine so badly. I kissed down the soft lines of her neck until I reached her chest and tugging at the bottom of her T-shirt, I pushed it up over her breasts.

"Charlie, what about the bet?"

"What bet?" I pulled down the cup of the lacy bra she was wearing and put my lips around her pert nipples, sucking them into my mouth. She let out a groan and her back arched off the back. Trailing soft fingers down to her leggings, I slipped them beneath her waistband until I was met with lacy knickers. Her breath shuddered as she parted her legs for me.

"God I've waited so long for this Beth."

Sliding a finger further down, I touched her clit before parting her folds. She was soaking wet. I sucked hard on her nipple, and Beth let out a cry. I sipped my finger inside, soon adding another to the party.

"Oh God, Charlie."

Thrusting in and out and stroking her walls with the tip of my fingers, I pushed her towards the edge. With one foot on the bed and her broken leg out flat she moved herself up the bed and held on to my head.

"Oh, shit Charlie!" Beth moaned, she gasped and held on tighter, and as my thumb rubbed her bundle of nerves, she hit her climax. Her orgasm coated my fingers, and she writhed on the bed until she was doing down.

I pulled my hand out of her leggings.

Her eyes opened, but I didn't realise she'd moved so far across the bed when suddenly she was falling off the edge.

"Ahhh." Her body hit the floor with a thud.

Celibet

My laughter burst out as I saw her lying on the floor holding her head. I looked over, still laughing.

"It's not funny Charlie."

"It's fucking hilarious." Before I could help her up, though, I licked my fingers clean and winked. Her eyes widened with shock before I followed her to the floor, hovered over her and took her lips with mine in an earth-shattering kiss.

Chapter Forty-Eight

BETH

I landed with a thump on the floor and Charlie chuckled at me. I wanted to swing for him, but he came down and stopped me in my tracks with a kiss that stole my breath and my heart.

My body hummed with longing, but my foot was throbbing, and although I was enjoying the feel of Charlie against me, I couldn't ignore it.

"Charlie, my foot…" I muttered, and he growled low in his throat, pressing a gentle kiss to my lips.

"Fuck, I forgot. Sorry, baby. Are you okay?"

"No. It really hurts. Can you help me up please?"

He smirked at me and then pushed onto his knees, letting me see how turned on he was. He reached down and helped me to get back onto the bed. Once I was safely situated, he grabbed a pillow and lifted my dodgy foot,

Celibet

replacing it gently. His eyes glittered, and he leaned down, kissing my leg from the knee up and making me shudder. His fingers tugged at the waistband of my leggings and began to take them down my legs.

"Lift," he commanded in a throaty whisper, and I shifted so he could pull them down. His fingers grazed my thighs and legs and my whole body trembled in response.

His eyes blazed and he pressed a soft kiss to my thigh and licked his lips.

"Charlie," I moaned, and he blew out a breath onto my clit, making me almost convulse off the bed as the sensations rocked through me. His tongue darted out and he licked down once and then back up, my fingers curling in his hair and holding him there.

Just as he began to press more firmly, his mobile began to ring in his pocket. He groaned and pulled back, plucking it out and rolling his eyes. "What is it Jack?" he asked, frustrated as he ran his fingers through his hair. Jack was his agent and a good friend, but his timing sucked.

"Okay. When? Tuesday! I got it…Yeah fine! See you tomorrow!" He hung up and roared out in frustration as it started ringing again. "I swear to fucking God, this is a nightmare!" He spun around and moved away from me, walked out then closed the door, leaving me wet, uncomfortable, and horny in his bed.

I closed my eyes and then heard his voice rising in anger in the hallway.

"I don't care! I'm not acting like we are together. That's not okay!"

My ears strained as I struggled to hear his next words.

"I've already said I'll be there, and I'll be cordial to her, but I'm not hurting the girl I love for publicity."

I heard the living room door open, and I decided to give him his privacy, even though I wanted to go to him and see what was wrong. My body thrummed with need, but my foot was aching, so I quickly popped the painkillers from the bedside table and drifted off to a dreamless sleep, waking up in the morning to an empty bed.

There was a note propped up on the nightstand.

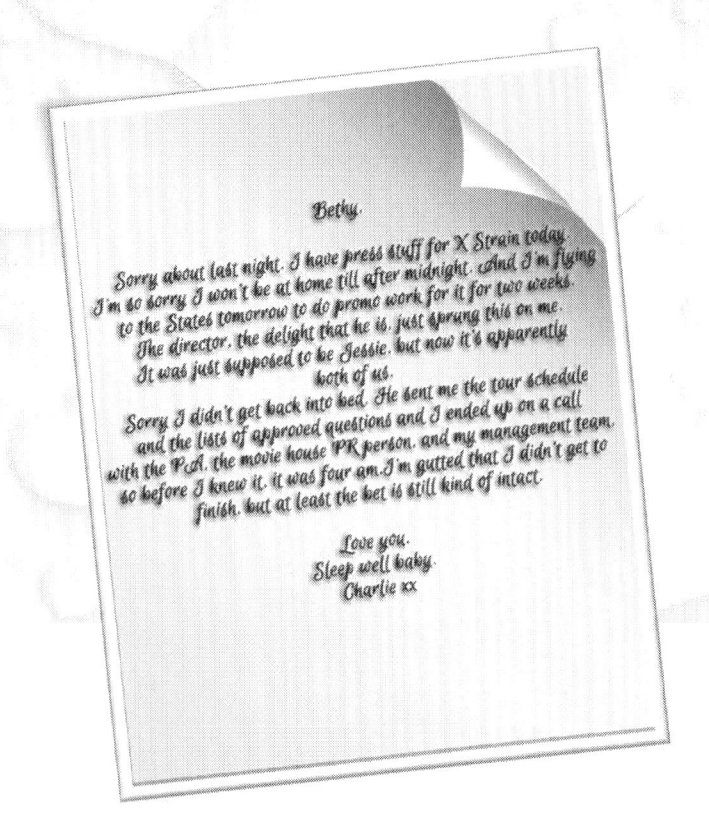

> Bethy,
>
> Sorry about last night. I have press stuff for X Strain today. I'm so sorry I won't be at home till after midnight. And I'm flying to the States tomorrow to do promo work for it for two weeks. The director, the delight that he is, just sprung this on me. It was just supposed to be Jessie, but now it's apparently both of us.
>
> Sorry I didn't get back into bed. He sent me the tour schedule and the lists of approved questions and I ended up on a call with the P.A, the movie house PR person, and my management team. So before I knew it, it was four am. I'm gutted that I didn't get to finish, but at least the bet is still kind of intact.
>
> Love you.
> Sleep well baby.
> Charlie xx

Celibet

I read the note and sat up, seeing my boobs were hanging out of my top and I had no bottoms on. After righting my tits, I lifted my leg gingerly and put my boot on before pulling some of Charlie's workout shorts and making my way through to the sitting room.

My eyes darted around as I walked into the kitchen and saw a new coffee maker there. Charlie really was the sweetest. There was a note on top.

*I bought this at five am, baby, since I'm not going to be around to make you coffee.
Love XX*

My heart thumped in my chest, and I set my cup up, popping in a pod as I leaned back and took a selfie on Snapchat where my top clung to my body, my nipples were hard and Charlie's shorts were snug on my ass. I had my arm wrapped over the coffee maker. It was quirky and funny, but I was happy with the result, so I quickly saved it and sent a message to Charlie.

Thanks for my coffee maker. I love it.

He quickly replied and made my body quiver in excitement.

Charlie: What? More than me?

I chuckled as I sent him the picture and he sent me back a message that made me laugh out loud.

Fuck me, Bethy babe. Your tits look amazing, and seeing you wearing my shorts has given me a boner, so thanks for that. We're about to go on air and my cock is standing proud.

My coffee was ready, so I grabbed a pan au chocolate from the counter and walked into the sitting room with it, my mobile and my mug.

As I sat down on the sofa, I pushed the button and the new tv loaded up.

What channel are you on?

He didn't text back, so I assumed he was on the air. I quickly scanned and found him on BBC breakfast with Jessie Lewis at his side. He looked gorgeous, and his smile as he spoke about the movie was breath-taking. Jessie sat looking demure beside him but answered the questions with a small smile. She openly flirted with Charlie, and when the reporters asked if there was any truth to the rumours about them, she answered before Charlie could.

"I think that's our private business, and we don't share things like that publicly."

Charlie's smile froze as she leaned over and pressed a small kiss to his cheek, leaving a lipstick mark there, blushing as she turned back to the camera.

The sight of it made me feel sick, and I knew that Charlie was furious because his hands were fisted in front of him.

He still answered in the same way as before, but the tension never left his shoulders or his eyes, and when the interview was over, he texted me straight away.

Charlie: Fuck, Beth. She's just gone and basically told them we're fucking. I'm so sorry.

My heart hammered in my chest as my anger overwhelmed me. He was spending two weeks with her, and she'd just led everyone to believe they were actually together.

Hey, it's okay. We know the truth. Just ignore her.

For a few seconds there was nothing, but then another reply came and made me smile.

Charlie: It's like trying to ignore a shark circling you, smelling your blood. But I swear, once this is all over and I've filmed in Spain and the premiere has been, we are going away for a week. Book some time off and let's go abroad somewhere or to a cottage where I can get you to myself. Gotta go, babe. Love you, C xx

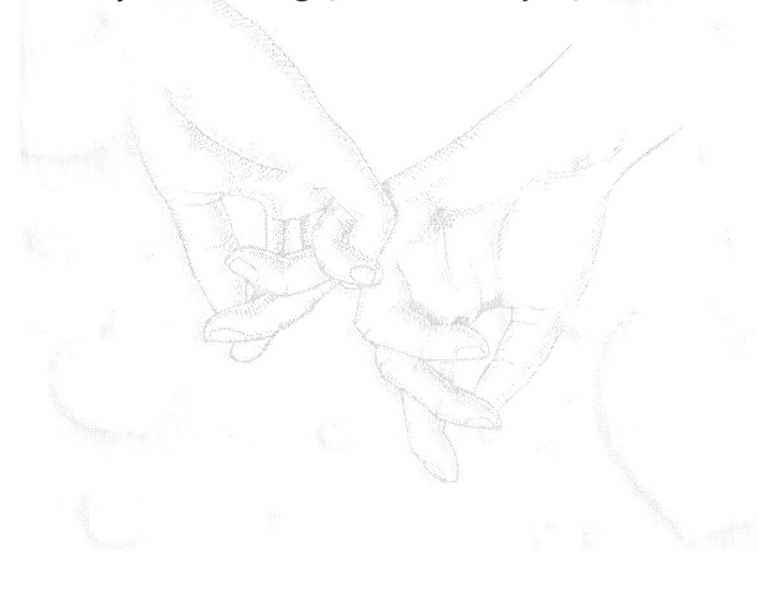

Chapter Forty Nine

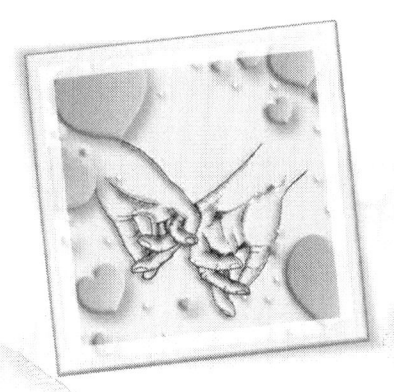

CHARLIE

As soon as the interview was over. I smiled at the presenter, a fake one albeit, but mainly for appearances. Jessie's hand was still on my knee, and I knew there was fuck all I could do. The cameras were still rolling while they changed scenes. The presenter sighed as soon as the camera turned from us. "Thank you so much, guys."

I nodded politely and abruptly stood from my chair. Jessie's hand slipped from my knee and I marched off set. I snatched the earpiece from my ear and slammed it on a speaker as I walked out, plucking my phone from pocket replying to Beth's message.

Pushing my phone back into my pocket, I made it back into my dressing room and slammed myself down on the chair. I was beyond angry: I was fucking furious. I was just getting myself settled—we were just getting settled—and that bitch had to try and ruin it.

A small knock came on the door. I ignored it. I didn't want to talk to anyone. I leaned back in my chair and closed my eyes. The doorknob turned anyway, and I opened my eyes, waiting in vain to see who it could be. I could have had three guesses but as the door opened further, I knew I'd only need the one.

"That was a little rude, don't you think, Charlie?"

"Rude?" I questioned. "I haven't even touched on rude. What made you think by doing what you did, did us any favours."

"Oh, Charlie, you're so naive. Pretending we're a couple makes the fans go wild. Fans always want their co-stars to have a real relationship. I mean, we almost did back in Paris…."

I shoved my body out of the chair and it rolled backwards, hitting the table with force. I spoke as close as I could in her face. "Yeah, I haven't forgotten what you did to me. Maybe in the next interview, I'll tell them what a cheating whore you are. What do you think your fans would think then, huh?"

Her face changed from smug to her jaw tensing in less than a second.

"I'd like you to leave."

My phone went off again in my pocket, and I silently dismissed her, turning away, and giving her my back as I walked back to my chair, sat down and spun it the other way so I faced the wall.

Celibet

A wide smile pulled at my mouth when I saw Beth's name again. I quickly opened the message.

Jessie huffed and left slamming the door behind her.

Beth: Aw, Charlie. Is she that bad? Let me know when the premiere is so I can buy something new and get my hair done. I miss you already. I'm not sure I can go 3 weeks without seeing you. Beth xxx

Charlie: She's a serpent. Full of venom. As soon as I get the date, I'll let you know. It premieres here in the state's first, so any pictures you see, please, please don't believe them. It'll all be a publicity stunt for Jessie fucking Lewis. C xx

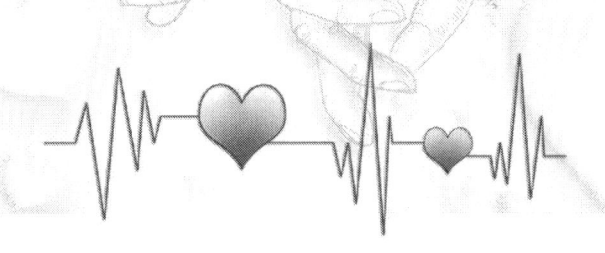

Before the next interview, I made sure Jessie knew that I wasn't joking about what I'd said before. Even if it made myself look bad, I didn't care. I didn't like underhandedness, and I made sure my agent knew about it, too.

We were set up for the next interview, and when we went on set, I separated the chairs just enough so she couldn't do what she'd done last time and kiss me. I didn't want her hands on me let alone her lips.

The presenter never missed a beat and raised her eyebrow at me. "Anything I should know before we go onto air?"

"Nope," I answered smugly.

We sat waiting and listened to the producer call down.

"In three, two…" He held up one finger, nodded and the presenter came in all smiles and introduced us. Every time she tried to ask about the relationship between us, I shot her down and turned it back to the movie. Jessie was fuming. She was trying her hardest to make it look like I was joking or that we'd had a lover's tiff.

Like fuck. She wouldn't show me up again.

My agent and the director were going mad. The director had wanted this to be a success, and he'd believed that Jessie and me pretending to be a couple would do that. In the end, I told him and Jack that if they wanted someone to do that then they could pull me and get the sound guy in—he'd be able to tell a good story. Not quite so glamorous for her, though.

Did I care? Not a fucking chance in hell!

By the end of the week, I'd had enough. I was homesick. I missed Beth. I hated Jessie fucking Lewis and her diva attitude.

Celibet

I miss you so much. I've had enough of it here now. Oh, and the bet can fuck off, too. When I do see you again, I'm going to devour every fucking inch of that glorious body and make you scream. Love you. C xx

Chapter Fifty

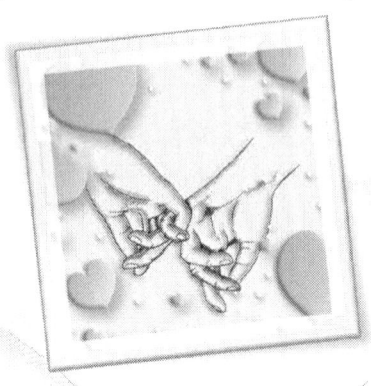

BETH

The last week and half without Charlie were long, but my foot was healing well. He was beginning to lose his patience with Jessie. She was acting as though he'd broken her heart, when the reality was that she's hurt him.

When Charlie text me, which was quite a lot, as they moved between interviews and promo work, he was becoming more and more frustrated.

Jessie was convinced that he would succumb to her charms and was constantly trying to get in his pants.

By the Friday of the second week, the day he was due to fly home, he called me to tell me that instead of being able to spend the weekend with me like we'd been

Celibet

planning, he was going to have to fly straight to Costa Del Sol for filming.

I was home alone with a migraine and had spent most of the day in bed or in the bathroom.

"And you can't get out of it?" I asked in a whiny voice as he told me about the filming moving up a few days.

"No, I can't babe, I'm sorry. I miss you so much, but the LA premiere for X Strain is in a few days and they want to ramp up the publicity and then the premiere in London is a day later. It's on the Friday twenty-fifth so make sure you have the day off, because I'm going to pamper you and then take you back to a hotel and make you come over and over again."

I smiled because he was excited about that, but then a knock sounded on his dressing room door and he opened it with a growl.

"What the fuck do you want?" His words were cold, and his voice sounded muffled and distant.

"I wanted to pick up where we left off last night…"

I didn't hear the rest because the phone cut off. My head told me she was just trying anything to get him into bed, but why had he hung up?

What was going on?

Beth: Charlie what happened there? I got cut off.

He didn't reply in the next half hour, and my head began to throb worse than before. I turned my phone volume down and climbed into bed with my eye mask on as the full weight of a migraine hit me. I'd already taken everything I could, but nothing was touching it. I tried to relax and drifted off to sleep, waking hours later feeling much better.

I checked my mobile and saw six missed calls from Charlie and four text messages.

Beth, answer the phone. I swear on my life nothing happened.

Beth, please! I need to talk to you.

Bethy-babe, I love you! Please talk to me.

Bethany, I swear to you that I haven't been with her in months. I'll come home and everything will be fine. I promise. I love you so much, babe.

I tried to call him, but it went to answerphone. I left him a message, asking him to call me back. I set my ringer onto loud and went into the kitchen to make myself something to eat and have a coffee. Padding through the quiet flat, I popped a pod into the coffee maker as I shoved some bread in the toaster.

My mobile was beside me, but I didn't hear from Charlie as I ate my toast and drank a few mouthfuls of coffee. My body was still achy from the headache, so I pulled the comforter over me and drifted off to sleep on the soft couch.

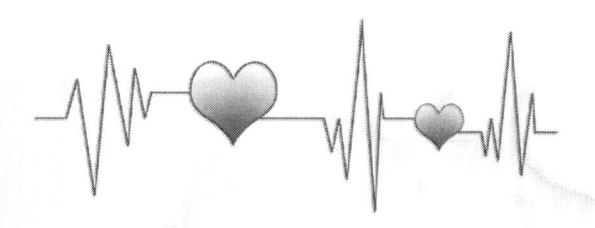

I woke up hours later when the door of the flat burst open and a harassed Charlie ran through the flat, calling my name.

His panic had me flailing about on the sofa, and I managed to fall flat on my face as I scrambled up to go after him. I could hear the panic in his voice as he ran, and I picked myself up from the floor just as the living room door opened again.

"Beth, I swear nothing happened with us. She knew you were on the phone and then my battery died, and by the time I got back to the hotel it was hours later."

He moved towards me as he spoke and pulled me into his shaking arms. His whole body shuddered as I wrapped my arms around his waist and buried my face in his neck.

"I love you so much, Beth. Please believe me." The pain behind his words made me peek up and a tear rolled from his eye and splattered onto my cheek.

"Charlie," I breathed as I reached up to cup his cheek, wiping at the tears that rolled from his eyes as he looked down at me. "I never doubted you. I knew you'd never cheat on me or ruin us for a quick fuck."

His shoulders softened and he leaned down, holding my gaze as he kissed me firmly and lifted my legs from the floor.

"Wrap your legs around me, babe."

"I can't. We can't. I'm on my period."

"Fuck my life. Are you kidding?" His voice was low and full of tension, and he chuckled as I shook my head.

"Every time I want to get you naked, something stops us. Every damn time."

I giggled at his crestfallen face and pressed a soft kiss to his swollen lips. "Why don't we just go to bed and hug for a while?"

I didn't feel much like sex after my migraine anyway, but when he led me back into his room and took his top off, my eyes widened. A new tattoo with the infinity symbol was now over his heart.

It had Roman numerals on the right side, and he grinned as I traced it with my fingers.

"Come on, Bethy-babe, let's go to bed."

He climbed in with a sigh and patted the bed beside him, pulling me down when I just stood watching him and enjoying the sight of him back in his bed where he belonged.

"I'm flying back to Spain at nine am, so can you set an alarm for six please."

Celibet

I did so and snuggled down to sleep in his arms for the six hours I had. I'd missed him so much, and I wished Aunt Flo had decided to visit on Monday instead, but there was nothing I could do.

He pressed a soft kiss to the back of my head and muttered against my neck, "God, Bethy, I've missed you so much."

His lips licked and nipped along my neck, and I turned to face him, kissing him with all I had.

He broke us apart and whispered against my flushed cheeks, his lashes and curls brushing my skin. "We have to stop or I'm going to flip you over and fuck you hard."

My heart soared and my blood thrummed around my body, making me want to say screw it, but I didn't want our first time together to be when he was exhausted, and I was on my period. It was supposed to be special, and this was not special, although knowing he'd flown halfway across the world to make sure I knew he hadn't cheated made me fall even deeper in love with him than ever before.

I pressed a soft kiss to his lips, watching as he lay down and closed his eyes.

Within a few minutes, he was asleep, and for a bit, I watched him sleep before I snuggled down in his arms and let my body relax enough for me to drift off to sleep.

When my alarm went off in the morning, Charlie quickly turned it off pressing a soft kiss to my forehead.

"Stay in bed, babe. I'll see you in a week. Love you." He kissed my lips and parted them with his tongue, plunging it inside my mouth and fucking it with his tongue for a minute. Then, he pulled back and peppered my lips with soft kisses before he tugged himself out of my arms.

"I have to go. Go back to sleep."

He turned and left the room. I woke again sometime later to the sound of the flat door closing. Rolling over to go back to sleep, I came face to face with a bear on the bed with a note attached.

My fingers shook as I opened it.

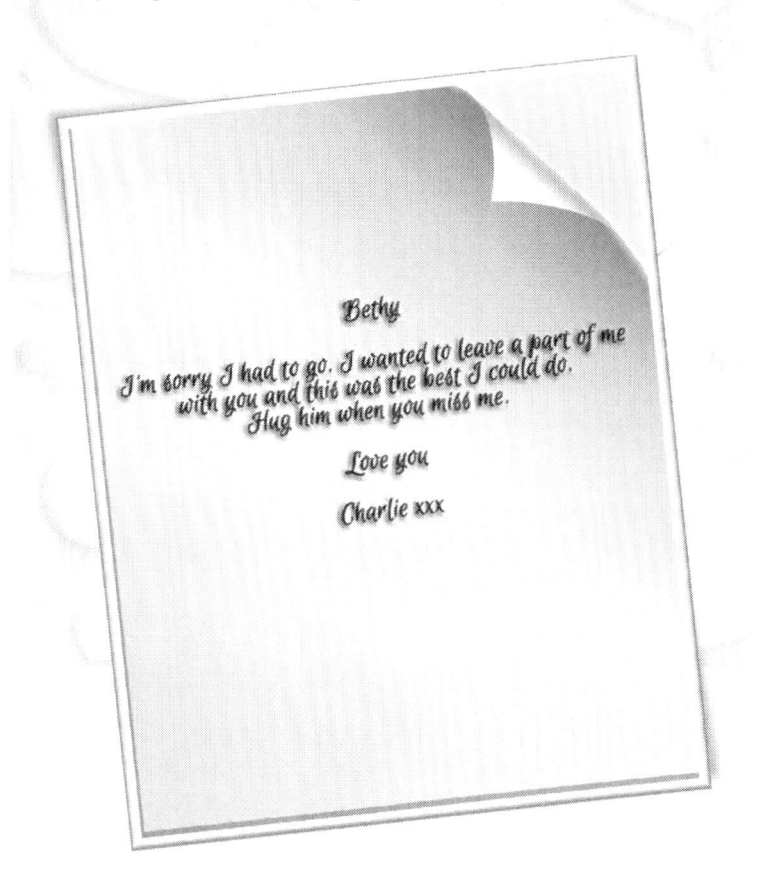

> Bethy
>
> I'm sorry I had to go. I wanted to leave a part of me with you and this was the best I could do.
> Hug him when you miss me.
>
> Love you
>
> Charlie xxx

Celibet

I wrapped my arms around the bear and the scent of Charlie's aftershave enveloped me. I wished it were him wearing it, but I guessed the bear would do until he was back in his bed with me.

Chapter Fifty-One

CHARLIE

I landed in the Costas at eleven a.m. Spanish time. The sun was beating down as I got off the plane and walked across the tarmac to the shuttle bus. Peter, Mia, and Liz met me in the airport, and we went on to the hotel. On the way there, I rang Beth. I knew she'd want to know I'd landed safely.

She picked up on the third ring.

"Charlie! Hey." Her high-pitched tone made me smile.

"Hey, baby. You okay? Did you sleep well?"

"Hm, thank you for my bear. I love him. Oh my God. You spoil me so much."

"You deserve it. I just wanted to let you know I landed and am now on the way to the hotel, then we'll be going straight to location, so I probably won't get a chance to

Celibet

ring til tonight." Peter smirked at me from the driver's seat as I spoke to Beth, and Liz made a comment from the back. Something like, 'sucker' I think. I raised my middle finger over my shoulder, and she laughed.

"That's okay. I'm glad you rang. I miss you already."

"I miss you too. I need to get going, we'll be out in the sticks soon, so I'll probably lose reception. I'll text you when I can."

"Bye, Charlie. Love you."

A proud smile tugged at my lips. Finally, I had my girl. "Love you, too." I cut the call and shoved it into my pocket.

"Charlie James you are so under the thumb," Liz said, laughing from the back.

"Hey, I don't care. Beth and I have been friends so long, then it was like the world and its dog was against us being together. I don't give a shit how corny I sound."

A hand rested on my shoulder and rubbed gently. "Ignore her, Charlie," Mia mused. "I think it's lovely."

I turned to my side and looked behind me. "Thanks, Mia." I smiled softly.

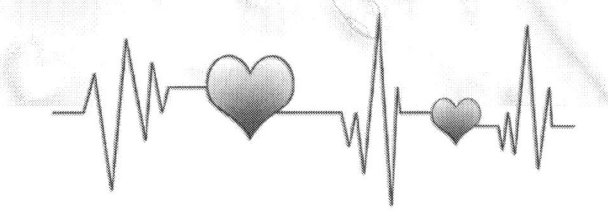

Once we'd arrived on location a couple of hours later, Peter confirmed we'd probably only be here three days maximum. We'd need some individual scenes shooting and some individual for me and Mia then he could get some scenery setting done. He knew about me having to get to LA for the premiere, and he really was cool with me cutting this short. It was just Sod's law that everything had come around at the same time.

Mia and I started our scenes and I realised how much I loved to work with her. She was calm, she never got stressed and she was a natural for the camera. We laughed and joked between scenes, and I couldn't wait for filming to start.

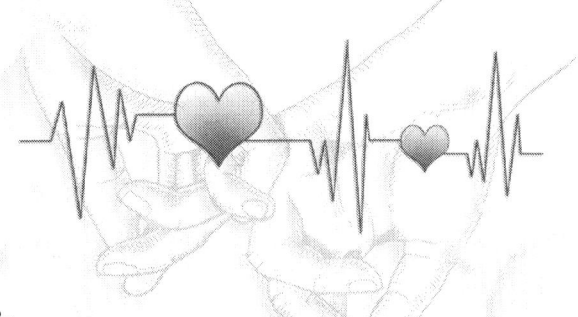

After three days in the sun, relaxation, and friendly faces, it was time to jet back to LA and face the diva.

There was no one at the airport this time, though. Instead, I jumped a cab to the hotel to drop my bags and knowing that the premiere was on Friday, I had to get a tux. I was tired, my body drained, but I had to keep going.

I was to meet Jessie at the TV studios for the last interview, and by the time I'd arrived I was ratty and short-tempered.

Celibet

Jessie picked up on it right away, but I didn't give her anything. I smiled for the cameras, and I was overly nice to the host, which pissed Jessie right off, especially since I'd barely said two words to her. She knew I was still angry with her from before I went back home. When, yet again, she'd tried to make Beth believe we were something more than we're not. I didn't have to go back home, and I'd known in my heart that Beth wouldn't believe her, but I did anyway. After everything we'd already been through up to now, I wasn't prepared to take that risk.

Every now and then, Jessie would put her hand on my arm as we were talking about the movie but, very subtly, I'd shrug her off. She was majorly pissed off by the time the interview was over, but fuck it. I was happy since I had the last laugh.

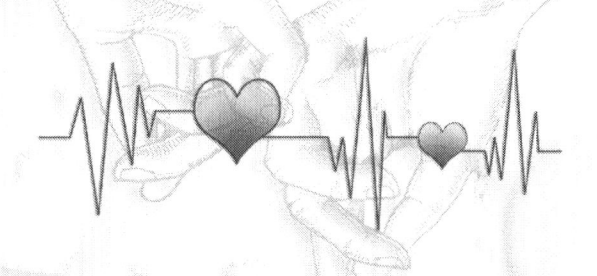

Camera's clicked, lights flashed, and microphones were stuffed in our faces as we got out of the limo and made our way down the red carpet. Jessie lapped up the attention, but so did I if I was honest. I was just craving to have Beth on my arm, not fucking Jessie.

She linked arms with mine, and I smiled for the cameras, but as soon as we were out of shot, I removed her. Presenters from various entertainment channels thrust their microphones in our faces, asking for a few words, but once we were inside, I made a point to keep as far from Jessie as I could.

Right now, all I wanted was to be on a plane home and heading to see my girl. I knew that was all that was going to get me through the night.

Chapter Fifty-Two

BETH

I spent the days Charlie was in Spain filming with my dad, Callie, and Bessie.

I also went shopping with Callie on the day of the LA premiere and bought a gorgeous green dress with silver sequins on the bodice. It was low cut at the back, and I bought a basque from Ann Summers with a matching thong in a pale green that went perfectly with it.

Callie convinced me to buy silver Choo's and a gorgeous silver clutch that were too pretty to pass up. As the day of the premiere dawned, I waited anxiously for Charlie to get back from the States, but his flight was delayed, and he was going to have to go straight from the airport to the premiere.

Jack was going meeting him at the airport with his tux and his hairstylist, but in the meantime, he'd text me and told me he'd be sending a car for me and Callie to meet him there, too.

I had plucked, pruned, and shaved every inch of my body, and my boot had come off because my break had healed well.

Callie dragged me to the hair salon where they had set my hair in loose waves with silver clips that kept it off my face. The girl also did my nails—a French manicure with silver studs on them.

When we went back to the flat, I felt amazing and when I pulled my dress over my underwear, a bubble of excitement sat low in my stomach. Callie had done my makeup, and when I looked in the mirror, I didn't see the frumpy girl I'd been with Wanker: I saw a pretty curvy girl in a gorgeous dress who's eyes sparkled and who deserved to be happy.

I went out into the sitting room and Callie whistled.

"Wow, babe. You look amazing." She handed me a glass of wine and I sipped at it with nerves bouncing around my stomach. I was waiting to hear from Charlie because his flight was due to land any minute. I hadn't realised I was bouncing my knee up and down until Callie reached over and put her hand on my leg.

"Beth, it's fine. It'll be amazing."

I met her eyes and saw excitement on her expression. She was in a long, red dress that was split to mid-thigh and her long brown hair was pinned up with wisps hanging down over her face.

"I know. I'm just nervous. What if his flight doesn't make it? What if he doesn't make it back in time?"

Callie took my hands between hers and gave me a gentle squeeze. "Beth, it's—"

My mobile rang, cutting her off, and when I plucked it from my bag, I saw it was Charlie.

"Hey," he muttered in a soft voice when I said hello. "Are you ready for tonight?" I could hear the promise in his voice, and after the last few weeks of phone conversations that had got dirtier and more erotic, I was ready to feel his hands and his tongue all over me.

"I'm so ready." My breathless whisper caused him to laugh. He sounded so off.

"Okay then. The car is on its way. You'll pick me up before heading to Piccadilly Circus and we'll arrive together." He sounded matter of fact and I wondered why he sounded distracted, but before I could ask him, he said bye and ended the call.

Tears burned my eyes at his brush off, but I swallowed a few deep breaths and slipped my feet into my new Choo's, just as my mobile rang again.

"Miss Beth, I'm your driver, Toby, and I'm outside."

I thanked the man and quickly stood, walking with Callie towards the door. She held onto me as we walked down the stairs. I had to concentrate so I didn't fall because I was a bit wobbly on my feet in heels, and my sore foot was aching by the time we reached the limo. We climbed in to see a bouquet of pink stargazer lilies on the back seat.

Callie popped the champagne and poured us a glass each, flopping down beside me as we made our way through the streets of London.

We made small talk as we drove towards the airport to pick up Charlie, and my fingers shook with nerves as I sipped on the Moet provided.

As we pulled into the airport, the car door opened, and Charlie jumped in with Jack. Charlie was in a dark grey suit, with a light grey shirt and black tie and he looked breathtaking. His eyes met mine and he held my gaze, making my insides melt and my panties soaked as he mouthed 'hi' at me.

I mouthed it back and he grinned widely as his eyes wandered up and down my body.

When his eyes met mine again, they were blazing as he leaned over and ran his finger down my arm. "You look breathtakingly beautiful." His tongue darted out to moisten his lips and my eyes tracked the movement.

I wanted to kiss him, but Jack touched his arm and Charlie turned to face him.

"Okay, so it's autographs and then photos and then the movie. Don't answer questions about you and Jessie or about you and uh, Beth. Jeff has decided that you're single and available but dating around."

Jeff was Charlie's manager, and he was an arse. I really didn't like him at all. I never had.

Charlie turned and met my eyes and I saw the disappointment in them before he shook his head and smirked at me. I knew that smirk. That was Charlie's 'fuck

Celibet

it all to hell' smirk, and I knew he wasn't about to follow Jack's directions. He was about to stick two fingers up to his management company and possibly crash his career for me.

As we reached the street before the premiere, I leaned over and kissed his cheek before whispering in his ear, "I am so proud of you babe, but you need to do what Jack says. We both know the truth, and that's all that matters. I don't care about what people think."

Charlie turned and brushed his lips against mine. His hand snaked up my back and he held my mouth captive against his, pushing his tongue into my mouth. His reverent kiss and the need I felt pulsing through me almost undid me, but it was his whispered words that melted my insides.

"I love you, Bethy. So, fucking much." He pressed another small kiss to my lips and then leaned on my head, taking a few deep breaths as the car pulled up.

The screams were deafening, and when Charlie climbed out of the car, they got impossibly louder. He helped me out and was walking with me until Jack stepped between us pushing Charlie forwards.

"Remember, autographs first, then photos and then press," I heard him call out to Charlie as he went into actor mode and moved towards his fans, smiling, and taking photos as Callie and I watched.

Within moments, he was joined by Addie Ascot and Jessie. Jessie went right over to him and pressed a soft kiss to his cheek that made his fists curl. My fists curled, too, and Callie put a steadying hand on my arm, shaking her head when I met her eye.

I watched as they posed for photos and answered questions and then Charlie was back by my side. He pressed a soft kiss to my cheek as he put gentle pressure on my back and began to lead me towards the interviewers.

Once we were there, he stepped forwards again and his spot by my side was taken by Jessie Lewis.

"So, you think you can hold him? You do realise that someone frumpy and dumpy has no place in our world." Her words, said with a smile, made me freeze and I turned to look at her and saw her smirk widen.

"You know I slept with him in LA two nights ago, but hey, he's committed to you. Ask him where he got the scratches on his back if you don't believe me."

With that she was gone, and I was left shaking with fury and hurt, but when Charlie stiffened as she reached him, I knew she was just trying to hurt me. Charlie wouldn't ruin us for her. There was no way. She was just being a fucking jerk, and I wasn't going to let her destroy this night for us.

I watched as they did more interviews and Charlie brushed off her advances, laughing and joking with the interviewers as she became more closed off.

Just as he reached the last ones and we moved down to stand to the side of him, my foot gave out and I landed with a thump on the floor at his feet.

Jessie started to laugh and said in a carrying whisper, "I guess some people aren't supposed to be in the spotlight, huh."

Celibet

The journalists around her laughed, but Charlie came over and helped me up, pressing a scorching kiss to my lips before he turned back to the press. The guy interviewing him asked who I was, and Charlie turned to him, then turned back to me and kissed my forehead.

"She's my girl, and she's recovering from a broken foot, which is why she fell over."

Jessie had appeared by our side by then and Charlie turned to glower at her as I burst out with, "No need to be a fucking jerk about it."

Charlie burst out laughing and every journalist who heard me laughed with him making my face heat with embarrassment. I wanted the ground to swallow me whole, but Charlie held me firmly to his side as he answered the questions from the press. He never once let me go until we were safely inside.

Chapter Fifty-Three

CHARLIE

I wrapped up the interviews and curled an arm around Beth's waist, guiding her in and leaving Jessie to walk in behind us.

As soon as we were behind closed doors, Jack pulled me off to the side. "What the hell are you doing, Charlie? You know what Jeff said…"

"Shhh," I ordered. "I told you when I was going to L.A. I would not be seen as being with that fucking woman. I might be an actor, and I know most actors don't give a fuck who they screw… that's not me, at least not when I'm with someone. I at least have some morals. Now do your fucking job and keep that bitch as far away from me as you can until I can get out of here," I seethed as the anger

Celibet

bubbled up inside of me. "Because after all this shit and tonight, I'll be looking for a new management company."

Spinning away from Jack, I joined Beth again and we took our seats. If he didn't like that shit, then he wouldn't like what I had up my sleeve next.

When the movie was over, Beth and I made our way out and with her safely in my arms the doors opened, and the flash of cameras started all over again. One of the press, I think she was from T.V Choice, called out, "So, Charlie, when are you going to introduce her to the world?"

"Are you ready for this? If not, we can go exclusive another time. You'll be in the limelight after tonight."

Beth stood a little taller and brushed her palms over the bodice of her dress. "I'm ready, Charlie. I want us to be exclusive." She pushed up to her tiptoes until her lips were at the shell of my ear. "Plus, I want to see Jessie's face when you do it."

I smirked and dipped my head. "You're a wicked woman, Bethany Matthews." I planted my lips on hers and took her hand, pulling her with me to Sophie from TV Choice magazine.

"Hey, Sophie."

"So, come on. Who's the lucky lady that's caught the eye of Charlie James? We all want to know."

I glanced at Beth and a wide smile took over. "This is my best friend, Bethany Matthews." Joining our fingers together, I brought her hand to my lips. "She's been my best friend for seven years, but I'm hoping she'll take the next step with me."

"What?" Beth asked, confused as I glanced at Sophie. I saw a grin light up her whole face and then she turned the mic and the spotlight onto Beth.

I dropped to one knee and took the box from my inside pocket. "Bethany, I want to marry you. I want to spend the rest of my life worshipping you. I want us to go on his crazy ride together because I couldn't envision anyone being by side but you."

"Yes!" she squeaked. She cleared her throat before answering again. "**YES**. I'll marry you, Charlie. Of course, I will,"

I scrambled up from my knees and wrapping both arms around her back, I lifted her from the ground and spun her around. She framed my face with her hands and kissed me, right there on the red carpet.

"Well, there you have it, folks: Charlie James is a taken man." The camera's flashed again all around us. I managed a glimpse at Jessie, and the fury on her face was epic. I believe I got my revenge.

"Can I just say on behalf of TV choice, congratulations to you both."

Beth expressed her thanks and I winked and pulled Beth along to the limo.

I placed the ring on her finger when we got in and kissed her again.

"Charlie," Jack called as he sat on the opposite chair. "You know you've probably kissed a whole lot of sales away after that stunt with Jessie and then proposing. Why couldn't you play the game for tonight?"

Celibet

"Fuck you, Jack. I don't give a fuck. I'm sick of everyone sucking up to a prima donna like her. I've never gone by the book. I am my own man. If you don't like it's tough shit."

I clasped Beth's hand in mine while she talked happily with Callie.

"Oh my god, Charlie."

My eyes turned to hers.

"My dad. He'll go mad seeing that on the television."

I chuckled at the fright on her face. "He knows. I told him before I came back to Kent for you that I was going to marry you one day, and let's face it, your dad knows I don't do traditional."

We sat in a bubble of bliss for the rest of the ride to the hotel for the after party. Apart from Jack of course: he was sulking. Fuck him and Jeff. As soon as Monday came, I was looking for new management.

The limo came to a stop.

I turned to Beth first. "Are you ready for more pictures?"

"Yes."

For the first time in a while, Beth looked confident. She was breath-taking. My heart stuttered in my chest when I realised that I got to have this woman for the rest of my life. "I love you so much Bethany Matthews, and I can't wait to make you my wife."

A tear rolled slowly down her cheek, and I brushed it away.

"I love you, too. I can't wait to be your wife. I can't believe it."

"Let's go wow this after party, then I'm going to devour your whole fucking body."

Jack stepped from the limo first, then Callie. The flashes and the clicks of the cameras began again. I got out of the limo before Beth and took her hand helping her out. Once Beth was out of the car, I scooped her up in my arms and carried her to the doors of the hotel.

Chapter Fifty-Four

BETH

My heart was still hammering as we walked into the hotel lobby, and I couldn't believe what had happened. I was engaged. En-freaking-gaged to Charlie.

My body floated into the room where the after party was, and I saw a lot of celebrities mingling around with people I didn't know.

The atmosphere was electric, and Charlie went straight into actor mode as we made our way through the room.

He led me to a table in the back and popped open a bottle of Moët as the music started.

"I have to network for a bit, but I'll be back soon." He gave me a kiss full of the promise of more and then poured a few glasses of ice-cold champagne, handing them out before he turned and began to move through the room.

I watched him as desire uncurled in my body, and I glanced to see Charlie talking to Austin Grant. They were both laughing and joking as Jessie walked over to them both.

Charlie ignored her, but Austin seemed to talk to her until she spun around and tossed a glass of red wine all over Charlie.

I was up and out of my seat before I even knew what I was doing. Charlie was spluttering and shaking with fury, but when I reached them, he touched my arm and shook his head.

He turned to face Jessie and growled at her in a high clear voice.

"Guess you really are a fucking jerk huh?" He spun around and began walking towards the elevators that were outside the room we were in.

"Guess he left you behind…" she tittered, and Austin glanced between us as I stepped right into her space.

"Looks like it, but guess what, jackass: he's my guy and he always will be. Just because you can't have him doesn't give you the right to ruin his night."

Her eyes widened and she brought her hand round to my cheek, but just before it made contact, Callie grabbed her and spun her around, making her lose her footing and fall over.

"Beth, why don't you go after Charlie and I'll deal with this jackass."

I glanced at my friend and saw her smile at me and nod towards the door. I grinned and spun away, heading

Celibet

towards the doors when Jessie caught up with me, I stood for a moment wondering how people like her thought they could just do whatever the hell they wanted and get away with it. Her team must have been busy paying people off because she was a raging maniac.

"He's mine," she screamed at me as she grabbed my shoulder and spun me around. I burst out laughing at her before shrugging her off and rushing to the elevators.

Charlie was nowhere to be found, so I went to the check in desk and waited for the receptionist to get off the phone. She ignored me completely as she chatted with whoever was on the other end about hairstyles and dresses, so I cleared my throat and she finally looked up.

"Can you," I began but she held a manicured finger up, stopping me and went back to her call.

"Excuse me!" I said loudly.

She rolled her eyes, saying goodbye to whoever she was on the phone to before she looked up at me and said in a sickly-sweet voice, "How can I help you?"

"Hi, I need the room number for Charlie James."

"Uh huh, sure you do. Sorry, we don't give our guests room numbers out. If he wanted you to have it, he'd have given you it."

I was about to say something to her when Jack appeared by my side.

"It's okay. Give her the other key please."

The girl snorted and shoved it towards me. I gave Jack a one-armed hug and went across to the bank of elevators, pressing the button. As I stood waiting with my foot tapping, Callie came over and gave me a hug.

"Congrats again, babe. I'm going to head home."

The lift arrived and I stepped away from her, pressing the button to the fourth floor. As the elevator moved, I kicked my shoes off, hiked up my skirt a little, before bending to pick them up.

I reached the fourth floor and moved along the corridor with butterflies in my stomach and my heartbeat pounding in my ears. I reached four zero four and saw it was a corner room. My hands shook as I took the key card and inserted it into the slot, pushing the door open with slowly and stepping inside.

I didn't know why I was so nervous. I'd had sex before, but never with Charlie, and although we'd both had a fumble with each other, we hadn't really broken the bet yet.

My breathing sped as I heard the shower running, and I pushed the door open wider to see

My body thrummed with excitement, and I didn't want to just watch him in the shower. I wanted to taste him, to suck him down my throat and drive him wild with my tongue.

I unzipped my dress and let it pool on the floor by my feet before I climbed into the shower still in my basque and thong. Charlie started in surprise when I touched him, and his eyes darkened as he took my body in.

The basque pushed my tits up and pulled my waist in, but it also made me feel sensual and sexy in a way I'd never felt before. My fingers brushed his cock, and he pulled me under the water with him, kissing my lips with reckless abandon as his hands moved all over me.

Celibet

His fingers twisted at my nipples and caused a jolt of lust to shoot right through me as his tongue caressed mine.

"Beth," he moaned as I ran my fingers along his cock and gave him a gentle squeeze. His moans encouraged me, and I dropped to my knees, sucking him into my mouth. Hearing his hiss of breath and feeling his fingers tighten in my hair, I twisted my hand on the base of his cock and sucked him in as far as he could go.

"Oh, my God, babe!" he groaned as his head hit the tiled wall behind him, but I didn't stop. I sucked a little harder and moved my hand faster until I felt the veins pop before his cock shot his load down my throat.

I licked every drop and then leaned back to look up at him as the shower water ran down my body.

"Beth," Charlie whispered hoarsely as I looked up at him, "seeing you on your knees, wearing that and looking sexy as fuck is one of my biggest ever fantasies, but now I want to taste you."

"The bet," I began, and he growled, leaning down to pick me up.

"Fuck the bet, I don't need a fucking Celibet. All I need is you."

He spun me around and dropped to his knees at my feet before lifting my left leg and pushing it over his shoulder.

"My turn," he muttered, moving my thong to the side he buried his tongue into my wet heat. "Fuck, you taste better than I thought you would," he moaned, and then his tongue darted up to lick my clit before he plunged it inside me.

My pulse began to quicken, and he pulled back to look up at me.

"Play with your nipples," he commanded as he inserted a finger inside me and licked and sucked at my clit as his finger fucked me. I twisted my nipples almost to the point of pain, and before long, my legs began to tingle. I writhed in his face and on his hand as my orgasm burst through me, causing my legs to shake and my body to shudder.

As it started to recede, Charlie stood and picked me up, pushing his cock into me and stilling as we both took each other in. This was it for us.

I knew as he started moving inside me that this was where I wanted to be and that he would always be my best friend first. I couldn't wait to become his wife, and I was excited to see what the future would bring us.

The Celibet was over, and we'd both won but lost, and I was so grateful that we made that stupid bet because it had given us each other.

Epilogue

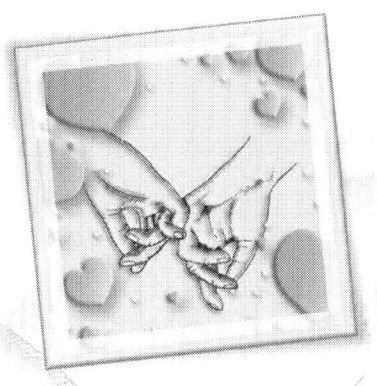

CHARLIE
Six Months Later
December

The first flakes of snow started to fall as I entered the massive marquee to wait for the woman of my dreams. Red and white roses scattered around the entrance and down the makeshift aisle.

It was hard to believe we had actually got here at all, but you know what they say: nothing in life is easy, and you have to work for what you want. Jesus. They weren't kidding. As usual, though, we got through it. Someone once said that friends can't be lovers. I never got that at first.

Over the seven years Beth and I had known each other, we'd gone through so many phases and one was denial. Rather than act on anything, we'd carried on screwing around with different people, thinking we were happy. But every single woman I'd dated, or even just hooked up with, never compared to Beth. After what had happened with Warren, it had really been a wake-up call for me. Luckily though, we hadn't heard nor seen anything of him since he'd made bail. He was currently under investigation for the charges that were made against him. Hopefully, he'll be going down for a long time and we would never have to see or deal with him ever again. Not that he'd get within an inch of my wife ever again anyway. I'd make sure of that.

It had only been six months since I proposed to Beth, but since the premiere, life had been somewhat crazy. I'd taken some time out to spend with my girl before I had to go down to Cornwall to film Wandering Warrior. I was gone for six weeks, and it was the hardest six weeks of my life. The only upside of it was that we were in the same country. If she'd needed me, I could've been back here within hours.

My half-brother, Lincoln, clapped me on the back and I turned around and smiled.

"You ready for this?"

"More than ready."

"Good. Come on, we better get changed. I'm not sure Beth would approve of you in shorts. Plus, man, it's fucking freezing out here. Who the fuck gets married in the winter?"

I nodded and took one last look at the garden. I knew that once I was in Beth's presence, I wouldn't notice one damn thing.

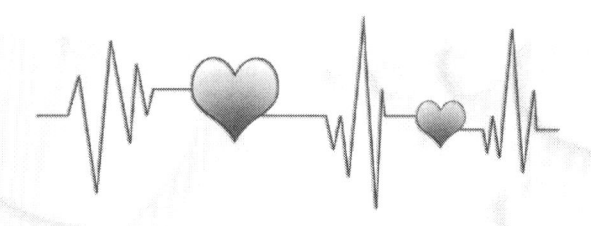

Beth

stood in front of me. My eyes swept over her body in that stunning gown she was wearing, and I brought my gaze back to her face, looking into her sea-blue eyes. I let myself sink into her depths, drowning in her beauty.

"Do you, Charles Lewis James, take Bethany Matthews to be your wife?" the minister said as the ceremony progressed.

I'd got so caught up in my head I forgot he was talking.

I held her hands in mine and brushed my thumbs across her knuckles. Her smile stretched across her mouth, and it lit up her whole face. I pushed the ring on to her finger and over her knuckle until it sat pretty against the solitaire engagement ring, I'd bought her from Tiffany's.

"I do," I said loudly so everyone could hear.

"Bethany."

She glanced to the side to look at the minister.

"Bethany Matthews, do you take Charles Lewis James to be your husband."

Beth nodded frantically before glancing back at the minister. She did the same with my ring until it wouldn't slip over my knuckle.

"It won't go on…"

Discreetly, I covered her hand with mine and together we pushed it over my knuckle, and I smirked.

"I do."

I smiled wide at the minister and nodded before I let him know he could go on.

"I now pronounce you husband and wife."

A relieved sigh fell from my lips, and before the minister could say anything else, I had her face in my hands, planting my lips on hers.

"I love you so much, Beth."

Even though I knew all our family and friends were around, all I wanted to do was scoop her up and take her to bed, but I couldn't. I softly licked inside her mouth and gently nibbled on her lips.

At the side of me I could hear the minister saying, 'you can kiss the bride', but I was way ahead of him and had already sealed that deal.

She fisted the lapels of my suit jacket and tugged me closer before she pulled back an inch and said against my lips, "I love you. More than anything in the world, Charlie James."

Clapping and cheers started from behind us, and we turned to face everyone. There were smiles galore as I

Celibet

wrapped my arm around her middle. She looked beautiful in her ivory gown.

I turned to my best man, Lincoln, and shook his hand. We walked back up the aisle together, nodding at the guests.

As we reached the top, Evan greeted us with a smile and a kiss for his daughter.

"Congratulations, you two. I'm so proud of you, sweetheart. And Charlie, there wasn't a man on this earth good enough for my baby, but you… You proved yourself worthy, and I couldn't be happier." He held out his hand, and as soon as I took it, he pulled me in for a hug and clapped my back.

As I pulled from Evan, a hand tapped my shoulder. I turned around to see who it was and saw my dad. "Dad. I'm so glad you could make it."

"I wouldn't have missed this for the world." He did the same as Evan and hugged me tightly, clapping my back before he loosened his hold on me and sidestepped me to see Beth.

"Weston. Oh, my goodness, I'm so glad you're here." Beth squealed as she launched herself into his arms.

He chuckled as he hugged her. "So, I see you and Mum didn't sit on the same side?"

"No. She might have possessed me if I'd sat near her. Plus, she sat on your side, and I decided in honour of you and Beth, that I should sit on Beth's side." He looked over my shoulder. "Oh god," Dad exclaimed. "Here she comes. It's too late to hide."

"Dad," I said sharply and turned to face my mother.

"Charles…"

"Mum." I cut her off. "Please call me Charlie, just for today, for me…please?" She huffed but ignored me. "Congratulations to you both." She kissed my cheek and moved towards Beth. "Bethany. You look very pretty." She did the same by kissing her cheek and stood back. As she glanced away, I took in her disdain for my dad and knew it was time to make a quick getaway.

I took Beth's hand and pulled her into my side. "We better go mingle with the guests."

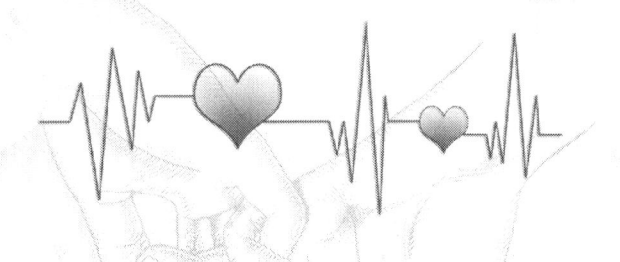

The day was going amazingly. We'd had food, drink and now it was time for the first dance.

Inside the marquee, there was a makeshift dance floor with scattered round tables. Evan had hired caterers to serve us and there was a DJ at the front.

The opening notes to our first dance began, and I knew that was my cue.

"Could you please raise a glass to the happy couple, Charlie and Beth."

I pulled her to the dancefloor with me and with her head in my hands, I leaned down and kissed her lips before

Celibet

taking her hands. I twirled her around as Bill Medley and Jennifer Warnes sang about having the time of their lives. Beth's smile never faltered, but as mid-song approached, we parted. She kicked off her heels and ran towards me. With my hands hugging her waist, I lifted her above my head. I held her for about a second, and my legs buckled. We fell, not so gracefully and landed on a heap on the floor, laughing loudly. Her lips met mine and she kissed me.

"Oh my god that was so cool. I love you, Charlie!"

Our guests cheered and clapped as the DJ said congratulations and changed to another song.

"I love you so much more, Mrs James!"

We were helped from the floor, and after another kiss we parted. I went to the bar for a shot, while Callie kept Beth on the dance floor.

While I stood at the bar with my dad and Evan toasting our marriage with shots of tequila, Beth's friend—and I used friend lightly—Chris joined us.

"Hey man." We clapped hands as he smiled. "She's one in a million. Look after her."

"She is. And you have no problem with that, I assure ya."

"Callie's looking good, though. Red suits her."

I smirked at him before grabbing the bottle of tequila and a shot glass and pouring him one. I handed it to him before pouring myself one, holding it up in the air. We clinked glasses and knocked the shots back.

Beth joined us at the bar after a while, and I wrapped her up in my arms while Callie dragged Chris to the floor.

I gazed into my wife's eyes and saw home. She was my home, and it didn't matter where I was located to film, she would always be my home. And from the moment I met her, I guess I'd always known.

"Happy Christmas, sweetheart."

She looked up and smiled. "You've made all my Christmases come at once, Charlie. I love you."

"You're the best bet I ever made."

I wrapped her up in an embrace. I'd make sure I'd never let go of her.

We hadn't really needed a silly bet, but if it hadn't been for the celibet, we never would have owned up to our feelings for each other.

Now, I get to spend the rest of my life with the girl of my dreams, my best friend, in every sense of the word.

The End

Celibet

Stacy McWilliams & Sienna Grant

Playlist

I Want it That Way – Backstreet Boys
Thorn in my Side – Eurythmics
Kiss Me – Sixpence None the Richer
Dive – Ed Sheeran
The Day we Caught the Train – Ocean Colour Scene
Gold Digger – Kanye West/ Jamie Foxx
Dirrty – Christina Aguilera
Can't Fight this Feeling – REO Speedwagon
Never too Much – Luther Vandross
You Are the Reason – Calum Scott
Feels Like Home - Chantal Kreviazuk
You Are The Sunshine Of My Life – Stevie Wonder
(I've had) The Time Of My Life – Bill Medley/ Jennifer Warnes

Celibet

Author Bio

Sienna Grant is a British writer from the West Midlands in the UK, who decided to step into the world of writing and has since never looked back.
She started her journey with contemporary romance as she loves a happy ever after, but has since sampled different genres and has pushed every boundary she has set herself. From contemporary romance to suspense, teen and young adult but also stepping into the darker world of Mafia and women's fiction.

When she's not writing, she's a wife and mother to three children, two of which are now grown up and starting their own lives and a 16 year old that's just stepped into the wide world of working life.

Sienna loves to read most romance when she can, but always with a hint of realism.

Celibet

Stacy McWilliams & Sienna Grant

Social Links

Facebook Page:
https://www.facebook.com/AuthorSiennaGrant

Facebook:
https://www.facebook.com/sienna.grant.18

Readers Group:
https://www.facebook.com/groups/1037307393047407/

Goodreads:
https://www.goodreads.com/author/show/15613594.Sienna-Grant

Instagram:
https://www.instagram.com/authorsgrant

Twitter:
https://twitter.com/authorsgrant1

Author Bio

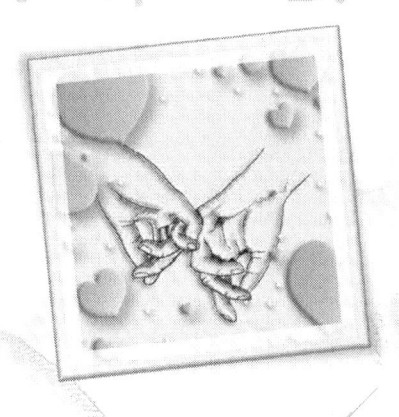

Welcome to the rollercoaster world of Stacy McWilliams.

Stacy McWilliams is a Scottish Author who loves romance. All of her books have a romantic element and her books will keep you on the edge of your seat, make you want to throw your kindle around and her characters will make you either love them or loathe them.

Reviews

"...on the edge reading..." Destroyed by Deception
"...hold on tight and hang on for the ride." Black Mercy
"...captivated from the start..." Candlelight
"...kept me intrigued..." Luminosity
"brilliant paranormal story that pulls you into her world of demons and teenage romance." Ignition
"What can I say... I was left wanting more... More Hunter, more Savannah, just more of everything."-Pride

Stacy McWilliams & Sienna Grant

Contact her on Facebook or Instagram and she will message back.

If she's not writing, looking after her three boys or spending time with her hubs, she's reading or watching TV shows such as Lucifer, The 100 and Supernatural.

She's working on new materials and is hoping to release three-four books in 2020. Also check out her Facebook page for updates on any signings she's attending.

Social Links

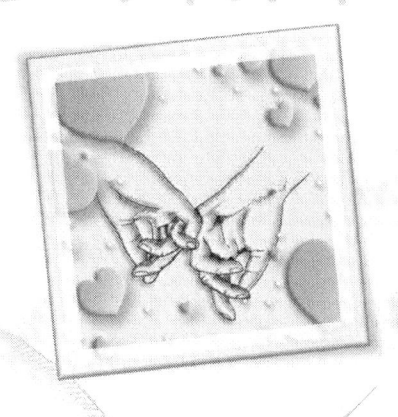

Goodreads:
https://www.goodreads.com/author/show/9796198.Stacy_McWilliams

Facebook:
https://www.facebook.com/authorstacymcwilliams

Twitter: http://www.twitter.com/@stacemcw

Instagram: https://www.instagram.com/stacemcwilliams/

Website: http://authorstacemcwilli.wixsite.com/author

Printed in Great Britain
by Amazon